HOW IT ENDS

"I don't think I have loved a book as much as this one in a long time."

—Reading Is Bliss

"Reading this elegantly written novel is like looking through a kaleidoscope with a different picture in every chapter."

—Metroreader

"Amazingly well-written . . . had me in tears more than I would like to admit."

—My Book Views

"Wonderful and sad at the same time."

—Chick with Books

"*How It Ends* just blew me away. . . . If you haven't read any of Laura Wiess's books, this one is the perfect place to start."

—Katie's Book Blog

"A unique coming-of-age tale that explores some of the most fundamental human bonds and experiences."

—Book Soulmates

LEFTOVERS

"Like her equally gripping debut, Wiess's suspense story delivers an outsize jolt of adrenaline. . . . Although the 'best friends against the world' theme is not new, Wiess's clear insight . . . and her layered storytelling bump up the subject to a much more challenging playing field."

—*Publishers Weekly*

"A riveting story. . . . I love this book."

—Laura Fitzgerald, national bestselling author of *One True Theory of Love*

"Dramatic and disturbing. . . . A captivating book that will keep you turning the pages."

—Teens Read Too

"Reading Blair and Ardith's story is like scratching a mosquito bite—you can't stop scratching until it bleeds. And as much as it hurts, you won't be able to put *Leftovers* down until you finish it."

—BookLoons

SUCH A PRETTY GIRL

Chosen as one of the ALA's 2008 Best Books for Young Adults and 2008 YALSA Quick Picks for Reluctant Readers

"Brilliance comes in a small package. . . . In the character of Meredith, Laura Wiess has created a girl to walk alongside Harper Lee's Scout and J. D. Salinger's Phoebe."

—Luanne Rice, *New York Times* bestselling author of *What Matters Most*

"*Such a Pretty Girl* hooked me on page one, and Laura Wiess's masterful prose kept me turning the pages. This is the first book in a very long time that made me say, 'Wish I'd written this.'"

—Ellen Hopkins, *New York Times* bestselling author of *Fallout*

"Wiess has created a spunky heroine—tough, darkly humorous, yet achingly vulnerable. . . . A nail biter of an ending. [A] gutsy and effective thriller."

—*Kirkus Reviews* (starred review)

"A gritty, terrifying novel about a father's abuse of power and trust. . . . A page-turner that ultimately sends a startling message of empowerment. . . . Extremely satisfying."

—*Booklist*

"Powerful. . . . Mature teens who enjoy realistic fiction with an edge will devour it."

—*VOYA*

"Strikes just the right balance between hope and despair, and Meredith's will to survive and ability to take action in the face of her terror are an inspiration."

—*KLIATT*

"*Such a Pretty Girl* is a riveting novel and Meredith is a wholly original creation: a funny, wise, vulnerable girl with the heart of a hero and the courage of a warrior. This gut-wrenching story will stay with you long after you finish the last page."

—Lisa Tucker, author of *The Promised World*

"Beautifully written and painfully real. Laura Wiess has crafted a gripping story that is heart-rending—and important, with a capital 'I.'"

—Barbara Delinsky, *New York Times* bestselling author of *More Than Friends*

Ordinary Beauty

laura wiess

GALLERY BOOKS   MTV BOOKS

New York London Toronto Sydney

For Stew, with love,
and
For my sister Suzanne,
without whom my heart would be so lonely.

Acknowledgments

It's always a pleasure to thank my agent Barry Goldblatt for his excellent advice and support, and my editor Jennifer Heddle for her guidance, insight, and her amazing ability to ask just the right questions. Working with you guys is the best.

A deep curtsy goes out to production editor John Paul Jones, copyeditor Victoria Mathews, publicist Erica Feldon, and art director Lisa Litwack, for lending their talent, skill and enthusiasm to the creation of this book.

Love and thanks to Sue Dial and Jane Russell Mowry, who were brave enough to read the first draft and report back, and to Bonnie Verrico, Wendy Gloffke and Shelley Sykes who were never too busy to offer support, or to listen to my writer's angst.

Next time, ladies, the coffee's on me.

Much love and thanks go to Stewart Russell for his support, patience, and especially his encouragement, which gave me the room and the freedom to disappear into this book and not come out again until I was done. It was exactly what I needed. I am truly a lucky girl.

And to my family—Barbara, Bill, Scott, Suzanne, and Paul—who have always been my rock solid foundation and the core of my heart: Thank you, forever.

Children's talent to endure stems from their ignorance of alternatives.

—Maya Angelou

Betrayal, though . . . betrayal is the willful slaughter of hope.

—Steven Deitz

Ordinary Beauty

Chapter 1

Walking up Churn Road at one in the morning is not the worst part of my life right now, which, since the road is nothing more than a mile-long rutted, frozen, unlit dead-end dirt track through the woods, really ought to say something.

I tuck the warm, grease-stained bag of leftovers close against me and train the dull beam of the flashlight on the uneven ground ahead, trudging past thick stands of barren trees and the hungry wild animals that slip like shadows among them.

What's worse than the walk is the cold, and how the roaring wind hurls itself down the mountain, rattling branches, numbing skin, and pelting me with snow as hard and stinging as sand.

I nestle my chin lower into my jacket and plod on.

What's worse is owing Marisol, the other busgirl, a lot of gas money for driving me eleven miles out of town and dropping me at the Route 40 intersection for the last eight nights, then having to walk another mile up the dirt road alone just to crash at Harlow Maltese's dump of a trailer after ten straight hours of busing tables full of Dug County families together for the holidays. What's worse is overhearing their laughter, watching them hug hello and kiss good-bye, seeing glowing couples holding hands, and friends talking for hours. Seeing all those townies and their kids home from college wearing their new Christmas clothes, spending money on appetizers and entrées and dessert and coffee, ordering exactly what they want and having it brought to them fresh and hot. What's worse is that flash of recognition in their eyes as I pass with a blank face and an armload of their leavings, and their not-quite-quiet-enough, *Isn't that Sayre Bellavia? You know, Dianne Huff's kid?* And then the speaking looks that follow, the women sliding casual hands down the backs of their chairs to make sure their purses are still hanging there, the sudden calculated interest in the men's sly, gleaming gazes.

What's worse is busing a table of Bowden and his friends, and having him not look up at me once, even though we'd skipped school together the Monday before Christmas vacation started, gone over to Snö Mountain so he could ski and I could fall down all day like the rank amateur that I was. He'd paid for everything— my ski rental, lunch, a movie afterward—and then on the way home we'd parked in the deserted ball field outside town and he'd kissed me, sweet at first, then harder and crazier until the windows steamed up and there was nowhere left to go but the backseat.

Which is when I sat up, said it was late and that I had to get home. He laughed, not nicely at all, and said, *C'mon, Sayre, who do you think you're kidding?* And I could feel myself go cold inside, and said, *What's that supposed to mean?* And he looked away, ran a hand through his disheveled hair and said, *You know what it means. Don't make me say it.* And with attitude in my voice I said, *No, go ahead, say whatever's on your mind.* And he got mad at seeing the night end without a better return on his investment, I guess, and so without looking at me, said, *Nobody's waiting for you anywhere.* And when I didn't reply, just sat there numb and receding, he made an aggravated sound, started the car, and roared out of the ball park, taking me back to the dingy, low-roofed, four-room cabin where Candy, me, and my mother were staying.

What's worse is that in Dug County your parentage is either your blessing or your brand, and the lines are drawn early. Their reputation becomes your reputation the moment you slide out into the world, your future charted and indelibly stamped with how high you'll rise or how far you'll fall, and no one will ever forget your beginning or be surprised by your end. Your reputation will cut and mold you, and its legacy, like your last name, will remain as constant as your shadow, always two steps ahead of you and one close step behind, and—

Something rustles in the dark woods beside me. I stop, heart pounding, tuck the bag of food farther under my arm, and run the quivering flashlight beam along the tree line. The shine catches a lone, golden-eyed bobcat, big and thick furred, tufted ears high and huge, clawed foot raised in midstep.

We stare at each other.

The bobcat's nose twitches.

I shouldn't do this, but it's hungry and so I inch my hand down into the bag and slowly remove the first thing my fingers close around, which turns out to be a big, fatty wedge of pork. I flick my wrist and the greasy chunk of meat lands less than two feet in front of him. "Now go," I say, voice hoarse.

The wind gusts, swirling my hair and ruffling its fur, but the cat doesn't move.

Doesn't even blink.

I keep the beam trained on its still, angular face and holding my breath, slowly walk backward up the road. After the eighth step, when there is distance between us, the bobcat snatches the pork, wheels, and vanishes into the night.

I exhale. Wipe my hands on the bag. Turn forward again, knees shaking, and catch my foot on a hump of frozen ground. Stumble but don't fall. Was that a sound? I shine the light along the deserted wood line. No, just the wind. I'm all right. Bobcats don't eat people, it's too cold for bears and rattlesnakes, and the coyotes haven't howled up here in a week, so just keep walking, Sayre. Don't run. Prey runs. And watch your step. If you get hurt, you're on your own.

What's worse is that Bowden was right. There isn't a person out there who would miss me if I was gone.

laura wiess

The wind howls, and high overhead the bare branches click like chattering teeth. I round the bend at the icy creek. Startled, three does snort in alarm and, white tails waving, break up the bank beside me. I scan the swaying tree trunks ahead, searching hard for the flat shaft of fluorescent light from Harlow's kitchen window.

There.

I find it, and keep moving. The snow stings my skin and peppers the bag of food, which is no longer warm. I smell the smoke from his woodstove, hear a faint snatch of music, and finally pass his mailbox bolted on top of an old truck axle. Head up the slope, skirt the broken-down riding mower, the three-legged chair, the piles of junk car parts, the cracked pink toilet, and the battered Kenmore washing machine anchored to the ground with ropes of bare vine, dormant honeysuckle. Switch off the flashlight to save what's left of the batteries, then trip over an empty plastic flowerpot and switch it back on.

Nothing.

The light's gone dead.

What's worse isn't knowing that Harlow will be drunk when I get there because when Harlow's off his meds he's *always* drunk, but that if it's a mean drunk he'll throw me out. No matter that he and my mother have been drinking buddies for a couple of years now, and he knows I don't have anywhere else to go. No matter that I've barely slept since a furious Candy tracked me down six days ago on Christmas to tell me my mother was in the hospital, that my feet ache, my eyes are grainy, and my thoughts scattered and stupid, and that right now giving up would be far easier than going on. No matter that without me Harlow would have no food, and neither would his crippled-up dog or that scared, skinny little feral kitten holed up in the frozen dirt under his trailer.

No matter anything because I'm Sayre Bellavia, and I have to take what I can get.

I weave through the rubble, snagging the leg of my jeans on a sheaf of rusty metal, bruising my hip on the handle of an old plow, stubbing my toe on something I can't even name. The pain throbs but I'm too exhausted to care, and a dull thought rises: Hasn't it always been this way?

No. Not always.

The worst of all is knowing that it hasn't always been this way.

Out ahead, the kitchen light lifts the path of darkness to gray. I follow it up the wooden steps and shove the dead flashlight under my arm, then flex my stiffened fingers and open the door.

Chapter 2

The stereo's on and the living room is loud, hot and stifling, ripe with the punishing scents of unwashed dog, smoke, and sour, fermented yeast. The only working bulb left in the overhead light flickers and dozens of houseflies buzz against the ceiling, resurrected from their windowsill graveyards by the unnatural warmth.

Dozer, Harlow's near-blind and grizzled old bulldog, is lying on his side up against the avocado green lounge chair. He doesn't lift his massive head or even open his bleary eyes, only draws a great, snuffling breath at the smell of the food in the bag and thumps his screw tail once to acknowledge my arrival.

Harlow is laid out in his lounge chair, eyes closed, sparse, gray hair in scraggly strands across his bald spot, damp tear tracks down the side of his face, an empty bottle of tequila wedged in tight beside him, a can of beer in his hand, and bits of fluffy white stuffing from the holes in the chair clinging to his faded brown work pants. Empties fill the wastebasket in front of the end table, and three sweating, unopened cans sit within reach. So does his shotgun, and a new mail-order skinning knife.

The tequila wasn't here when I left this morning.

"'. . . his love lives on, he knows she's gone . . . and she will never come back . . .'"

He never buys tequila. That's Candy's poison, and if she was here again . . .

"'. . . *she will never come back . . .*'"

The record is warped and hilly, horrible on the stereo, which is an old garage sale turntable with a static volume knob, bad speaker wires, and a dull needle.

"'. . . *she will never come back . . .*'"

Harlow crying is not a good sign.

"'. . . *she will never come back . . .*'"

The album is skipping.

Irritation crosses his face and he sweeps a sloppy hand toward the end table where the stereo is, sending the needle screeching across the vinyl and knocking the last three beers to the floor. "Goddamn piece of shit," he mumbles and drains the rest of the can. Drops it over the side of the lounge, barely missing Dozer.

The turntable needle rides the center of the album, *cha-chunk, cha-chunk, cha-chunk.*

Harlow sees me.

"I brought food," I say, heading for the kitchen table and trying to gauge his mood as I open the bag. The bittersweet love song is a nightly event, his own personal sound track to a heartbreak that, according to him, is the greatest sorrow of his life and one that can never be eased. He's told me his version of the story every single night I've been here, not knowing or caring, I guess, that I already know the parts he's leaving out, and so I've lain awake on that couch, bone weary but too tensed up to sleep and he's lain in that lounge chair, drunker than anything but still unable to let it be . . .

"*She was young, a pretty little girl from a good, churchgoing family and I . . . well, I had a bad reputation, you know, being hotheaded and cocky and a Maltese to boot, so her mama was always keeping a close eye on me. She was a real Christian, though, and she gave me plenty of chances to do right by her daughter. I see that now. I* didn't before," he said, looking at me with the same childlike earnestness every single time he told the tale. "That girl loved me more than anybody ever did, and she begged me to straighten up, but I was arrogant, and besides, I didn't think she'd ever really do it. Leave me, I mean. But she did." He closed his eyes and the exhale deflated him. "I couldn't see the truth of it, you know? I was too pissed off to see my own part in driving her away and so I went a little crazy . . . And I never saw her again."

I sat there in shock that first night, unable to believe what I was hearing, mad, scared, astonished at all the pieces of the story he was leaving out, sick at even being in the same room with him and trying hard not to let him see any of it on my face. Of all the things he could have said, all the stories he could've told, I'd never expected this one, and if it hadn't been snowing and I'd had anywhere else to go, I would have stood right up and walked out. But I didn't and so I was stuck listening to the insanity of Harlow Maltese, the man my mother had known the truth about, yet still befriended. The man she and Candy had partied with, wheedled money from, gossiped about, and laughed at behind his back, mocking his size, his smell, his occasional fruitless attempts at sex, saying how his mind might be willing but his flesh just wasn't interested, no matter their efforts, and how all that beer had ended up pickling more than just his brain.

As if *that* was the worst thing about him.

"I used to think I would see her again," he said, opening his eyes and swiping a tear off his grizzled cheek. "I thought maybe she'd forgive me and we could start a new life together but now . . ."

I folded my arms across my chest, my face carefully devoid of all expression.

He looked at me for a long moment, then down at himself. Plucked at the stained and holey 9TH ANNUAL COYOTE HUNT T-shirt stretched tight across his enormous belly, touched his tongue to the rotten front tooth that was giving him so much trouble, studied the can of beer welded to his hand. Looked back at me with eyes so full of resignation, so naked with defeat, that I had to look away.

"*Well, that point is past,*" he said quietly.

I don't listen anymore when he tells that story. Now I just lay in the dark and watch him drink himself senseless, watch the end of his cigarette smolder as he talks, and pray he doesn't fall asleep, drop it into the lounge chair, and burn us both to death.

"I'm not real hungry." He smears a trembling hand across his face and tries to sit up. The lounge's footrest mechanism is shot, and four times he slams it down before it catches and holds. He starts to rise, sways, and thumps back down. "Christ. Bring it over, will you?"

"Sure." I unwrap the remainder of the food that wasn't sold by closing time: the outside slice of a ham, some ziti, cold French fries, a charred slab of pot roast, some mashed potatoes and gravy, and a chicken breast returned for being too spicy. "Here." I give him the chicken, ziti, and mashed potatoes, along with a pack of plastic utensils I swiped from the restaurant because Harlow only has three forks and they've laid dirty in the sink since I got here. The ham and French fries go to Dozer, who wolfs them down and then struggles painfully to his feet and goes in search of the toilet for a drink.

"What're you doing with that?" Harlow says through a mouthful of food, craning his neck as I open the last piece of tinfoil and start tearing the pot roast into bite-size chunks.

"Nothing," I say, shifting to block his view.

"You're feeding that goddamn cat," he says, taking a slug of beer.

I shrug, keeping an ear to his tone of voice because when he's drinking, you never know what's going to set him off and if it happens, I want a running start. Everything I own is in the canvas tote bag hanging by the door, where it's a quick grab on the way out.

"You're not doing it any favors, you know," he says, forking up a piece of chicken and stuffing it in his mouth. "Jesus, that's spicy. You got to turn your efforts in the right direction. How's it ever gonna learn to survive on its own if you keep feeding it?"

"*She's* an orphaned kitten," I say. "There's nothing wrong with feeding a kitten."

"It has to fend for itself," he says, like he doesn't even hear me. "That's the way of nature, Sayre. Only the strong survive."

Oh, like you? I think, watching him devour the food *I* brought. "So you're saying I should just let her die," I say, trying to keep my voice neutral.

He swallows hard and belches. "I'm saying it's a cat, and there's a million other ones out there just like it. You planning on feeding them all?"

"I don't know." Dear God, he has to shut up because I can't do this right now. My nerves are frayed, my eyes are burning, and all I want to do is feed the cat, wash up, and crash. I need to ask him about the tequila, too, but I'm afraid to hear the answer.

"You can't save the world," he continues, scraping up the last of the ziti from the paper plate. "You can only save yourself. That's just the way it is. Trust me, I know. Your mother knows, too."

My mother. "Yeah, you're right," I say, crushing the tinfoil closed over the small pile of pot roast and heading for the door. "My mother's always been really good at that." I flick on the porch light and slip outside, catching my breath at the furious wind and the whipping snow, and hurry down the steps to the kicked-out hole in the trailer skirt. I glance back to make sure he hasn't followed me, then get down on my knees and grope around in the hole until I find the old Savarin coffee can. I couldn't keep it here in summer because this hole would be crawling with rattlesnakes but now, in winter, it's perfect. I quick pull it out, fumble today's tip money from my pocket, stuff it in the can and slide it back into the hole, off to the side where it can't be seen.

Harlow has asked me every single day when they're going to pay me, and I've lied and told him they pay every two weeks, and that only the waitstaff get tips, not the bus people. I know he believes me because if he didn't, he'd be patting me down the minute I walked through that door, and God forbid he discovers I've been holding out on him.

I crouch and call a soft *kitty kitty* as I open the tinfoil.

A dirty pink nose comes into view, poised at the jagged edge of the trailer skirt, then a wide, scared green eye and a scruffy white ear. She's a scrawny thing, maybe four months old, all fluff and fear, a lone white kitten born feral and abandoned. She's skittish from being cussed at by humans, growled at by Dozer, and hunted by everything with teeth, claws, or a beak, but maybe, I hope, still young and hungry enough to be gentled.

"Come on, kitty," I murmur, and moving slowly, reach into the tinfoil and toss a piece of beef to the frozen ground in front of her. "Come on."

She snatches it up and swallows it whole, watching me, tense and wide eyed.

"Good girl," I say, moving only to throw her another piece of beef, and another. "Don't worry, I'm not going to hurt you." My legs are cramped, my feet are freezing but I stay crouched, waiting, watching and murmuring a steady litany of reassurance because any sudden move will make her run. "We should find you a name. Let's see, what's white? Snow, eggs, paper . . . coke. No, that was Candy's pit bull's name and it's just . . . ugh. So, maybe Snow. Ice. No. Cloud. Fog. Mist. Misty." I pause, considering. "Misty. I like that. What do you think?"

I talk until the pot roast is gone then stay a moment longer, hand outstretched, waiting to see if she can be coaxed closer. She hasn't fallen for it so far but it's only been a week, so maybe . . .

She gazes up at me, wary.

I blink my eyes slowly like I've seen mother cats do when they're content. Keep my fingers, slick with the lingering scent of beef, steady in the air. Keep my voice soft and low, saying, *Come on, Misty, come on.*

And she does, just a little, stretching her neck out so that her cold little nose touches my fingertips. Retreats as if shocked by her own bravado, then does it again, this time venturing a quick, scratchy lick. And then another. And then—

There's a huge crash in the trailer and Harlow bellows, swearing a blue streak.

"Oh, hell." I rise automatically and when I look back, Misty is gone.

Chapter 3

I find Harlow lying on the kitchen floor next to an over-turned chair. He's on his back, one meaty arm thrown across his eyes and Dozer creaking around next to him, whining and snuffling his cheek. The room reeks of fresh ammonia and the front of his pants is stained dark.

God, not again. "What happened?"

"I tripped over the goddamn dog, what does it look like?" he snaps without moving his arm, as if by not being able to see me, I won't be able to see him, either. But I *can* see him and it's not good. His cheeks are flushed, his hands are white-knuckled fists, and he's breathing hard. Too hard. "Frigging tequila."

"Oh yeah, that." I ease back a step, in case he comes up swinging. "Where'd you get it?"

"Where do you think?" he says.

"Candy?"

"Give the kid a prize." He snorts and shakes his head, scrubbing his hair against an old spaghetti stain dried to the ratty linoleum. "And next time you see her, you tell her I don't want her coming here without your mother anymore. Every time she does, something goes missing. She stole my goddamn penny jar today, the one I kept right there by the door, and who knows what else. Bitch." He ruminates a moment in silent outrage. "And then she wouldn't even go down to the mailbox and get my check, and I *told* her walking was hard on me. Your mother would have got it for me if she was here." He cracks a bloodshot eye. "She would have. She always did before."

"I believe you," I say, my tone noncommittal. "So, what'd Candy have to say?"

He doesn't answer.

"Hey. Harlow." I nudge him with my foot. "What'd she come by for?"

"She brought news of your mom," he says without looking at me.

"And?" I say, trying not to sound too impatient. "Let's hear it."

"Jesus, let me think a minute so I can remember it right," he says, smearing a grimy hand across his florid face. "You know, calling her yourself would be better."

"Yeah, well," I say because he has no phone, I have no cell, and the closest pay phone is nine miles from here, down the mountain and through the woods at the factory. Had I known earlier that Candy wanted to talk to me, I could have called her from work but it's too late now. "Come on, Harlow." My stomach is in knots and if he doesn't quit being stupid drunk and answer me soon, I don't know what I'm going to do. "What did she say?"

He sighs. "Ah, shit. You ain't gonna like it."

No surprise there. I've never liked anything Candy had to say.

"Uh, she said to tell you—Jesus," he groans as Dozer settles his front paws and massive head on his stomach. "Get off me, you fat load." He gives the dog a mighty shove, and with a yelp Dozer tumbles sideways into the wall and smacks his nose.

Immediately, it starts to bleed.

"Oh, for . . ." Frustrated, I knuckle my forehead. Take a deep breath. Turn to the dog and pat my leg. "C'mere, Dozer. Come on. Let me see your nose."

The dog glances warily at his master, and whimpering, lies down beside his leg. Snakes out a tongue and licks at the trickling blood.

"Hey!" Harlow whacks the dog's quivering flank. "Quit whining and grow a pair already, will ya?"

Now, I learned a long time ago how to be quiet on the outside while I'm freaking on the inside. How to turn away like I don't see all the things that need to be seen, just to keep the peace. How to lie low and act like I want nothing, expect nothing, and hope for nothing so I don't become more trouble than I'm worth. I'm five months short of eighteen and I know how to be cursed and ignored and left behind, how to swallow a thousand tears and ignore a thousand deliberate cruelties, but it's two o'clock in the morning on New Year's Eve and I'm mad and scared and bone tired and really, really sick of acting like I'm grateful to be staying on a hairy, sagging, dog-stained couch in a junky, mildewed trailer with a fat, dangerous, volatile drunk who sweats stale beer and wallows in his own wastewater, and who doesn't think there's one thing wrong with taking his crap life out on his dog, who comes bellying back for forgiveness every single time, no matter how rotten the treatment—

"Oh yeah, now I got it." Harlow squints up at me. "Candy says you need to quit jerking around and get your ass down to the hospital because your mother's not gonna be around too much longer and she wants to see you, so you need to get past all your prima donna bullshit and act like a daughter again because this time it's for real."

Chapter 4

"Did you hear me?" he asks when I don't respond.

"No," I say, which is wrong because of course I heard him, heard Candy's message delivered just as hard and sharp and hateful as if she was standing right in front of me, slapping my face.

I heard it, and my first reaction is a fierce, panicked *no*.

No, I am *not* jerking around. I left because my mother wanted to be free of me my whole life, and now she's getting her wish.

I'm not going back.

I'm not.

I can't.

I mean, I couldn't even if I wanted to, not after what happened between us the week before Christmas Eve, the raw, unforgivable night that drove me out the door in a move I never thought I could or would make.

So no, there's no going back and no, I am *not* getting my ass in gear just because Candy says to. She's my mother's best friend, not mine, and that's been obvious since the night she said, "Oh, c'mon, Dianne, this party's gonna kick ass and we're not missing it just cause of her. Jerry's kid is old enough to babysit. Just leave her, she'll be all right."

And I was, if you don't count Jerry's kid tying me so tight to a kitchen chair that my hands turned blue, force-feeding me vinegar and Cheerios, and then leaving me sobbing in my own puke until the next morning when Jerry, whoever the hell he was, finally stumbled home from the party. He spanked me for making such a stinking mess, called over and woke Candy up, and told her to tell my mother to come get me before he set me outside and shut the door on my howling.

Three and a half hours later when no one had claimed me, he loaded me, swollen eyed, snuffling, and exhausted into his truck and took me to the site of the party, where we found my mother, Candy and five guys outside drinking beer, eating hot dogs and playing poker.

I got spanked again that day, for ruining Candy's car seat on the way home with my soggy drawers.

I was what, five?

And no, Candy's wrong when she says my mother isn't going to be around much longer because that's the same exact thing my mother says every long, cold, lonely winter, after she either takes *less* than her normal forty-three Vicodins a day to kick off a really ugly withdrawal, or takes *more* so she's barely breathing and one step from comatose. Either way, the payoff for the last six winters has been a strategically scheduled trip to the emergency room where, for at least a couple of days, she gets a clean bed and hot food, free drugs, sponge baths, and people taking care of her round the clock.

This is the first winter since we left Beale's house that I haven't walked in and found her either sweating, panicked and throwing up, or cold, blue, and collapsed, and had to run to find her phone to call the ambulance.

No, this year that terrifying moment was Candy's Christmas gift.

"All right then, listen," Harlow says. "Candy wants you to get your ass in—"

"I heard you," I say.

"Yeah?" Scowling, he props himself up on one arm and gives me a look. "Well, you're not moving too fast and I'm not seeing any tears, so . . ."

No tears?

He hasn't got a clue.

"Why did you do that?" I cried on the slow walk out, violating all the rules and taking my mother's arm in a desperate, bewildered gesture. "That was your only chance, Mom, and you blew it on purpose! Why?"

Oh, God, I can't go see her. I won't.

And I'm not a prima donna, unless that means someone who desperately wants better and more than she has, who lives with just one beautiful, golden memory as proof that it hasn't always been this way—

"Hey!" He reaches over and whacks my leg. "I'm talking to you."

I see him down there on the floor, drunk, sweating, stomach bulging out from under the bottom of his T-shirt, pants smeared with Dozer's blood, and it's like he's not real anymore, he's just another past somebody in the long, dark list of past somebodies my mother's gone off and left me with.

"Ah," he mutters, struggling to his knees. "I knew this was gonna happen." He pulls the overturned chair closer and, using it as leverage, hoists himself to his feet. Panting, he swipes his hair from his eyes and wipes his hands on his pants. "Get your stuff together and come on."

My stuff. Oh God, my stuff. Where is the ruby velvet blazer? My gaze snaps to the canvas bag hanging by the door and suddenly, dizzy with dread, I lurch over and grab it from the hook. If Candy stole the blazer along with Harlow's penny jar, I might as well lay down and die right now, as that blazer is the only thing I've managed to hold on to all these years, the only thing my mother hasn't taken and sold to get high, the only thing we have left of Beale and that time when we were a family.

Frantic, I sink to the floor and rummage through the bag, pulling out underwear and my other jeans and sweater, mascara and socks . . . There, on the bottom, my fingers grope the familiar soft worn velvet, brush against the small white Queen Anne's lace flowers Beale's mother Aunt Loretta had embroidered on the lapel.

"I hope you won't think it's silly, but in the language of flowers, Queen Anne's lace represents sanctuary, and that's what I hope you and Beale and Sayre always find in each other, Dianne," Aunt Loretta had said, smiling as she patted my mother's hand. "This is a one-of-a-kind piece now, and when Sayre grows up you can hand it down to her, and then she can wear it, too. That's how family heirlooms begin."

"Hey." Harlow nudges me with his foot. "Come on. Put your stuff away and let's go."

I gaze blankly up at him. "Where?" And why is he wearing his coat?

He jingles the quad key. "I'm gonna take you down to the end of the road. The factory changes shifts at three and this way, once you're out on the main drag, somebody heading to work will pick you up and get you that much closer to the hospital."

"Oh." He actually thinks I'm going to hitchhike down to the hospital tonight, thirteen long and lonely miles in the frigid cold and whipping snow, in the dark, alone, and exhausted just because Candy gave the order? "Uh, not tonight. I'm really tired. I'll go in the morning." The minute the words leave my mouth I want to take them back.

"In the *morning*?" he echoes in a tone so ominous a chill rips through me, and I start shoving things back into my canvas bag. "You're gonna wait until the *morning*? She could be *dead* in the morning, or don't you even care?"

"I care," I say, fumbling to latch the bag and stand up again.

"No, I don't think you do," he says, shifting his weight from foot to foot. He's wearing lug-soled hunting boots and one kick would be devastating. "If you cared you'd be moving heaven and earth to get down to that hospital." He shakes his head. "You got a real cold streak, you know that? There's something missing in you, kid. You're more concerned about that cat than you are your own flesh and blood."

"No I'm not," I say, rising on trembling knees and slinging the bag's strap over my shoulder. I edge sideways and snag my purse from the table. I want to give the place a quick once-over to see if I'm leaving anything but I don't dare take my eyes off him. I can always steal another toothbrush. What I'm worried about is getting my money. "And you don't have to go out in this cold to give me a ride, Harlow. It's all right. I'll just walk." Sweating, I reach behind me for the doorknob.

"You see, you got no concern for anybody but yourself." He steps closer, his eyes small and red and mean with drink. "Here I am trying to do you a favor and you throw it back in my face. What am I, a piece of shit? My feelings don't mean anything?"

"No, that's not what I meant." My heart is pounding and I can hear the weird wobble in my voice. "I just—"

"Then get on the goddamn quad!" he screams, spittle flying and his rank breath hot in my face.

He grabs my arm, opens the door, and shoves me through. Excited, Dozer rushes past me, bloody nose forgotten. The wooden porch is slippery and I almost fall, barely finding the railing in time. The snow lightens the darkness and I go down the stairs fast, hoping for a chance to grab the coffee can but he's right there on the porch behind me so I have to go over to his four-wheeler instead. It's an old battered Honda, the only vehicle he has, and it's covered with snow. I quickly brush it off and climb on, sitting as far back on the seat as I can.

He climbs on in front of me, clumsy and slow. Turns the key and the motor chugs but doesn't start. He curses and tries it again and again while I sit behind him shivering, trying not to breathe him in, trying not to move a muscle while he gets angrier and angrier, trying not to freak when Dozer sticks his nose into the hole in the trailer skirt and barks like thunder.

"Sic 'em!" Harlow snaps, and then to me, "If I see that cat, I'm shooting it."

Misty.

And then the engine *vrooms* to life and he shifts gears and the bald tires spin and we're creeping through the littered yard to the mailbox where he pauses, snags his government check, then moves onto the road where he guns it and I have to grab on to his waist or be thrown off backward. The frigid wind is searing, my eyes are tearing, and every couple of minutes I have to duck my head and hide behind his massive shoulders just to clear my vision.

I *have* moved heaven and earth to be with my mother. I have. I've stuck by her through hell, tried to help, to be near her, make her smile, save her, tried to keep up when she walked away, to be good enough and not cause trouble, trying trying trying, but it was useless, she's impossible to reach, and you can't get close to someone who doesn't even like you, who doesn't want to hear what you think or know how you feel, who at best tolerates you because you're useful and at worst betrays you in a way you can still hardly bear to think about.

How can you make someone love you when they won't?

How long are you supposed to keep trying?

We roar down the road with Dozer barking and limping frantically along behind us, jouncing over ruts, fishtailing over slick, snow-covered ice. Harlow laughs and spins the quad, almost sending us over the bank and down into the dark ravine. My stomach lurches, queasy. My hands are numb and my head is pounding.

He slows to make a turn and I peer straight up the mountain to where Sunrise Road is, the high road, the road where Beale lives, the road I haven't been up on *once* since we left when I was eleven.

Doesn't *that* make me a real daughter, Candy? Following my mother's unspoken orders, never asking questions, knowing, without her even saying, that they will never be answered, finding out the hard way that she will never, *ever* talk about what happened? That I live knowing it doesn't matter to her if the open wound inside me never heals, that we left Beale without saying good-bye but with a bag stuffed with things that didn't belong to us, things my mother decided were our due and I didn't even know we had until we landed back at Candy's, and she and my mother went through it all to see what they could pawn. The first to go was Aunt Loretta's beautiful amethyst promise ring, which bought them two cartons of cigarettes, a case of vodka, three dozen painkillers, and a bag of Doritos.

The only thing my mother took from our time with Beale that was actually hers was the ruby velvet blazer, and scared that it, too, would be hocked, I stole it out of her bag one night when she was out.

She never mentioned its disappearance, so I have no idea if she ever even missed it.

I haven't talked to Beale in six long years, so I still don't know why he never had us arrested. Maybe he was too deep in mourning to even care. Or maybe by that point he was just glad to see us go, whatever the price.

That thought still hurts, and is why even if I did have the chance to ask him, I wouldn't. How could I ever face him again, knowing how badly we'd betrayed him, how we had robbed him of so much, and left him to suffer the aftermath?

How could I face him, knowing my mother had threatened him with the unthinkable?

No, my life hasn't always been this way.

We reach the deserted, main-road intersection. Harlow stops the quad and stands so I can climb off. Watches as, shaking with cold, I step away and fumble to shoulder my purse and canvas bag. "You should have worn gloves."

"I don't have any," I say, unable to stop myself from glancing at his.

For the first time all night, his mouth thins into a smile. "Yeah, well, life's a bitch and then you die, right?" He revs the engine, turns the quad in a wide, slow circle back toward Churn Road, and pauses beside me again. "Okay, look. Uh, tell your mother I said she'd better hurry up and get out of there so we can hang out again, okay? Tell her it sucks without her." He hesitates, then tugs off his gloves and hands them to me. "Will you do that for me?"

"Sure." I fumble them on and the lining is still warm from his fingers. "I'll tell her."

"Good," he says, and heads back up into the woods.

How I Came to Know Harlow

When I was ten, after we lost our home to foreclosure but before the wondrous year we lived with Beale in a haze of unaccustomed happiness, before the inevitable, irreversible destruction of all things good and promising, my mother and I ate our meals down at the Mission of Mercy soup kitchen on Main Street behind the Shell station, along with Dug County's other down-on-their-luck unfortunates.

The Mission was nothing on the outside, a cinder-block building squatting on a barren, graveled lot strung with potholes in the front and spent .22 shell casings in the back, a grim reminder of its years as a no-frills dog pound, when being homeless did not get you a hot meal and a supportive Unitarian blessing but a one-size-fits-all choke collar, a walk out into the weeds, and a bullet to the head.

On the inside, though, through those smudged and crooked doors life trudged on. Up until I met Beale, the only love I can remember came from my grandma Lucy, and then from Miss Mo, a retired Walmart cashier and street preacher from outside Atlanta who'd turned foster parent and mission volunteer, a short, stout, shelf-bosomed lady with kind eyes, generous hands, and a voice that made my name sing like a hymn.

She would smile when she saw me and ask how I was doing, like she really cared, like she was so happy to see me again that she would hold up the whole line just to hear, and while I squirmed and blushed and stammered an answer, she would wink and slip an extra pancake or scoop of mac 'n' cheese onto my plate.

One morning, when a junkie in line started freaking out over some invisible torment and using his bony elbows like javelins, Miss Mo leaned right over a steaming vat of home fries and talked him down before he could do more than bruise me, catching him up in a safety net of comfort words and soothing him the way you would a panicked dog.

"Lord have mercy, that boy needs more than this place can give him," Miss Mo said, after he finally calmed down and reeled off. "How you doing, honey? Did he hurt you?"

"No," I said, rubbing the tender spot on my shoulder where his elbow had hit the hardest. My knees were still shaking, but that would pass. It had before. "I'm okay."

She gave me a disbelieving look and glanced across the dining room to where my mother was hunkered down at a back table shoveling in her breakfast, oblivious. "Someday that woman's gonna look up and see what she's got," she said, as if to herself. "And, Lord, I just pray it isn't too late. You hang in there, Sayre. Sometimes the hardest people to love are the ones who need it the most." She handed me a plate heaped with scrambled eggs and Tater Tots, winked, and became my benevolent Miss Mo again, seeing promise everywhere, and nourishing the world one plate at a time with a faith that never seemed to waver.

She nodded and I nodded back, as though we had reached some profound agreement, and I took my tray and wove through the hot, crowded room to a seat near my mother who, jamming the last bit of toast in her mouth, leaned around the frail old wino trembling between us and with crumbs clinging to her lips, said, "Why the fuck does it always take you so goddamned long to eat?"

So maybe Miss Mo knew what she was talking about, but maybe she didn't because she was murdered that night, ambushed in the carport right outside her house, punched, kicked, and stabbed in the stomach with a bone-handled skinning knife, then left on the dirt to die by her daughter's psycho ex-boyfriend Harlow Maltese, who was off his meds, blind, raging drunk, and blaming her for their breakup.

He was arrested staggering down the side of Route 40 with the knife in his belt and her blood under his fingernails. He spent the next five years up at the county mental hospital, and then went on to a local halfway house because the Maltese clan, trouble though they were, had lived in Dug County since the Civil War, and around here deep roots, no matter how diseased, still counted for something.

When he got out he started working construction and drinking again, got laid off, and claimed a bar stool down at the Colonial Pub, where he met my mother. The town of Sullivan had twenty-eight hundred residents in it then, too big to know everyone but still small enough for word of Harlow's return to get around, and most people crossed the street when they saw him coming. My mother had never spoken to Harlow before but she knew him by sight, knew exactly what he'd done, and still she smiled, sat down next to him, and said that first hello. Still she took him back to Candy's cabin to party, the hard gleam in her eyes daring me to protest, to make a scene over the side she'd chosen, but I was almost sixteen by then, my face trained to the shape of an indifferent mask, and so all I said when my mother introduced him, while my stomach roiled and cold sweat broke out along my hairline, was, "Well, if it wasn't for him, you never would have met Beale."

That twisted truth had haunted me for years but I hadn't known I was going to say it until it came out. The shock was mutual but the instantaneous rage at my speaking that forbidden name was hers, so the slap I got across the face, then her whirling and dragging him back out into the night was not unexpected.

"Could you be any fucking stupider?" Candy said, casting me a scornful look, grabbing her car keys, and following them.

I didn't care: I'd chosen my side, too. I'd loved Miss Mo, her kindness, her strong, safe hugs and generous smiles, and so the tears in my eyes were not from the lingering sting of the slap but instead, from the small triumph of the stand.

Chapter 5

I wait until Dozer's barking fades and the quad's taillights disappear into the trees, then bury my gloved hands in my pockets and start walking along the main road carved into the base of the mountain. There are no streetlights or sidewalks, only woods; a craggy, stone wall of mountain rising up on one side; and sporadic guardrails and plunging banks covered with pine trees and mounds of briars on the other.

The wind is at my back, pushing me forward into a long, two-lane tunnel of darkness. The snow crunches under my feet. The strap on the canvas bag digs into me. There's a blind curve up ahead and I don't want to get caught in the middle of it, so I glance over my shoulder, see a pair of headlights cresting the hill a ways back, and walk faster.

Candy says my mother wants to see me, but that's a lie. My mother has never been able to stand the sight of me, hates that she was stupid and careless and got caught, that my father was just some anonymous out-of-state guy staying at a friend-of-a-friend's hunting cabin for the weekend with a bunch of other guys who came up to party and maybe kill something. Well, he didn't get the deer he'd been hoping for but he did get the party, and I'm a daily reminder that he left one tipsy, fifteen-year-old local girl named Dianne with something to remember him by, and then disappeared into the Monday morning sunrise without a backward glance.

I don't know where my last name, Bellavia, came from—it's one of the million topics my mother won't talk about—but Sal Marinelli, the old guy down at the pizza place in town, says that where he comes from, *bella via* means "beautiful way" in Italian, and it's obvious just by looking at me that it's so.

I think Sal had better get his eyes checked.

My mother was beautiful before she got so screwed up, and I know I don't look anything like her. I take after my father, I guess, or at least have the same dark brown hair and eyes that my mother seems to remember him having, but she never made that sound like a beautiful thing, only a regrettable one. Plus, I'm tall and pretty strong from walking everywhere and carrying heavy bus trays, so I look capable, I guess, and not like I need to be taken care of.

And I think it's pretty telling that when I was born, my mother didn't give me her last name. She could have, seeing as how she was Big Joyner and Lucy Huff's only child and sole hope of passing it on to the next generation, and from what I hear Huff used to carry some very respectable weight in Dug County.

Well, until my mother did everything she could to destroy that.

I stop and glance behind me, eyes watering in the wind. The first set of headlights has been joined by a second set about a quarter mile behind them. Great. I've already started into the blind curve and there's no shoulder on this side of the road. If the first car swings wide, not even flattening myself against the side of the mountain will help. But if I cross the road then they won't know I need a ride, and will blow on past.

I think I'd better stay right where I am. Any farther into the curve and they won't see me until they're right on top of me.

I stamp my feet, trying to get some feeling back into them.

I wish my coat was red instead of black and had a hood, but this was the only one the mission had left that fit me.

The headlights grow closer, illuminating me.

Shivering, I stick out my thumb.

Brake lights flare and the vehicle—an SUV—slows.

God, I hope it's only one person. A woman would be best but they don't usually stop for hitchhikers at almost three in the morning. Unless they're the do-gooder type, who want to save me from being just another unidentified broken body pitched out and left on the side of the road. That would work.

The SUV pulls wide of me, straddling the centerline, and the passenger window goes down. A rush of raucous music and hot air sour with smoke and alcohol hits me, and a middle-aged guy with a beard sticks his head out and grins. "Need a ride?"

Shit. There are four guys in the car, and there's no way they're going to work down at the factory. More likely they just got kicked out of the Corner Tavern after last call. Shit.

"Come on, we'll take you anywhere you want to go," the driver calls, his voice thick with laughter. "Hell, I might even have enough fuel left in this old tank to take you all the way around the world."

The backseat explodes in rowdy hilarity.

Okay, yeah, no. "Thanks anyway, but here comes my ride," I say, glancing back at the next car coming and stepping away from the passenger door. I want them to leave, and fast, so this next car still half a mile back will stop.

"That ain't your ride, that's Mike and his girlfriend following us home," the passenger says, then hawks and spits into the snow. "You better jump in before you freeze your pretty little ass off." He turns to the backseat. "Make some room for her, will you?" He laughs. "There ain't no room on your lap, Charley. Your belly's too fat."

And now there's a third car, way back at the hill but moving fast.

"No, my ride's coming, I can see it," I say, shaking my head and pointing past the second car, which is slowing behind the SUV. "Thanks anyway." I shove my hands in my pockets and start trudging up the curve just to get away. I would cross the road but that looks like I'm scared and that's definitely not the message I want to send. I keep walking, walking, walking, shoulders hunched and heart pounding, until finally the SUV revs and blows past me, shortly followed by the second car. I keep my head down, watching from under my hair as their taillights round the bend and disappear, then I stop and let out a shaky exhale.

That could have been bad.

My mother used to hitchhike everywhere, sometimes with me trailing along, and it had gotten us into some iffy situations, the kind where the guy driving the truck pulls over into the woods or a field and my mother tells me to get out and go sit on the bumper until she calls me. I didn't know what that was about and I would go stand by the back of the truck, memorizing the license plate, writing my name in the dirt with my shoe, crouching and studying ants, coughing at the smelly exhaust clouding out of the tailpipe. Once, they even forgot I was back there, I guess, because after twenty long minutes of waiting they started to drive away and I had to yell and wave my arms and run after them just to get them to stop.

I used to wonder what would have happened if I hadn't shouted, and just let them leave. Would my mother have remembered me and come back, or would she have stayed silent and just kept going? And what if Beale had been driving by and found me sitting on a bank of violets near the road and crying? He would have stopped for me, I'm sure, and taken me back to his farm where Aunt Loretta would have washed my face and brushed my hair and fed me cookies and milk, and tried to find out my name.

But I wouldn't have told them. I would have said I was an orphan and been so good they would have stopped asking questions and just kept me.

My whole life would have been different, not just one beautiful year of it.

I would have been warm and fed and wanted. There would have been supper on the table and my own bed in my own room. Aunt Loretta would have helped me with my homework and I would have helped her cook and feed the chickens and pick the raspberries and sell the pumpkins. I would have made every one of those barn kittens my own, played in the pond, washed my hair, showered and brushed my teeth every morning, waited for the school bus and watched the swallows soar to greet the day.

I would never have been dirty and smelly and wearing outgrown clothes that were so tight they chafed my armpits and rode up my butt. I would never have been one of the poor kids on the free school lunch program, and would never have had to beg the school nurse for tampons because I didn't have any money to get them. I wouldn't have stolen used bras from the Salvation Army bins, leftover food from the grocery store Dumpster, bedded down in the backseats of cars, or watched my mother sell every single thing we ever had that was worth something.

I glance up into the snow-swirled darkness to where Beale sleeps.

I would have had a father, sort of, and another grandmother, sort of.

Just no mother.

And no baby sister.

My chest tightens.

I can never see Beale again. My mother has made sure of that.

I pick up my pace, walking faster because all this time the low rumble that's been humming in the background is louder now, much louder, and that's the third car coming and somehow I ended up smack in the worst part of the blind curve. I glance back and see its headlights sweeping round, hear the engine roaring like this guy's in a hurry, and all of a sudden I know I'm in the wrong place and there's nowhere to go, I can see by the headlights' path that he's swinging wide and there is no shoulder here so I step out into the road to try and run across even though that means I won't get the ride. I try to do it fast but I'm cold and clumsy and the canvas bag is heavy, and I'm only three steps into the lane when the pickup comes barreling into sight. The headlights blind me and my heart surges so hard I gasp with the pain of it and stop dead, knowing a terror so great it freezes the night with hard crystal brilliance.

And then the headlights veer away and the truck whips by and it's blue, a blue truck with spinning tires that spray wide arcs of snow as it skids past. The headlights flash over me one last time then fly up into the bare-limbed trees as it pitches backward over the bank.

Chapter 6

The sound of impact stuns me, the shrieking and squealing of crashing metal, and the final loud, dull *whumpf*. From somewhere over the bank a tree branch cracks, sharp like a gunshot,
snapping me out of my paralysis.

I start across the road, shaking so bad each step takes too long,
looking both ways before I cross the centerline, which is crazy and
stupid but I do it anyway. The wind is easing and the snow lessening, but the flakes are bigger and wetter and fatter. There's a weird
sound carried on the wind, a low, ugly noise that makes the hair at
the back of my neck prickle and the closer I get to the bank, the
louder it is.

Someone is moaning.

I follow the tires' tracks to the edge, and peer over.

I see the headlights first, about thirty feet down the bank. The
truck is there, rammed sideways into two pine trees that have
stopped it before it fell too far. The driver's window is shattered, all
spiderwebbed glass, and a big branch has fallen on the hood.

Something moves inside the cab, against the shattered glass.

A guy's face, pale and smeared with blood.

My knees go weak, and sudden, shimmering silver speckles float
in front of my eyes. Help. I have to get help. I take a deep breath,
then another. The faintness recedes. I turn, take three steps into the
road and stop. Help from who, Harlow? He's the closest one on

this stretch of the road but he's at least two miles away and doesn't even have a phone and by the time I got there . . .

"Oh God, help," I say, frantically looking around for another set of headlights but the road stays dark. I step closer, scared to go right to the edge. Clear my throat and call, "Are you all right?"

Silence, and then a weak, "No," from the truck.

"Is it only you? Are you alone?"

"Yeah."

"Can you climb out of the truck and come up here?"

"No." Silence. "My head's bleeding and my knee is . . . ow, *God*."

"Do you have a cell phone?" I call, crouching and wringing my hands.

Silence.

"*Do you have a cell?*" I shout, standing right back up.

"Jesus, you don't have to yell," he says, slurring his words. "Yeah, somewhere."

"Is it in the truck? Can you see it?" I ask and when he doesn't answer, I slip the canvas bag and my purse from my shoulder, wishing they were any color but black and setting them at the spot where the skidding tire tracks barrel over the edge. Dug County is teeming with hunters keen on following signs, and I'm praying the next car by is one of them. "Okay, listen. I'm coming down. We have to find your phone."

No answer.

Great. I take one last look around and lift my foot to step over the edge of the bank. Then stop. The ground is an unforgiving slope, and thanks to the snow, the only place where I can actually see what I'm stepping on are the tire tracks. There's little to hold on to, a sapling here and a clump of briars there. What if I lose my balance and fall? What if I get there and he's already dead? Or dying? What do I do if he's dying?

I don't know, I don't know.

Paralysis sweeps in, anchoring me in place.

I can't do this.

I can't watch someone die. Not again.

The shimmering faintness is back.

I can hear myself breathing.

I shouldn't go down there. I should just stay here and wait for someone to come . . .

Stupid. No one ever comes.

I put my hands to my face. Cover my eyes.

It doesn't stop the panic.

What if I get down there and then a car goes by up here but doesn't see the tracks in the snow or my bags? Then we lose our only chance at help.

So stay here and wait for help.

No, go down there and do something.

I take another deep breath. Pat my arm until the panic recedes.

There has to be a way. There has to be.

I scramble back to the bags and brush the snow off of them. Unzip the tote and rummage for the ruby blazer. It's not a bright red but it's better than black, an eye-catcher in a landscape of nothing but white and brown and gray. I tie the arms of the blazer through the tote's straps. Nickel-size snowflakes settle on the velvet, snowflakes that look a lot like fragile, lacy flowers.

"Some people think Queen Anne's lace is nothing but a weed," Aunt Loretta says, walking me along the field's edge, careful to watch for snakes, "a waste plant not fit for a flower garden, but don't you believe them. That kind of shortsightedness will stop you from ever appreciating any of life's ordinary beauty, and that would be a shame, Sayre, because Mother Nature does not make junk." She pauses, the breeze blowing her short, silver hair from her forehead, and cups one of the fluffy white umbrella-like flowers in her palm. "Queen Anne's lace may look delicate but it has a tough stem, strong roots, and the ability to not only survive but to thrive in even the meanest environment. That may not sound impressive, Sayre, but trust me, those things count for something. . . ."

All right. All right. Get a grip.

You have to *do* something.

I rise and look around.

I wish I knew what time it was. If it's still not three then maybe waiting up here on the road for someone to come by on their way to the factory would be better than disappearing down the slope, but if it's already past three, then the odds of anyone coming by are—

The guy in the truck groans.

"I'm coming," I call, although I have no idea what I'm going to do once I get there. Steeling myself, I set one foot down sideways over the bank. There's no real foothold, I can tell, nothing to stop me from rolling all the way down.

I sit, hang my legs over the edge, and start down on my butt. The ground is frozen and unyielding but every time I slip I somehow dig my heels into a rut and stop before I end up out of control. A handful of firmly anchored sticker bushes stop me once, a rock to brace against a second time. There is no sound but my own ragged breathing.

"Jesus," I mutter, glancing at the truck. The grille is hanging off, the hood buckled, and the smear on the window is awful, a deep, crimson-black stain across a sheet of crackled glass.

Beyond it, a pale face is streaked with brighter blood. Two dark, glazed eyes watch me from under a swatch of wet, matted hair.

"Almost there," I call again in a voice high with false cheer. "Just hang on, okay?"

He blinks and nods slightly. Winces and closes his eyes.

"Don't fall asleep," I say because the one thing I know is that people with concussions shouldn't be allowed to go to sleep.

He nods again, just a little, but doesn't open his eyes.

"Hey!" I snap. "Did you hear me? You can't fall asleep!"

He groans and his eyes flutter open. "You yell a lot." His voice is slurred and muffled behind the shattered glass. "I'm cold."

"I know it's cold, but I'm almost there," I say, which doesn't make any sense but it doesn't seem to matter because he nods again, and lifts a bloody, swollen hand to his face. Two of his fingers hang mangled and crooked off the side.

"Shit!" he blurts, jerking back in shock when he sees them. "Oh God, that's bad. Gross. I can't move them. God, that hurts. How the hell . . . I can't even . . ." He gazes at me, stricken. "Don't leave me here."

"I won't. I swear." I let go of the sticker bush I've been holding on to and slide a few more feet down the bank, bruising my tailbone on a rock and filling my jeans' legs with snow that burns my bare skin. "Almost there."

And then a dull rumble surges and stops, the side of his truck lights up, and a car door slams somewhere above and behind me.

I turn, heart racing, and stare up the bank.

A figure steps into the light.

"Help," I croak, and then louder, "Help!"

"Sayre?"

It's Candy.

Chapter 7

"Oh, my God, Candy, yeah, it's me," I cry, jumping up and waving, slipping and falling back into a crouch to hold my balance.

"What the hell is going on? Are you all right?"

"I'm fine," I call, swiping a shaky hand across my eyes. "Can you—"

"What happened?" She hunkers low at the edge of the bank, a squat, misshapen silhouette in the headlights, and stares down at me. Her face looks sunken, her pale eyes rimmed with shadows, and her thin, scraggly hair whips wild in the wind. "Well?"

"I was walking and he swerved not to hit me and went off the road."

"Is he alive?" she asks.

"Yeah, but his head's bleeding and he hurt his knee—"

"I know that truck. That's Ben Greenwood's boy Evan," she says, rising again. "He'll be all right. That whole family has hard heads. Now, come on up here. We'll send the ambulance back for him when we get to the hospital. Hurry."

I stare at her, certain I haven't heard right. "What?"

"Your mother was conscious again for a little while, and I told her I'd find you and bring you back with me," she says impatiently. "She wants to talk to you. Now, come on. You can try to call EMS as we drive, if there's any friggin' service out in these goddamn boondocks."

I blink. Look over at the truck, at those dark, scared, pleading eyes and then back up at Candy. "We can't just leave him here."

"Can he walk?"

I look back at the truck. The guy—Evan—tries to sit up higher in the seat. He groans and a single tear rolls down his cheek, cutting a bright, fresh path in the drying blood.

"No," I say. "Not by himself but maybe if we both—"

She exhales, harsh and impatient. "If he's hurt that bad, moving him will only make it worse. There's nothing you can do. He has to wait for the ambulance and the sooner you get up here, the sooner we can call them." She pulls her cell from her jacket, studies it, and shakes her head. "Nope, no service. Now come on."

"But I promised I wouldn't leave him," I say.

"Jesus Christ, I don't need this," Candy mutters, clenching her jaw and staring off down the road. "Look, your mother's in a bad way so I'm not real concerned about *him* right now, okay? As soon as we get to the hospital we'll send the—"

"Candy, I can't just—"

"Goddamnit, Sayre. Get your ass up here *now*."

"I will, I promise, but he has to come, too," I say, voice shaking. "If you would just come down here and help me get him out of the truck—"

"No!" she yells. "I'll leave you both here, I swear to God I will, because if you think I'm gonna let my best friend die alone in that goddamn hospital just because her asshole daughter thinks I should climb down a cliff and maybe kill myself just to rescue another little asshole who was probably driving too fast and—"

"Please," I say, wringing my hands. "Please come down here and help me."

"Oh, for . . . I'm telling you, he'll be *fine*," she shouts.

"No he *won't*!" I scream, losing it. "He's hurt and bleeding and if he hadn't gone off the road he would have hit *me* instead, do you get that, and I'm not just going to leave him here!"

Silence.

"Fine. It's your funeral." Candy shrugs, steps back, and suddenly my canvas bag and purse go flying past me down the bank and hit the side of the truck.

"Hey!" I shout, and scramble the rest of the way down the hill to snatch the blazer out of the dirty, torn-up snow. "What the hell? I—"

She turns and disappears.

The car door slams.

The engine revs.

The headlights veer off, brighten the road, and soar away into the distance.

I turn in disbelief, and meet Evan's stunned gaze. "Oh my God. She left us here. She drove away and *left* us here!" I pace a few steps, knuckling my forehead, and stop, finally noticing Evan worrying his bloody bottom lip. "I don't believe it."

"Uh . . . do you think she'll call someone?"

Yes. No. "I don't know. I hope so." I take a deep, steadying breath because if I don't stay calm, it's all over. Look at my bags lying in the snow, at the rumpled blazer in my arms. "I better go put this stuff back up there on the road, just in case. Maybe somebody else will come by and see it." I bend and lift the canvas tote, feeling a hundred years old. "I'll be back."

"I'll be here," he says and another tear slips down his cheek. "Sorry."

"Me, too," I say, and start slowly back up the hill.

How I Came to Know Candy

My grandmother Lucy Huff was a gentle, wounded woman of reminiscence and routine who found pleasure looking backward rather than forward, and every night when the supper dishes were done and she was tucked into the corner of the couch with an afghan across her lap, Cricket, the old blue parakeet dozing behind her in his cage, and her second glass of coffee brandy almost empty, she would lean back, her gaze distant, and begin with something like *You know, Sayre, where's there's life, there's hope* or *I was taught never to hate the person, only the behavior* or *Every family needs a peacemaker, someone who will sacrifice their needs for the good of the others . . .*

With that said, she would then launch into any one of a hundred martyred tales of past trials, punctuating each with a sigh and a satisfied *But I never gave up. I kept trying, and it always worked out.*

When she got to the one about how my late grandfather Big Joyner Huff had betrayed her with upward of four local ladies, always adding *And I use the term* lady *very loosely,* and him returning to her afterward, shamefaced and bearing bejeweled gifts, hat in hand and humbly asking to be taken back, she would tease the ever-present tissue out of her sleeve, dab at the corners of her damp eyes, and say *What else could I do? He was a big man with big appetites, he was used to getting his own way, and I loved him. He always promised he'd never be unfaithful again and I always believed him. And besides, where would I have gone and what would I have done? He was my whole world. No, for better or for worse my place was with him.*

She said that once in front of Mailey Biggs, one of her old school friends come back to Sullivan for a visit, and Mailey gave her an incredulous look over the rim of her teacup and said, "No offense, Lucy, but for better or for worse did NOT mean better for him and worse for you."

My grandmother goggled at her.

Mailey Biggs sighed and said, "Not to speak ill of the dead but take off those rosy glasses for a minute, will you? I mean, you're talking to *me*. That man was a dog, pure and simple, and he didn't care who he hurt as long as he got what he wanted. Hell, he came on to *me* that night I babysat Dianne while you two went to that Christmas ball over in Hamlin. Remember how he dropped you off at home and came alone to pick her up? I hustled him out the door, of course, because you were my friend, but there were others I know who didn't." She shook her head and set her cup down on the table. "He was a selfish man, Lucy, and from what I've been hearing, the apple hasn't fallen far from the tree." She sniffed. "*Di*-anne dumping her child on you and running around wild with that no-good Fee girl, getting into nothing but trouble."

I perked up at this because Dianne was my mother, and Candy the Fee girl.

"She's what, twenty-two now? That's not a child anymore, Lucy. That's old enough to know better. She should be working steady and making a life for her daughter." She sent a vague wave in my direction. "It's a crying shame, because Dianne was a good baby before Joyner went and spoiled her. *Anything for my little princess.* Remember him saying that? She could do no wrong in his eyes, not even when she *was* wrong. He let that child get away with murder, and my God, the way she talked to you." Mailey clucked her tongue. "If my Annie had ever shown me such disrespect, her father would have grounded her for a month. But not Big Joyner. He made every excuse for her and threw you right under the bus at the same time. Shameful."

"He was a good father," my grandmother said faintly. "He was very generous."

"Guilt money," Mailey Biggs said with a snort. "Lord have mercy, how many times did you call me up crying while the princess was pitching a hell-on-wheels tantrum because her daddy had promised he'd be home to help her with her homework or take her shopping and instead he'd stay out till all hours drinking and whoring around and leaving you to make up some lame excuse for him?"

"Well, they were very close," my grandmother said, fiddling with the cuff of her blouse. "Naturally she was disappointed."

"Disappointed enough to give you a black eye?" Mailey said with a shrewd look.

"That was an accident. She just didn't like to be controlled," my grandmother said, and catching sight of Mailey's raised eyebrows, said in a rush, "I don't know why you're dredging up all this unpleasantness now. Joyner is gone, God rest his soul, and I will miss him until the day I die, and I would appreciate you not coming in here and stirring up the past. He was a good husband and father, and that's the way I prefer to remember him."

Mailey Biggs studied my grandmother's flushed face for a moment. "All right, Luce. If that's how you need to remember it, then have it your way."

I was seven when Mailey Biggs said that, not old enough to understand everything but old enough to remember most of her words and my grandmother's stiffly polite reaction, which was to rise, pick up both teacups, and thank her for stopping by.

And so Grandma Lucy's stories continued, but after Mailey Biggs's visit she started drinking *three* glasses of coffee brandy and even darker tales would surface, snatches of memories dragged from the shadows about a daughter who was moody, critical, and impatient, whose assessing gaze often made her uncomfortable, and who, despite her best efforts, she just couldn't get close to.

"She would run to her daddy for everything, like she had no use for me at all," Grandma Lucy said, idly swirling the brandy around in the mug. "I was sitting at the kitchen table once, crying after an argument with Big Joyner over . . . well, over one of his lady friends. Do you know, she'd had the gall to show up at my front door with a tie pin he'd left at her house—a tie pin *I* had given him for his last birthday—and I told her to leave my husband alone or I would call the sheriff and have her arrested for harassment. Well, she must have run right back and told him, because he got furious with me and we argued and he walked out. Probably hurried right back to her, too."

Cricket, the parakeet, pecked at the little blue bell in his cage, making me jump, but Grandma Lucy didn't even seem to hear it.

"My goodness, I'll never forget this," she continued, her gaze dark and distant. "Dianne must have been listening the whole time because once Joyner left, she came right into the kitchen and gave me this awful look of disgust—she was fourteen then, and filled with nothing but scorn for me anyway—and said, *You do it to your-self, you know. He's never gonna stop because he doesn't have to. Don't you get it? He has all the power. He* knows *he can do anything to you, and all you'll do is sit there and cry, boo hoo hoo, and then take him back anyway. God, you're so stupid, Mom. Why won't you see? You love Daddy more than he loves you, it's that fucking simple, and that makes you the weaker one.*" Grandma Lucy's voice was trembling. "And then she shook her head, hard, and put up her hands as if to block the sight of me and said, *You know, I can't even stand to look at you sometimes. I swear to God I would rather die than be like you.* And then *she* walked out, and didn't come home that night. Later, when Big Joyner got back, he was angry with me for letting her go." She sighed. "It was a very difficult time."

She went on about my mother, a child who'd never cared if she hurt people, blamed others for her bad choices, blossomed early, and disregarded every rule. A girl who was chased by many a boy, came home drunk for the first time at thirteen, caught in school with coke at fourteen, suspended, immediately reinstated and the record expunged thanks to her father's intervention.

"I told him she should have to take her punishment, but he wouldn't stand for it," my grandmother said, slumped on the couch and staring at the last of the brandy in her glass. "He was furious at me for even suggesting it. He said Dianne swore the cocaine wasn't hers, she was just holding it for someone and that she was going to college when she graduated and he would be damned if she had to carry around any kind of black mark on her record and blah blah blah . . ." She waved a drunken hand. "She was right there listening the whole time, of course, looking like butter wouldn't melt in her mouth, but I knew the truth." She struggled to sit up and pointed a finger at me. "People think Joyner was so smart, but he wasn't. Not when it came to his daughter. Mailey was right about that. Dianne was never held accountable for anything. People thought I let her have her way, but let me tell you, there was no *let* involved. Her father was the only one she'd listen to, and even then, only when it suited her."

I glanced at the framed school picture of my mother sitting on the other end table. It was her sophomore year photo, the last one taken before she'd had me and dropped out. Her hair was cut short, bleached white-blond, and she was peering out from under heavy lids, blue eyes gleaming like she knew far more than she was telling. She looked wicked, disturbing, and beautiful.

"She would make her helpless-little-girl face and do her "Oh, Daddy," snuggly routine and he would fall for it every time. Stupid man. He always got her out of trouble, and between you and me," Grandma Lucy's voice grew hushed, "I think it ruined her. I do. She's a bully and a liar. Even her guidance counselor at school said she had an antisocial personality because she just didn't care about anybody but herself." She nodded at me, grave and owl eyed. "Of course I didn't dare mention that to Joyner, as he would have stormed down to that school and raised holy hell, and gotten the counselor fired for even suggesting his daughter was flawed, but I believe that counselor was right. Oh yes, I do."

I stared at my late grandfather's posed, studio portrait hanging above the mantel. His face was florid, his chin high, and his chest puffed out. He looked like a rooster.

"Dianne always said I was so stupid and weak but I'm not the one who screwed up my life, am I? No, not me. Not good old pitiful, stupid Mom. No sir." She nodded at me, smug. "I kept trying, and I made it. She hasn't made anything except a baby and a mess. So who's the smart one now?"

I lived with my grandmother until she died when I was almost eight, and these tipsy, rambling monologues were pretty much how I learned about my family history.

Well, and eavesdropping on my mother and Candy.

Pieced together, I learned that before my mother turned fifteen and went to the hunting cabin where I was conceived, before five months later when she and Candy shoplifted the pregnancy test from Dell's Drugs to confirm the cause of her increasingly rounded belly, before I went on to be born and ruin her life forever, my mother, Dianne, was a surprise late-in-life baby, a difficult, pampered only child with a successful future all mapped out. She was a pretty, possessive, strong-willed daddy's girl who loved her big, burly, indulgent father deeply, and her passive, long-suffering mother in a scornful and irritated three's-a-crowd kind of way.

This might not have become such a problem had Big Joyner Huff been able to stand alongside his wife and say no to his daughter, then stick to his word through the resulting teary eyes and trembling bottom lip, the pouting and pleading, and finally the cold, accusing stares, icy silences, and her ability to make life miserable for everyone involved.

But he couldn't, so thanks to my grandfather's inflated ego, guilt, deep wallet, and reluctance to be seen as anything but a benevolent god in his daughter's eyes, he became putty in her hands.

Until the night she brought Candy home with her as an insurance policy of sorts, to guard against her parents totally freaking when she told them she was seven months' pregnant.

Now, there are three different versions of this story—my grandmother's, my mother's, and Candy's—but all three are alike in one aspect: that the next morning my mother found Big Joyner still sitting in the exact same leather chair they had left him in the night before, his Johnnie Walker black still in the glass, his bottle of heart pills on the floor next to him, and dead.

I had no chance of welcome after this tragedy, and according to Candy, who is chronically ignorant and enjoys telling this part of the story way too much, it's a miracle I wasn't born deformed by my mother's grief, with fetal alcohol syndrome or whatever degree of messed-upedness came from recklessly hard, nonstop partying, the kind that's vodka and beer and coke and meth, spoons and needless and pipes. The kind of partying that left my mother numb so she wouldn't have to think, wouldn't have to feel, wouldn't have to remember that the last thing she'd shouted at her stunned and devastated father before storming up to her room with Candy in tow was, *You're such a fucking hypocrite! So I screwed around and got caught. So what? I learned it from YOU.*

It didn't matter that the autopsy revealed time had run out naturally for Big Joyner's fatty, enlarged heart, and his last five months had been nothing but borrowed time anyway. It didn't matter that he'd kept the condition a secret from everyone so as not to be treated like an invalid, and disregarded most of his doctor's dietary orders.

Nothing mattered but that he was dead.

My mother was stoned for the wake, and didn't make the funeral.

And according to their stories, during labor my mother had screamed and sworn and said all kinds of terrible things including,

I hate this fucking thing! Get it out of me! while Candy was right there in the delivery room holding her hand, gagging, and going, *Okay, that's really gross* as the sight of me crowning made her throw up all over her own feet.

I learned that my mother breast-fed me for three days, then said the hell with it, turned me over to Grandma Lucy and a bottle, quit school, and left with Candy, and that my grandmother, drowning in grief and with an unwanted infant to take care of, didn't even try to stop her. I learned that my incredible disappearing father had no name other than That Asshole, and when the infamous hunting cabin was finally sold to new out-of-towners, my mother shrugged and said, *I should have burned that friggin' place down a long time ago*.

For seven years I lived a stable, routine existence in the blue house in town with Grandma Lucy, her memories, melancholy sighs and absentminded affection, her Michael Bublé CDs, ambrosia salad, and *Wheel of Fortune*. I had clothes, food, a bedtime ritual, Sunday school and a few friends, Halloween costumes and Easter baskets, a bookshelf in my room, winter boots and a chair at the kitchen table. The blue house was my home, and Grandma the woman waiting there for me, and I guess I could have loved her like a mother had it not been for the occasional whirlwind visits from Dianne, my real mother, the intense, unpredictable, dangerous, and exotic teen with the fast temper, smoker's breath, kohl-rimmed eyes, and backroom broken-heart-in-barbed-wire tramp stamp, the girl who showed up unannounced and destroyed our peace, rummaged through Grandma's purse for money, and strode around like she owned the place.

At first her visits unsettled me, left me nervous, angry, and strangely excited, but after a while, on those few occasions when she swept me up and sat me on her lap, left sticky, strawberry-scented lip gloss kisses on my face and fruity alcohol exhales in my nostrils, there was a stirring in my heart that made me brave and full of longing, made me plant shy kisses on her cheek, wind my arms around her neck, and bury my face in her shaggy, dyed-black hair, wanting to stay that way forever.

But the moment I gave in and clung she would withdraw and disentangle me, ignoring my cries to stay, tugging free of my stubbornly entwined arms, sometimes with the help of Candy, who didn't care if the jagged edges of her bad French tips scratched my skin or her cheap bracelets caught in my hair, and finally, impatiently, telling me to stop being so fucking needy and shoving me back at my grandmother.

I'd be upset for days after she left, having stomachaches, snapping at Grandma, bursting into tears for no apparent reason. I wanted my mother, then I didn't, then I did again. As I got older, I couldn't understand why I didn't see her more, why she didn't live with me like other mothers did with their kids, why I couldn't be with her.

When I asked that question on one of Grandma's good days, she would say something like, "Because she can't take care of you right now, Sayre, and besides, I would be so lonely if you weren't here. You don't want Grandma to be lonely, do you?"

On her dark days, when she was sunk in the murk of too much bitterness and coffee brandy, the answer would be more like, "If being here is so bad, then sure, go ahead, go pack your things and live with your mother. Make her take care of her responsibilities. See how she likes it. By all means, go ahead and go." And when, hesitant, I said, "But I don't know where she lives," my grandmother gave a rude snort and said, "Well, that makes two of us, so I guess you'll just have to stay here until she decides to come for you, and I don't see that happening anytime soon. Do you?"

The truth was no, because only three times did my mother and Candy—always Candy, too—ever come and take me away with them for the weekend.

Three times, in seven years.

I shouldn't have remembered that first time, given that I was not yet three, but I did remember parts of it, vividly. Grandma Lucy added to the story later, and at some point I heard my mother and Candy reminiscing, but there were fragments of that day that nobody knew but me.

My mother and Candy had hooked up with a couple of older guys, and thanks to good weather, a little gas money, and the rush of some kick-ass meth, they decided to head down to the Jersey shore. I don't know why my mother thought I should come along. Maybe she felt it was time to show me off, or maybe she wanted the guy she was seeing to realize what a great little family the three of us could be.

I remember crying at being pulled away from Grandma Lucy, and being wedged in the backseat between Candy and the second guy, who stunk of garlic. I remember Candy feeding me soapy-tasting beer to shut me up, and later waking up alone on a blanket in the sand, terrified by the roaring ocean and the seagulls swooping over my head, being hungry, thirsty, and nauseous, sweating and screaming and getting sand in my mouth and in my eyes, pushing myself up and toddling off into the crowd.

I remember the Asian lady in the green one-piece bathing suit who was sitting on the next blanket picking me up and taking me to the lifeguard, who finally called the police when no one came frantically searching for me. I remember an EMS guy with a ponytail and glasses checking me out for heatstroke, the cool water he gave me, the lotion he smoothed on my scorched skin.

Somebody must have given the police descriptions of my mother and Candy and the guys because the police tracked them down in a bar off the boardwalk and arrested the guys for the remaining meth.

I remember how my grandmother, who'd had to drive all the way to that police station for me and my mother and Candy, got a stern, embarrassing lecture from the cops because my mother was underage, drunk, and carrying a pretty convincing fake ID.

I remember my grandmother taking one look at me, then whirling and slapping my mother right across the face and shouting,

Look at this baby! How could you be so irresponsible? and my mother, cheek red and eyes crazy, screaming, *Don't you EVER touch me! I wish Daddy was here! I wish he was alive and you were dead!*

I remember the policewoman grabbing her arm and Candy taking the other one, and whispering something in her ear, some caution that made her furious but also shut her up.

That day, the one I was supposedly too young to remember, must have left a deep imprint because I still hate shouting, am afraid of the ocean, and will do almost anything to avoid the hollow terror of being left behind.

The second time they took me out I was four and my mother was nineteen. I remember standing in line with her at McDonald's, clinging to her leg and her prying at my hands, trying to dislodge me. I remember her getting mad because I wanted a plain hamburger with no onions or ketchup, and how she got me a regular one anyway and scraped off the ketchup but it was still there and I couldn't eat it without gagging, so all I had was French fries. I remember her leading me into a dark field with a big bonfire going and people everywhere, loud, thudding music and some guy smiling, holding a beer and crouching in front of me, taking my hand and hearing my mother say, *Go ahead, Sayre, give him a kiss,* but I didn't want to because his breath stank.

I remember my mother got mad at that, too.

I remember the two of them disappearing and me not being able to find them in the sea of legs. I remember being thirsty and picking up a glass and drinking, and people laughing around me. I remember falling down and skinning my elbow and crying, and someone who smelled like burnt leaves picking me up, putting me in the back of a car, and covering me with a jacket. I remember waking up scared and disoriented, crawling out of the car and walking back to the smoldering remains of the fire where it was quiet now and Candy was on her knees in front of some guy sprawled in a camping chair.

I remember her seeing me, and me saying in a little voice, *Candy,*

I don't know where's my mother and her lifting her head, pushing her hair out of her face, and saying, *Yeah, well, I don't know, either, so why don't you go look for her?* I remember starting to cry and saying, *Could I stay with you till she comes back?* and her, sloppy drunk, smirking and saying, *Sure, watch and learn, right?* I remember hurrying over while she lowered her head again and the guy closed his eyes and I stood behind her looking at how messy the back of her hair was and patting myself on the arm the way Grandma Lucy did when I was upset. Finally I went and climbed into a lawn chair by the dying fire and patted myself to sleep.

The third time I went out with my mother and Candy I was five and my mother was twenty, and that was the Cheerios and vinegar incident.

By the time I was seven I wasn't cute enough to show off anymore and my mother wasn't as pretty. She was skinny, too skinny, and pale, and had scabby lesions on her cheeks and at the edges of her mouth. She twitched and scratched and her eyes were sunk in dark hollows. Grandma was worried and kind of afraid of her, mostly because she would show up angry and tear through the house saying things like *Where's the money, Mom? I know it's here. You're too cheap to have spent it all. Daddy wanted me to have it, now where's the goddamn money?!*

I would hide under the dining room table and Grandma would watch as my mother rifled through her jewelry box taking whatever she wanted, while Candy paced and said things like *Didn't you used to have a sapphire ring, Mrs. Huff? Yeah, Mr. Huff gave it to you after he slept with that barmaid over at the Red Fox, remember? Now where did that go?* and making everything worse.

It was then, watching Grandma cry and sit, helpless as they stole all her stuff that I hated my mother, hated her and her ugly friend with her pale, watery eyes, tiny, yellow teeth and too-wide gums, hated that she and Candy were always together, that when she smiled and laughed it was always with Candy and never with me, and that she never talked to me unless she had to.

I hated that she blew in like a bad storm, wreaked havoc, and then blew out again, leaving a trail of wreckage in her wake. And sometimes I hated Grandma, too, for not being strong enough to stop her.

When I was almost eight, Mrs. Carroll the neighbor came to school and picked me up in the middle of the day. She told me Grandma Lucy had passed away in an accident, that she had fallen down and hit her head on the cement back-porch step sometime that morning, that my mother and Candy had dropped in and found her, and that they were very upset and waiting for me at home right now.

And so my mother inherited everything, including me, and that was how we all came to live together in the old blue house.

Chapter 8

I'm cold and tired, and the bank seems steeper now and more slippery, but thanks to Candy pitching my stuff over the edge, I have to climb up it again to make another distress signal. It's slow, hard going but I finally claw my way back to the top and drag the canvas bag into place at the edge of the snowy tracks. I don't know if my ruby-blazer signal is going to work anymore because Candy's tire tracks have crisscrossed and confused the ones going over the bank, making them way less noticeable.

She'd better call someone.

She really better or I don't know what I'm going to do.

I look up and down the curving road.

No headlights, just darkness.

"Come on," I whisper, wrapping my arms around myself. "Come *on*, somebody." My fingers are numb inside Harlow's gloves and my feet feel like chunks of frozen meat. How long am I supposed to stand out here waiting?

I glance back at the truck. See the ghostly outline of Evan's face through the shattered window. I can't tell if he's watching me or has passed out, but I wave anyway.

I wait, but he doesn't wave back.

That's not good.

I'm going to have to get into that truck and see if I can find his cell phone. Fast.

I crouch and fumble the ruby blazer back through the bag's handles. Spread it out to make it more noticeable. Is this futile? I don't know.

Maybe I should have just gone with her. Candy is petty and spiteful and a little nuts. Not a good enemy to have.

She could drive all the way back to the hospital without even trying to call anyone for help, and later just say she didn't have any cell service. She would do that, too, just to show me what happens when I cross her.

Candy's a Fee, from the back mountain ridge Fees, and they'll tell you themselves that they're a really badass crew. They hate the government, the rich, minorities, foreigners, gays—well, unless they're porn star Barbie-doll lesbians—vegetarians, suits, feminists, yuppies, cops, seat belts, and speed limits. They used to run a pretty profitable still but upgraded to a meth lab that blew up and left Candy's daddy, who was fresh out of prison and still learning the trade, blinded and burned over the top half of his body.

And rearrested, and sent back to prison.

Within a month Candy's brothers had stepped into the breach and rebuilt the lab.

My mother was their first customer.

There isn't an animal in these woods the Fees haven't poached, a bar in the county they haven't fought in, and a law they haven't broken. The men breed early and often, and Candy is the lone sister in a family of thirteen mean, hardscrabble, ridge-running brothers who walk through the world with fists clenched, chips on their shoulders, and nothing to lose.

"Hey . . ."

I blink and squint down at the truck.

Evan gives a slow wave, and I notice he's wearing a watch.

"What time is it?" I call, holding up my own wrist.

He lowers his head. Shakes his wrist. "I don't know. It stopped at twenty of three."

Damn. Now I *have* to find his cell phone. "I'm coming," I call and go back down over the edge of the icy bank. I'm moving too fast and slip near the bottom, sliding the last ten feet and almost going right under the truck. Instead, my shoulders hit the front tire and I grab on, haul myself up, panting, and step closer to the shattered driver's window. "Well, that's one way of getting back down here," I mutter, brushing the snow off my jeans. "Okay, now I need to come in and look for your phone. Can you slide over to the passenger seat?"

"Uh, let me see," he says slowly, and shaking, tries to shift by bracing the hand with the broken fingers against the wheel. "Oh, shit," he groans, going white and slumping back in his seat. "No. God, this sucks."

"Can you do it without using your hand?" I say.

"It was my knee," he mumbles, eyes closed and grimacing. "I can't move it."

"All right, let me think," I say, walking around the front of the truck just to make sure what I suspect is true. Although one of the trunks looks cracked, the pine trees on the passenger side are the only things holding the truck in place. They're white pines, notorious for being soft and dropping limbs but without them he'd have careened all the way down the steep bank to the bottom of the valley. They'd saved him, but now they also make it impossible to gain access to the passenger door.

But I really need to get into that truck, first to make sure he isn't bleeding to death or anything, second to find the cell phone and pray it works, and third because I'm so cold my knees are shaking and—

"Evan," I say, walking around the driver's side to the back-cab window. "This is a slider, right? I can get in through here." Excited now, I grab the side of the truck, step up on the tire, and haul myself over into the snowy bed. Examine the sliding window. "It's locked," I say, tapping on the glass. "Can you get it?"

"Let me try." He twists slightly, reaches his good hand back and fumbles with the lock. "Okay," he gasps, slumping in his seat.

"Okay." I pull off my gloves, wedge my numb fingers in the tiny crack, and slide open the window. "Wow," I say, looking at the size of the hole. "This is gonna be a close one." I drop my gloves onto the passenger seat, then strip off my coat and stuff that through, too. Stick one leg through the gap, then the other. Next my hips, which are the tightest fit. I scrape my backbone sliding in but I'm so cold I hardly even feel it. I slide the window closed, tug my coat out from under me, and, shivering, yank it on. "Whew." Turn to look at him and find him looking at me.

"You made it," he says.

"I did," I say and feel really bad because one side of his face is normal looking, dark eyed and with a nice mouth that seems made to smile, but the other side is ravaged, bloody and swollen. The broken fingers on his hand are horrible, and there's blood soaking through the knee of his jeans. "I'm really sorry about this."

"Yeah, well . . ." He shrugs and stares out the windshield. "I just hope that lady made the call." He glances back at me. "I couldn't hear everything you guys were saying, but she wanted you to go with her, didn't she?"

I nod.

"I'm glad you didn't," he says. "Thanks."

"You're welcome." I don't know what else to say or do so I just sit there like an idiot, self-consciously rubbing my fingers to work the cold out of them and flicking my damp, snow-tangled hair from my face. The truck smells like oil, old leather, and warm pennies, which might be the scent of his blood spattered across the dashboard and the fractured driver's window.

"So uh, where were you going, anyway?" Evan says finally, breaking the silence. "I mean it's a bad night to be out walking."

This is one question I really don't want to answer. "I was,

um . . . oh, wait. I have to find your cell!" I bend and run my hands along the truck floor until I find it. "Here. Now, please let there be coverage." Avoiding his gaze, I punch in 911 and wait.

Nothing.

Hang up, do it again.

The screen says SEARCHING FOR SERVICE.

I hold my breath.

The screen says SERVICE NOT AVAILABLE.

"Oh, come on," I mutter, leaning forward, setting the phone on the dashboard and trying again. "I thought 911 was always supposed to go through on these things!"

The call does not connect.

"I can't believe this," I say, sitting back in frustration.

"I can," he says, and the good corner of his mouth twitches into a brief, wry smile.

Oh. I was right. It *is* a great half smile, and I can't help smiling back. "Stupid question, but how do you feel?"

"Like shit," he says, tilting his head back against the seat and closing his eyes. "You wouldn't happen to have an aspirin or anything, would you?"

"No," I say regretfully, thinking how bizarre it is that less than two weeks ago I had over a hundred of my mother's Vicodin in my purse and no good use for them, and now when there *is* a good use for one, I have nothing.

"Not even, like, a Midol?" he says.

"No," I say, shaking my head.

"Really? I thought all girls carried that stuff."

I shrug because what am I going to say; that Midol costs money I don't have, so I just deal with it? That I have some weird, deep-rooted horror of taking pills, any pills, even vitamins, because I don't know what's in them? That watching my mother and Candy swallow handfuls of pills and still crave more has cured me of reaching for any of it, even aspirin?

"Sorry," I say.

"It's all right, don't worry about it," he says, shifting slightly and grimacing. "I just have to remember not to move."

I study him for a moment, taking in the undamaged side of his profile, his olive green jacket with the brown leather collar, the straight, longish brown hair tucked behind his ears, and the haze of stubble on his chin. His jaw is tight and his breathing is heavy, but I think it's more from pain than anger and suddenly, it seems very important to find out if I'm right. "You know, you're being really good about this."

He glances over. "What do you mean?"

"Well, you could be all pissed off and yelling or freaking out or, like, hating me or something . . ." I shake my head and gaze out into the swirling snow. "You do have that right."

"Why? I mean don't get me wrong, I'm not happy about total-ing my truck and screwing up my knee—it hurts like a bitch—but getting all pissed off isn't gonna change anything. What was I going to do, hit you? It was an accident. I just hope this baby can be salvaged." He reaches out with his good hand and pats the truck's steering wheel. "Glad my insurance is paid up."

"Yeah," I say huskily because I was right, he *is* calm and kind and reminding me of someone I used to know, someone who hurts my heart just to think about.

He glances over at me. "So, you work down at the Candlelight, right? What's your name?"

"Sayre," I say, surprised. "You eat there?"

"Sometimes," he says, closing his eyes again. "Sorry, but my knee is killing me."

"Is it broken?" I ask.

"Feels like it," he says. "Something's all torn up in there."

"Do you want to try to stretch it out? You could lay it across my lap," I say.

He shakes his head, wincing at the movement.

"All right," I say, trying to think. What should I be doing to help him?

I don't know.

But I *need* to know.

Think, Sayre.

The truck lights are on but the engine's dead, so we have no heat.

Harlow is two miles away and I could go back and get him but he has no phone and once we're tucked up in the woods at his place, there's even less chance of EMS finding us.

We could sit here and blow the horn until it dies, and hope someone hears it.

We could light the woods on fire and hope someone sees it and responds before it roasts us.

I could go back up on the road and try the cell again. Or light a fire in the middle of it, if he has any matches. That would make someone stop. Of course all the wood is cold and wet, and even if I manage to get a little fire going the wind is still wicked . . .

Or I could go throw wood in the road. Pieces big enough to make someone stop, and once they do, we can blow the horn and flash the lights and yell for help.

That might actually work.

"I have to go back outside," I say, putting his cell phone in my coat pocket. "Do you want me to bring in some snow for your knee, to maybe numb it?"

"Not yet," he mumbles without opening his eyes. "I can deal as long as I don't move."

"Okay."

Slithering out the slider window is easier than climbing in, and I'm back on the ground and zipped into my coat in a heartbeat, revved with a fierce determination to help him, to get back up that damn bank and block the whole road if I have to.

I tug on my gloves. Fight my way to the top of the steep, slippery slope and crawl out onto the road, panting. Stagger to my feet.

Wood. I need to find wood.

But first, I try the phone.

Still no service.

"Cancel *that* contract," I mutter, shoving it back in my pocket and crossing to the mountain side of the road where there's a rotten log frozen to the ground. I push, pull, and kick at it, but it won't budge. "Good, then stay there," I mutter, sweating, and move on to a big branch farther up the bend. This one is just lying there so I grab the thick part and drag it back, leaving it right in the lane by the tire tracks, near my bag. Trudge up and down the edges of the road, checking the cell, shoving it back in my pocket and prying loose as many branches and limbs from downed trees as I can, feeling shots of blunted pain as my nails are bent backward and knowing that when my fingers finally thaw again they're going to hurt bad, rolling rotted logs and dragging chunks of wood onto the pavement, laying it all out there in plain view where it can't be missed, can't be passed by, can't be ignored.

Ending up with a roadblock that nobody could fail to stop for.

I plop down, chest heaving, thirsty, exhausted, and sweating, on the side of the road. Scoop up a clean handful of snow and eat it, then another.

It's got to be at least four o'clock by now.

So much for Candy calling the ambulance.

I wonder what she told my mother when she went back to the hospital without me.

She would never tell her the truth, especially if it made her look bad. No, what she probably said was *I found that little bitch of yours on the side of the road with Ben Greenwood's boy, and she said she wouldn't come without him, so I left her there.*

"Great," I mutter, shaking my head and checking the cell coverage one last time.

Nothing.

Okay, then.

The factory has already changed shifts and the bars are closed. Tractor trailers roll all night long to move factory product, but I have no idea if they'd take this steep, winding road in this kind of weather. And it's not that I haven't been out on these roads in the wee hours with my mother and whoever's car we're in, with the bleary-eyed driver creeping along trying not to get busted for drunk driving, and me, at thirteen, sitting right there next to him to catch the wheel in case he starts weaving off the road, but that was usually on a weekend.

Today is New Year's Eve morning, and it's Tuesday.

I stare down at the truck's blood-streaked window, searching for movement.

Nothing.

Look up at the mountain, searching for even the tiniest pinpoint of light.

Nothing.

So that's it. I really am alone.

The old pain sweeps back, stronger than a memory should be, and behind the image that haunts me is the guilt, the knowledge that I did nothing, only stood paralyzed with terror instead of moving faster, reaching farther, trying harder . . .

But I hadn't.

If Harlow is right and there *is* something missing inside me, it's because that was the moment grief sank its jaws into my heart and tore loose more than it left. That was the moment the wailing began inside me, a sound that should have echoed out over the mountain until it was naturally spent and all grief was exhausted, and it should have been *all* of us, howling out our misery like coyotes in a mourning chorus, but it never was. Instead, the high road fell silent and we sat and waited and never quite looked at each other, and when the final word came we crawled away and hemorrhaged separately, each huddled in our own bottomless pool of unspoken pain.

Or at least I assume we did.

I did.

I wipe my eyes and look back down the bank at the truck.

I didn't know what to do six years ago, so I did nothing.

I still don't know what to do, but it's not going to be nothing anymore.

I've already seen what that gets me.

I push myself back to my feet and stand there, swaying. Look out at the piles of rotted stumps and broken branches and my footprints, hundreds of them, weaving in and out all around the roadblock, creating a silent scream for help.

Help.

I wipe my eyes.

I wonder what my mother wants to tell me.

It won't be *I'm sorry I gave you such a shit life, Sayre. I'm sorry about Beale and your baby sister. I'm sorry I never loved you. I'm sorry I love my painkillers more than you, my meth more than you, my drinking and guys and Candy more than you. I'm sorry for all those times I said you were just like your father and your father was an asshole. I'm sorry, I'm sorry, I'm sorry . . .*

If she would say any of that, just once, then maybe we could clear up a few other things, too.

Like why, since she's been peeing orange for ages, the whites of her eyes are tinged yellow, and she's weak and shaky and riddled with spider-vein bursts all over, and her muscles have wasted away, her temples are sunken, and her skin is stretched tight across her skull, since she *knows* she has liver problems, why then, *why* had she deliberately blown the transplant team's interview to get her evaluated and onto the organ donor list?

Or maybe she would tell me why, when living with Beale and Aunt Loretta and sweet little Ellie had been so wonderful, so much like a beautiful dream come true, with her clean and sober and Beale loving us and us loving him, with laughter and affection, warm beds and clean clothes and as much food as we wanted to eat, had she started drinking again and destroyed everything?

Or even more important, maybe I would find out if she'd ever, even for just one spontaneous, surprising second, loved me.

I look up the blind curve in the direction of the hospital, eleven snowy and treacherous miles away.

What if she *is* dying? What if I'm wrong about why she's in the hospital this time, and Candy is right? What if she dies before I can get there, and the last thing I ever said to her, no, flung at her, was, *You're sick, Mom, you really are, and I can't even stand to look at you anymore. You deserve what you get, so go ahead, hate me some more, do whatever you want, because I don't care. Merry Christmas. You're finally getting your wish. I'm out of here for good.*

And I was.

I did it, I left her to the things she loves most. I did the thing I never thought I could do because she'd betrayed me in the worst possible way, and I just couldn't take it anymore.

And what did I think would happen? Did I think she'd sit up and finally realize what she'd lost, and try to get clean again so we could start over?

Maybe.

Yes, hopefully.

I thought maybe it would shock her, my finally saying how I felt out loud.

I thought maybe it would matter.

I thought if I stayed within reach at Harlow's, maybe she'd come looking for me. Maybe she'd say *All right, let's try this liver transplant thing again, Sayre, because you know what? I'm only thirty-three and that's too young to die, especially without ever really knowing you.*

I thought maybe she would say that.

Instead, she went into the hospital, and if Candy's not lying, this time she won't ever come out again.

Chapter 9

I go back down the hill and shimmy into the truck.

Evan stirs, and opens his eyes. "You okay?"

"Yeah, just freezing," I say, wrapping my arms around myself and huddling in the seat. "I blocked the whole road, so if anyone ever shows up, they're gonna *have* to stop."

"She didn't call, did she," he says and it's an acknowledgment rather than a question.

"No, I'm pretty sure," I say, sighing and glancing at him. His head wound has stopped bleeding and it looks like he tried to clean some of it up because the dried, clotted blood is smeared from his hairline to his chin. Grisly. "I don't know what else to do."

"Just wait, I guess," he says. "What else can we do?"

"But you're . . ." I make a sweeping motion because I can't say *gross looking*. "You're hurt and there has to be something I can do."

"Talk to me," he says, closing his eyes. "Maybe it'll take my mind off my knee."

Talk to him. "About what?" I ask, pulling off my gloves and examining my throbbing fingers. Two of the nails are bent back below the skin, one is torn low, and a ripped cuticle is bleeding. I grit my teeth and quick flip the bent nails back the right way, my eyes tearing at the pulsing pain, then ease my gloves back on and gently tuck my hands up into my armpits. I sniffle, and say, "What do you want to talk about?"

"I don't know," he says with a faint shrug. "You're a girl. What do girls talk about?"

"Guys," I say, and then, "Themselves."

"Well, I don't really care about guys, so . . ." His mouth curves into a slight smile. "Come on, I'm a captive audience. Let's hear your life story."

"Ha." The snort comes out before I can stop it. "No, that's okay. The last thing you need right now is a horror story. Why don't you tell me *your* life story instead?"

He cracks an eye. "I already know my life story and it's boring."

"Boring isn't necessarily bad," I say, and mean it. "Were you, uh, on your way to work when you, uh . . . ?"

"Yeah, when school's on break I come home and work part-time down at the factory for extra cash," he says and points at a half-full bottle of Gatorade on the console. "Would you open that for me, please? And have some if you want." He waits until I unscrew the top and hand it to him. Drinks and hands it back. Watches as I take a cautious sip. "Have more."

"No, I want to make it last, just in case," I say, closing the top and putting it back.

"Just in case what, we're here for a week?" he says.

I glance at him, stung, and realize he's teasing. "Hey, you never know, right?" I gesture out the window at the fat, fluffy snowflakes. "If this turns into a real blizzard . . ." And then I sit up straight, struck with a thought. "The plow truck! They'll send the plow out to do the road before everybody leaves for work in the morning!"

"That's right," he says, nodding. "So then all we have to do is wait."

And then I'm struck with another thought, one not so bright and way more panicky. "What if the plow comes and doesn't stop, just plows right through the blockade? I mean, that's what plows do, you know? Plow stuff. What if they don't even hesitate? What if—"

"Hey, whoa, it's all right," he says, reaching his good hand over and touching mine. "They'll stop, and if they don't, when we see the headlights coming I'll just lay on the horn and you can get back out the window and start waving your arms and yelling and all. They'll see us, Sayre. Don't worry. We'll *make* 'em see us."

We'll make 'em see us.

His words bring tears to my eyes. "Okay," I say hoarsely, staring out the window at the long plunge down the bank beside me. He'd touched my hand, not in a bad way but like he'd wanted to reassure me, and I can't remember the last time someone did that. I clear my throat and look back at him. "Okay, so listen, you tell me the boring story of your life, and then I'll tell you the horror story of mine. How's that?"

"Hmm," he says. "I thought the whole point of this was to entertain *me*."

"So did you go to Sullivan High?" I ask, giving him a look and settling in.

He smiles again and gingerly tilts his head back against the seat. "Yeah, and now I'm in my last year up at SUNY-ESF. Uh, Environmental Science and Forestry, Syracuse," he adds at my puzzled look. "You?"

"We'll get to me later," I say because really, what am I going to tell him? That I'm a Sullivan high school senior with good grades and a crappy attendance record, thanks to never knowing where I'll be waking up in the morning or where the closest bus stops are? Uh, *no*. "Forestry, huh? Cool. So, what do you want to be when you grow up?"

The minute I say it a memory of Mrs. Grinnell, my fifth-grade teacher, flashes through my mind, of her asking us all that exact same question and me, eleven years old and fresh out of the tragedy at Beale's, looking right at her and saying with complete sincerity, *An orphan.*

"I'm getting my degree in Fisheries Science. I want to do something with the rivers, hopefully somewhere along the Susquehanna," he says, perking right up. "Did you know that the Susquehanna's over four hundred miles long, goes through three states, and provides about half of the fresh water to the Chesapeake Bay? You'd think that'd be a good thing, right, but back in 2005 it was named America's most endangered river because of the pollution."

I open my mouth to say *really?* but he barrels on.

"I mean, c'mon, what the hell are we doing here? The river dates back to what, the Paleozoic Era? It's managed to stay alive for sixty million years and now we're gonna kill it for cash?" He catches my puzzled look. "Manure? Chemicals? Hazardous waste spills? Factories spewing pollutants? Contamination? Gas-well drilling? Fish not safe to eat? Water tests taken upstream of the waste pipes instead of downstream where the discharge is so the toxin readings are inaccurate?"

"Ohhh," I say, nodding and stifling a grin. "You're going to be one of *them.*"

"*Them?*" he echoes indignantly, and catches my smile. "Wiseass. But yeah, I am. I mean, I grew up on this river, we camped on the islands, caught trophy bass and watched the bald eagles and it shouldn't be—" He tries to sit up higher in his seat, and groans. "Oh shit, I shouldn't have done that. My knee." A sheen of sweat breaks out on his forehead. "*Damn.* Uh . . . it shouldn't have to be jobs *or* clean water, you know? *Jesus.*"

"Can I do anything? Do you want to put snow on it yet?" I ask anxiously, leaning across the seat toward him. "I can go get some. It's right—"

"No," he says, voice strained and good hand white-knuckled around the steering wheel. "You talk. Just talk, Sayre."

Talk. Okay. I hunt frantically through my life, trying to find something that doesn't spell *Loser* and can't believe I can't think of one thing that—

"What were you doing out there so late?" he mumbles, eyes

closed and face pale. "I swear to God the worst minute of my life was coming around that bend and seeing you standing there. I really thought I was gonna hit you."

"I know," I say. "I'm really, really sorry." And then, because he wants me to talk and I can see how hard he's trying not to scream with pain, I go ahead and say it. "I was trying to get down to the hospital because my mother's in there and supposedly she's . . . dying."

He opens his eyes and stares at me. "For real?"

"I don't know," I say with a helpless gesture. "I didn't think so before, but now I think . . . maybe, yeah."

"That's what that lady was all pissed off about? Because you didn't go with her?" he says.

I nod.

"And you didn't go because I made you promise to stay with me." He rubs his forehead with his good hand, and the look he gives me is an unhappy one. "I'm really sorry. I didn't know. I never would have asked you to stay if—"

"No, really, it's all right, or at least it was then." I know I'm not making sense, so I take a deep breath and say, "My mother's been in the hospital before, like six times, and she's always come out again. I thought that's what was happening this time, too, only now I don't know. She's had liver problems for so long and she doesn't take care of herself at all, and she won't talk about anything with me . . ." My fingers are aching and absently, I rub them. "A week before Christmas she *had* to go to the doctor's because she was really sick and the doctor did these tests and said her liver was failing and that's why she was so vague and lethargic, because the ammonia was built up in her brain. So he quick set up an appointment for an interview with the organ transplant evaluation team to see if she was physically strong and emotionally stable and . . . and if she had a family support system to help her and I don't know, all the other stuff you have to go through just to be evaluated for getting on the transplant list . . ." My voice is wobbling and I can't stop it.

"Oh, man," he says softly. "I'm really sorry."

"They gave us all this paperwork before the appointment, and she didn't even read it, but I did and I knew she was in trouble . . ." I falter, not wanting to say this, God, I don't want to say this but it just keeps coming, "because to even *pass* the interview you have to be clean and sober for six months and committed to staying that way forever, and she wasn't, she hasn't been sober since we lived with Beale and that was almost seven years ago. The night before the appointment she drank what, I don't know, maybe a quart of vodka and took a whole ton of her stupid Vicodin and when we went there the next morning she just blew them all off, like she knew she wasn't going to make it anyway so why even try. When they explained that there aren't anywhere near enough donated livers for everyone who needs one, and so they don't usually give them to addicts who are just going to go out and wreck the next one, too, she just shrugged and said, *Well, that'd be me, guys, so let's just call it a day* and grabbed her cane and walked out." I look at him, miserable. "She just walked out and left me sitting there, and one of the doctors came over and said, *You have a rough road ahead of you. Is there anyone in the family you can turn to for help?* and I was so freaked that I couldn't even answer her."

Evan is very still, listening.

"And then after we got home she went and stole all the money I'd made busing down at the Candlelight and bought a mess more Vicodin." Oh God, my head hurts. "So I waited till she passed out and grabbed every pill that was left and took them back to her dealer and got my money back." My breath hitches. "When she found out they were gone we had a really brutal fight, and she told me some stuff I never knew, really bad stuff, and I got so upset that I left. And now she's in the hospital and is probably really dying this time, and I'm not there and it's not your fault, it's nobody's fault and that, Evan, is my shit life and aren't you glad you asked?" I meet his gaze with what must be a ghastly smile. "Now, not to change the subject or anything, but do the windshield wipers work?"

He blinks. "Uh, let me see," he says gruffly, turning the wiper knob.

They swish across the windshield slowly, clearing it.

"Now we can see headlights coming either way again," I say when he shuts them off. I can't look at him anymore because I know what I'm going to see, and I don't want to see it. Not from him. I'm sorry I said anything and I wish I'd never even opened my mouth.

"Good thinking," he says.

"Thanks," I say, staring out the passenger window.

"I'm sorry about your mom," he says after a long moment. "So you were heading down to the hospital when I . . . ?"

"Yeah," I say.

"In this snow? Couldn't you have called somebody for a ride?"

"I don't have a cell and there's no phone where I was staying, so . . ." I shrug. "I didn't really have a choice. It was either walk or don't go, you know?" There's no reason to explain how I was pretty much forced out of the trailer, and bringing Harlow, the infamous derelict town murderer, into this will only make it worse, so I don't.

I have to go back there, though, and soon. The thought fills me with dread, but my coffee can of money, all seventy-three dollars and forty-eight cents, is still under his trailer, along with little Misty—if he hasn't shot her yet—and I want them both.

"So what are you going to do?" Evan says hesitantly.

"About what?" I say.

"Well, I mean if your mom . . ." He shakes his head slightly, as if to erase the thought. "Do you have any relatives you can go live with?"

"No, but I'll be eighteen in May, so I guess I'll be on my own," I say, trying to sound as if it's no big deal and failing miserably because that's just one more mountain I'm going to have to find a way to climb.

"You're still in school?" Evan asks, sounding surprised.

"Good old Sullivan," I say with a crooked smile. "I graduate in

June." *If I make it,* I add silently, because right now my attendance record is not looking so good.

"You know what you're going to do after that?" he says.

I snort. "Are you kidding? I'd be happy just to—"

And then a sudden sharp, wrenching groan rumbles outside my window as one of the pine tree trunks rips loose from the sparse, frozen soil on the incline and the truck tips toward me, sending me sliding into the passenger door and Evan, yelling and swearing as his knee collides with the console, across the truck seat and crashing into me.

Chapter 10

"My knee," he grinds out. "Jesus, Sayre, don't move! My knee . . . oh *God*." He slams his good hand into the dashboard and tries to push himself up off me. His face is pale and the veins in his neck are corded with the effort. "Are we going over?"

"I hope not," I mumble from beneath his jacket, which is covering half of my face. "But I think it's time to get out of here, just in case." A curious calm has come over me, like everything bad that I've ever been afraid of is finally happening and I'm stuck right here in the middle of it again . . . only this time all that fear has somehow turned into white noise because when the worst actually happens, then there's nothing left to be afraid of, is there?

Or maybe I'm just in shock. That's also a possibility.

Moving carefully, I push his jacket off my face so I can breathe again.

"I can't move without twisting my knee," he says in a strained voice, trying to keep himself propped up off me with only one hand. "I can't do it, Sayre, I'll pass out or really screw it up and—"

"We're not going to screw it up," I say, touching his arm to get him to pay attention. "Listen. Your good leg is braced, right? Now, I'm going to put my hands here," I slide the other one up and flatten them both against his chest, "and I'm not going to move anything but my arms, okay? When you're ready, I'm going to push you up and back real slow, and when you want me to stop I will.

I'm not going to move my legs. I'm not gonna bump your knee."
I hold his dark gaze, keeping mine steady. "Okay? Think you can
do it?"

"I don't know," he says, the hint of panic still in his voice.

"You can," I say calmly, as his heart races beneath my hand.
"We'll just go easy. Ready?"

He takes a deep breath and exhales. "Shit. All right."

"I'm gonna start to push," I say and begin to straighten my
arms. He's heavy and I'm suddenly grateful for carrying all those
trays stacked with dirty dishes. "So far, so good?"

"Yeah," he grunts, jaw clenched. "Keep going."

I push some more and he braces his good hand against the back
of the seat, and hooks the forearm of his bad hand around the
steering wheel. He's sweating, muttering under his breath, and my
arms are beginning to tremble because they're not fully extended
yet and I can't lock my elbows until he—

"Oh Christ, my knee, stop," he blurts out.

"I don't think I can," I say. "You've got to keep going, Evan. Sit
up!"

And with a Herculean effort he does, pulling himself back into
the driver's seat and slumping against the door. I see his shattered
knee bump the steering wheel, hear his swift, indrawn breath and I
quick sit up, too, slide open the cab window, and shimmy up and
out.

I pull myself over the high side of the dangerously tilted bed to
the snowy ground, and reach for the driver's door. Yank it open,
completely unprepared for Evan's wild yelp and then he comes falling out at me backward, and I try to catch him but he's panicked,
thrashing and heavy, so I can only grab him around the waist as his
bad knee whacks the side of the truck, as he slides all the way out
and we both go down.

Chapter 11

"Evan?" I squirm out from under him. "Oh my God, I'm so sorry. I didn't think—"

He's unconscious, and his leg is lying at a hideous angle.

"Okay, oh God, that's bad, that's really bad," I whimper, leaning over him, my hands fluttering over his knee but too terrified to touch it, so instead smoothing the blood-matted hair off his forehead. The cut is nasty, puffy and angry looking, but it's still not as bad as that grotesque, swollen knee. "Evan? Come on, no sleeping. I need you. You have to fix your leg. I really don't think it should be crooked like that. Wake up." I pat his cheek over and over, and finally stop, my fingertips resting on his skin. "No, you know what? It's all right. Better you don't wake up until I figure out what I'm going to do with you." I look around, frantic because we're out in the snow and the wind, on the ground with the teetering truck right next to us, and we have no blankets and he can't climb but he can't just lie out here or he'll freeze to death.

I look up at the truck. It's tilted bad but—

Lights sweep the trees in front of me.

Headlights.

My heart leaps and I scrabble around on my knees and look up the bank.

It's the plow truck, slowing because of the branches in the road, and with a hoarse, desperate animal sound I push myself up and start waving my arms and shouting, "Help! Help! Down here! Help!" I reach up into the truck, grab the steering wheel and lay on the horn. The blare splits the night, splits my skull, and down on the ground Evan shifts and groans but I keep it going, keep shouting until the truck stops. I can hear the rumbling idle and it's the most beautiful sound in the world. "Down here! Help! Please, help us!"

And then a big, husky figure appears at the edge of the road and I let off the horn in time to hear the guy say, *Sweet Mother of God.* I run out next to Evan's still form and yell, "He's hurt! We need to get to the hospital! Please don't leave us here!"

"Stay right there," the man says and starts down the bank. "I'm coming."

"Oh, thank you," I say, only it comes out like a prayer and that's when I realize I'm laughing and babbling and the relief is so huge it makes my head spin.

"What's wrong with him?" the guy asks, picking his way carefully down the slope.

"He might have a concussion and a shattered knee and broken fingers but I don't know if that's all," I say, sinking down in the snow next to Evan and cradling his cold, limp good hand between mine. "He just fell out of the truck and passed out."

"Good," the guy says, striding the last few feet and crouching next to us, "because he isn't going to like this part at all." He slides his beefy arms under Evan's back and the curve of his knees, and ignoring my frantic warnings, grunts and rises, lifting him like he's nothing more than a little kid. "You go on up ahead of me."

"Okay, okay," I say, and reach into the truck, grab the keys, slam the door, and start up the bank. "I know you. You're Red Ganzler, right?" I would recognize him anywhere, partly because we've met before and partly because he looks like a lumberjack with his buffalo plaid jacket, fuzzy orange beard, and huge, meaty hands. But he's not a lumberjack, he's on the township road department and is the youth minister over at the Methodist Church, a fact my mother always thought was a real hoot, seeing as how he was a stoner in high school and the first thing he did when he got back from fighting in Iraq was to go on a five-day bender, the highlight of which was his skinny-dipping at noon in the creek off the Main Street Bridge, singing "California Girls" at the top of his lungs and unabashedly sloshing out of the water when the openly amused police showed up.

"Yeah, that's me," he says, huffing along behind me. "Listen, when you get up to the truck, clear off the backseat so I can lay him down."

"Okay," I say, trying to find the best footholds because Red has no free hand and if he slides backward or falls . . . "Be careful here. It's really slippery." I stop, watching him struggle, and when he gets close I grab his arm and try to help pull him along.

"Keep going, I'm all right," he says, glancing at me.

"Okay." I scramble the rest of the way up the bank and run to the truck, yank open the back door and with one sweep shove the crushed cigarette packs, empty Yoo-Hoo bottles, magazines, Yodels wrappers, old coffee cups, and newspapers down off the seat and onto the floor.

"Watch out now," he says, coming up behind me.

I dart around the other side of the truck, open the back door, and climb in. Red leans over and eases the top half of Evan onto the seat. I wedge my hands under Evan's armpits and pull until he's as far in as he can get.

"I hate to do this," Red says, grimacing and shaking his head, "but I'm gonna have to bend his knees to shut the door."

"No, wait," I say and making sure his head is still far enough in the truck, quick climb in and shut my door. "Here," I say, shrugging out of my jacket, wadding it up, and sticking it against the door. "Now let me see if I can pull him higher."

"No, you'll hurt yourself," he says. "I'll do it." He climbs into the back of the truck as I scramble between the front seats and plop into the passenger side. Red takes hold of Evan and, grunting with effort, slides him up until he's propped against my coat and both of his legs are stretched out on the seat. "There." Red shuts the door, then comes around and climbs back into the driver's seat. He picks up the township walkie-talkie and tells them he's coming in and taking two kids from an accident scene to the hospital. Waits until he gets confirmation and then says, "Now let's get moving."

"Wait!" I cry as he shifts gears and we creep closer to the road-block. "My stuff!" I throw open the door and slide out, run to where my bags and my ruby velvet blazer still sit, grab them, and am scrambling back up into the truck before the snow starts to sting my bare hands. "Thank you."

"Don't thank me yet. We still have to get down there in one piece." He studies my face for a moment, recognition dawning in his eyes. "Sayre, right? Okay. I knew I knew you. You all right?"

"Yeah, just freezing," I say, shoving the bag and purse down by my feet but keeping the blazer on my lap. The lacy, fragile snow-flakes are already melting and leaving glistening, tearlike droplets on the worn velvet. I brush them away before they soak in.

"Well, we can fix that," he says and turns up the heat. Shifts the truck back into gear, and lowers the plow. "Did you make that roadblock?"

"Mm-hmm," I say, holding my hands out in front of the heating vent. "We needed to make someone slow down long enough to see us."

"Smart," he says.

"Thank you," I say as the truck surges forward and all that debris I'd dragged out into the open is enveloped by a rising mountain of snow and swept aside in one steady push.

Without Grandma Lucy

Something set my mother off two days after Grandma Lucy was buried, but I didn't know whether it was discovering the bowl of leftover ambrosia salad in the refrigerator, or the "Children Learn What They Live" poem by Dorothy Law Nolte I'd brought home from Sunday school months ago and posted on the refrigerator with little fruit magnets.

It didn't really matter, as the end result was the same.

"Now what the hell is this shit?" my mother said, the covered bowl in her hand, the poem plastered in front of her on the fridge door.

I was sitting in my chair at the kitchen table because it was lunchtime, I wasn't even eight years old yet, and I guess I still thought someone was going to feed me.

"'If a child lives with criticism, he learns to condemn,'" my mother read, and her lip curled in scornful amusement. "Oh, for . . . Hey, Candy, did you know that if a child lives with hostility, he learns to fight? And if he lives with fear, he learns to be apprehensive?"

Candy pushed herself up off the couch and wandered into the room holding a can of Bud. "Yeah, so?"

"Wait, there's more," my mother said in a false perky voice and held up a finger. " 'If a child lives with encouragement, he learns to be confident, and if he lives with acceptance,' guess what?"

"What?" Candy said, smirking.

"He learns to *love*," my mother cooed, and with a sharp snort, pulled the poem off the fridge, scattering magnets all over the floor. "If this is the kind of artsy-fartsy bullshit my mother's been feeding you all this time then you're gonna be in for a really rude awakening, kid," she said, glancing at me. "Welcome to real life."

"That's from Sunday school," I whispered.

"What?" my mother snapped.

I could feel the tears gathering in my eyes because she'd crumpled up my paper and now there were banana and apple and grape magnets all over the floor. Candy was wearing Grandma Lucy's pink flowered bathrobe and had already spilled beer down the front of it and that was the last present Grandpa ever gave her and now it was ruined. The sink was full of empty, smelly, crusted casserole dishes from all the neighbors and no one was washing them or making me a peanut butter and jelly sandwich cut into triangles with potato chips and pickles and that's what I *always* had on Thursday, but no more, no more, just like no more good night kisses or clean clothes left folded on my bed or Cricket the parakeet because no one remembered to give him water, so he died of thirst on the bottom of his cage with his tiny, gentle feet curled into clawed fists, and instead of letting me say a prayer and bury him, my mother just took his body and tossed it into the garbage. "Sunday school," I said again, sniffling and not much louder than the first time.

"Jesus Christ, don't you ever do anything but cry?" my mother said, tossing the poem onto the counter, setting down the covered bowl, and peeling back the tinfoil. She stared at the ambrosia salad for a moment too long and then with one fierce motion the bowl went flying across the kitchen past Candy and hit the wall, splattering mushy pineapple and marshmallows and maraschino cherries and Cool Whip everywhere, knocking Grandma's clock to the floor, and breaking the bowl in two. "You know, I've always hated that shit," my mother said into the resounding silence, and started to laugh.

Candy joined her.

I sat frozen and aghast, barely breathing, nose running and tears pouring down my face.

"There she goes again," Candy said, snickering and jerking a thumb in my direction.

But instead of my mother laughing at me, too, my tears made her mad. Really mad because her face grew hard and her gaze cold and in a low, threatening voice she said, "Stop it right now. I mean it."

But I couldn't because the sorrow was too big, and it overwhelmed me. I was just beginning to understand that Grandma Lucy really *was* dead and nothing would ever be the same again, that the solid, familiar ground had crumbled and fallen away, leaving me in alien terrain, a rough and treacherous landscape with no familiar paths.

"Stop it," she said angrily. "I'm warning you, Sayre. Stop crying or I swear to God I'll *really* give you something to cry about."

That just scared me more, and sobbing, I moaned, "I want Grandma!"

She crossed the kitchen and had hold of me in a flash, her fingers digging into my arm, yanking me out of the chair with a jerk that snapped my head back and stole my breath, and started spanking me. "What did I just tell you? What did I tell you, huh? You think because my mother never spanked you that I'm not going to? You think you don't have to listen to me? If you want to cry, I'll give you a *real* reason to cry!"

"No, don't, let me go," I howled, shocked, twisting and squirming in her grasp, which only made her hit me harder. "I'm sorry, I'm sorry, ow, Mommy, I'm sorry, I'll listen, I promise, owww."

"Then next time I tell you to do something, you'd better do it," she ground out, releasing me and walking back to the fridge. "Now *shut up*."

I collapsed on the floor, gasping, my butt burning and stinging, my hair hanging damp and scraggly in front of my eyes, nose running, and my mind, oh my mind, was like a crazed, panicked animal darting, frantic, in a hundred different directions, wounded and searching desperately for safety.

"There's nothing to eat in this goddamn house," my mother said, slamming the fridge door with disgust and glancing at Candy. "Want McDonald's?"

"Sure," she said, heading for the stairs. "Give me five minutes to change."

I lifted my head, breath hitching, and swiped the hair from my face.

"Not you," my mother said, giving me a look. "I want this mess cleaned up by the time we get back. And don't you *dare* cry or you'll be punished even longer," she added, and grabbing her purse, she walked out.

I stayed where I was until I heard Candy go, too, and the car leaving the driveway, then burst into a fresh storm of weeping, and ran upstairs. I passed my mother's room, the guest room where Candy was staying, and my room because the one I really needed to be in was Grandma's.

I opened the door, intending to throw myself on the bed and beg God to send her back, but the sight stopped me cold.

The room had been ransacked, the bureau drawers emptied on the bed, the jewelry boxes opened, the books pulled from the book-case. Grandma Lucy's hope chest was open and all the old, delicate, handmade doilies she'd inherited from her mother were flung aside in piles. Her wedding veil was lying on the floor. The pictures of Grandpa and me on her night table had been turned facedown and instead of the room smelling like her lily of the valley cologne, it smelled like sweat, stale beer, and smoke.

"Oh no, Grandma," I whispered, sniffling and patting my arm. "Oh no."

I knew they'd been looking for money because that was all my mother had talked about since Grandma died. The thing was, I knew where Grandma Lucy had hidden some of her dollars because she'd shown me on purpose, and said it was our money, hers and mine only, and never to tell anyone about it, especially my mother.

I wondered if they'd found her secret hiding place.

I was afraid to go in and look, though, afraid they would somehow know I'd been in there, like my footprints would glow, telltale, on the carpet or my fingerprints on the doorknob or even worse, on the old mahogany bedpost knob that secretly unscrewed and had just enough room inside the hollow post to harbor a small roll of cash.

So I never looked, afraid I would somehow give the secret away, and ten days later I came home from school to see two guys with a big box truck carrying the mahogany bed out the door because my mother had sold it, along with the matching bureaus and the dining room set, all antique family heirlooms.

My mother was in the house, drunk and livid, because she'd finished going through Grandma's desk and had then gone down to the bank, where she'd discovered that Grandpa had lost most of his investments in one of the big banking scandals. The only funds left were a couple of small IRAs, Grandma's checking and savings accounts, and a savings account she'd started for me when I was born, which my mother promptly withdrew the money from and spent.

Home turned into an angry, scary place.

When Grandma was alive, I drew bright pictures of the two of us and Cricket the parakeet. Wore shiny pink rubber boots with daisies on them when it rained and had Hello Kitty pajamas. I took chewable vitamins every morning with my scrambled eggs and toast, and when I got sick she tucked me in under the prettiest crocheted afghan and fed me ginger ale and chicken noodle soup. I went to Methodist Sunday school and sang "Jesus Loves the Little Children," played with Mrs. Carroll's nieces whenever they came to visit, learned my ABCs, and always had bedtime stories. We watched cartoons and took the bus to Radio City Music Hall to see the Rockettes at Christmas. We went to the library every Friday night, then picked up Chinese food, went home, and curled up with our dinner and our exciting new books.

When she died, it wasn't just her physical presence that ended, but I didn't understand that at first. I had never gone without food or heat, clean clothes, or a set bedtime before, never even realized those things could stop, so I guess I thought that when my mother came back to the blue house to live, I would still have all those things, just not Grandma.

No one explained that it wasn't going to be that way, and so each unhappy shock—and there were dozens—was like a punch in the chest, leaving me aching, bewildered, and lost as to what to do next.

No one did anything for me, with me, or because of me anymore. I would be right in the room and it was like I wasn't even there. No matter the topic, the conversation wouldn't change, nor would the activity around me, which was usually my mother, Candy, and a bunch of guys doing stuff I'd never seen before.

I saw Candy grind a cigarette out on my grandmother's living room rug, take off everything but her thong, and dance on the coffee table, shaking all her lumpy flab and making some pimply guy kiss the mouse tattoo high on the inside of her wobbly thigh. I saw my mother lick the end of a needle before she stuck it in her arm, saw the needle go red with her own blood and then saw her lick the spot on her skin after she pulled it out. I saw screaming fights, naked people having sex on TV, Grandma's picture torn in half, and Candy slapping my mother, hard, across the face when she had passed out and wouldn't wake up.

The atmosphere was sharp, driven, and erratic now, and all I could do was swallow my fear and stay quiet in the background because I never knew what would get me in trouble. Sometimes it didn't take more than just the sight of me to ruin my mother's good mood and make me feel as sorry that I'd been born as she was. I started taking hot baths when everyone had gone out, not only because I always felt dirty but because the water was soothing and gentle, a place of warmth and peace.

There was no schedule anymore, no one helping me with my homework or making breakfast or even being around in the morning. I was on my own, so I started trying to figure out how to do it all for myself.

I kept going to school, most mornings hungry, sometimes wearing the same clothes as the day before and without brushing my hair or my teeth because I would wake up late, miss the bus, and have to run just to make it before the late bell. I was always tired, so it was hard to concentrate, and I started getting Ds in everything, even reading and penmanship.

Did anyone notice how badly I was falling apart, that I trudged around disheveled and neglected and lonely, or did they chalk it up to a little girl mourning her grandmother? I don't know, but some of the teachers seemed kinder and gave me extra help, which was nice because going back to the blue house and being ignored every day was hell.

No one cut the grass, trimmed the hedges, or shoveled the sidewalk when it snowed. No one cooked, cleaned, did laundry, or shopped for food. No one paid the bills until the water and electricity were cut off, and then swearing and furious, my mother would storm down to the local office and throw cash at them, cash she had from selling all the antique furniture and emptying Grandma's bank accounts. No one answered the phone when it rang because everyone knew it was either bill collectors or local busybodies. All of my mother's friends had her disposable cell phone number.

No one did much but talk, laugh, drink, fight, get high, get paranoid, hallucinate, sell more of Grandma's stuff, and have guys sleep over in their bedrooms. I discovered the sleeping-over part for the first time one morning before school when I was in the bathroom peeing, yawning and rubbing the sleep from my eyes when the door swung open and some tall, skinny, naked, hairy guy walked right in on me. I stared at him, frozen and mortified, and he peered back at me sitting there, mumbled, "Yo, sorry," and backed out again, leaving the door open behind him.

I saw him naked again, at least four more times, because he was Candy's boyfriend and he had moved into her room with her. His name was Sims and he didn't work, but Candy did down at the hardware store, and so she paid his rent to my mother, too.

He was always there when I got home from school, sometimes just him and my mother, sometimes them and other stragglers looking to party, and he always smiled and said hi. A couple of times he brought me back food when everyone went out to Mc-Donald's, and sometimes when I got home from school my mother would be passed out on the couch but he'd be awake, and we'd go sit on the porch and he would ask me things about school and my lack of friends. I would answer, shyly at first but then eagerly because he was doing what Grandma Lucy used to do, sit with me for a while, ask questions, and be interested in whatever I had to say. I was hungry, no, *starving* for someone to care and he was there with attention, smiles, and an occasional hug.

He talked about himself, too. He said he had a little three-year-old daughter who lived in Utah but her mother was a bitch and so he hardly ever saw her. He said he missed her a lot, and hanging out with me made him feel better. He looked so sad that on impulse I leaned over and gave him a kiss on the cheek, and then he hugged me and told me I was a smart, beautiful girl and if it was up to him, I would live like a princess and have everything I ever wanted.

And that was when Candy came home, screeching her old Ford pickup into the driveway and getting out with a hammer in her hand. My mother appeared, triumphant, beside us, and Sims slid his arm from around my shoulder and leaned away.

My mother called, "See? Didn't I tell you? They're out here every day, snuggled up together all cozy, hugging and kissing and telling secrets. . . ."

Candy came storming up the sidewalk with murder in her eyes and the hammer in her fist but she wasn't looking at him, no, she was looking at *me* and instinctively I leaned closer to Sims but he stood up fast and went inside, past my mother, who snickered drunkenly, swatted his arm, and drawled, "Busted."

"You keep your skinny little child ass away from him!" Candy shouted, coming for me, and as adrenaline surged and keen terror carved my senses, I could see everything as if it was all finely drawn in front of me: the crazy light in her pale eyes, the snarl pulling back her lips and exposing those meaty red gums, and the hammer clenched in her freckled, white-knuckled hand.

She was crazy, as crazy as my mother was when she started digging at the invisible bugs she felt crawling around under her skin, or accusing me of making her coffee with turpentine or taping sheets over the closet doors so Homeland Security couldn't send an airborne team in to steal the tinfoil she kept under the couch.

They were crazy. Both of them.

Candy charged the porch steps, and I dove off the side as the hammer came down, scrambled up, and took off running across Mrs. Carroll's yard and down the street with Candy huffing, puffing, and cursing behind me, and my mother yelling, "You get your ass back here right now, Sayre! I didn't say you could leave this property!"

But I didn't stop running for a long time, bulleting down side streets and dodging cars until finally, chest heaving and legs burning like liquid fire, I sank down on a curb behind the library and drew great sobbing, whooping breaths until I could breathe normally again.

I sat there as dusk fell.

Sat there as happy little kids came prancing out with armloads of books and watched as their mothers and fathers carefully strapped them into car seats and drove away.

Sat there as groups of junior high girls came out giggling and talking loud about going down to Sal's Pizza Place and glancing flirtatiously back over their shoulders at the group of junior high boys pushing and shoving and slouching along behind them.

Sat there as the inside lights went off and one by one the librarians got into their cars and left.

And when the moon was high and I was shivering with cold and exhaustion, a police car pulled up. An officer got out, shined the flashlight in my face, and said, "Are you Sayre Bellavia?"

I nodded, tears blurring my vision, and huddled even smaller because I knew what he was going to do, he was going to take me home and then I would be in for a world of hurt, that's what my mother and Candy always called it whenever they had to hit me, and that made me start crying in earnest.

"Shh, it's all right, come on," he said, and when I rose he opened the back door of the police car. I climbed in, and he shut the door gently, not like he was mad, and that made me brave enough to stammer, "Am I in t . . . t . . . trouble?"

"You?" he said, sliding into the front seat and glancing at me in the rearview mirror. His eyes were brown, kind, and maybe sad, too. "No, you're not in trouble." He pulled a small pad from his shirt pocket and glanced at it. "We've been looking for you. Your neighbor Mrs. Carroll called us earlier and said she saw a woman with a hammer in her hand chasing you down the street."

"That was Candy," I said, swiping a hand across my damp eyes. "She thought I was trying to steal her boyfriend."

His brows rose. "What?" He pulled out a pen and made a note on the pad.

I took that as disbelief and hurriedly said, "I wasn't, I swear, but she didn't let me say it. Me and Sims only talk and sometimes he gives me McDonald's and hugs me when I'm sad." My eyes welled up again. "I know he's Candy's boyfriend because he lives with us, but he's the only one who talks to me since Grandma Lucy died." I sniffled, and twisted my hands together in my lap. "I didn't mean to do anything wrong."

"Sims Pozorowicz?" the officer said, pausing in his writing and swiveling to face me over the seat.

I nodded. "Yup."

"He lives in the same house you do?" he said, and now his voice was different, harder and not as friendly. He made another note, then touched the little walkie-talkie pinned to the front of his shirt and talked into it. I heard my name, and Sims's, too.

"Uh-huh, since August," I said and then, "He sleeps in Candy's room."

"I see." He turned back to me. "Has he ever done or said anything that makes you feel funny, like uncomfortable?"

"No," I said, and then squirming a little because it felt like lying, "well, he curses a *lot* and sometimes he calls Candy a fat skank when she's not there . . ." I frowned, and thought harder. "Oh! And he has this really gross foot fungus and he always scratches himself here," I wrinkled my nose and pointed to my crotch, ". . . and sometimes he comes into the bathroom naked when I'm in there peeing, but he never means to, he just forgets because the door doesn't lock and he's drunk, and him and Candy are . . ." I stopped, blushing, because I'd never told anyone any of the things I'd seen and heard. I wouldn't even have known how to begin. "You know. Doing it."

"Sayre, how old are you?" he said after a long moment.

"I just turned eight." My stomach rumbled and I clapped a hand over it.

"Eight," he repeated softly. "The same age as my daughter. Tell me, did you have supper tonight?"

"Nope," I said. "No lunch, either."

"Why not?" he said and his eyes were kindly again.

"Because the only food we have is mustard, and I hate that," I said as my stomach grumbled even louder.

"All right, first let's get you something to eat," he said, facing front, pulling his door closed and glancing at me again in the rear-view mirror. "McDonald's sound good?"

"Uh," I made a face, "could I have pizza instead?"

"Sure," he said. "I kind of like Sal's pies myself."

And when we went into Sal's I found out that he was the policeman's uncle, and they laughed and joked and looked really happy to see each other, and that made me feel kind of left out because it had been so long since anybody was that happy to see me.

"And who is this lovely young lady?" Sal asked, peering over the counter and waggling his bushy gray eyebrows.

"Sayre Bellavia," I mumbled, tracing the tile pattern on the floor with my toe.

"Ah, *bella via,*" Sal said, nodding. "Where I'm from it means *beautiful way,* did you know that?"

"No," I said, gazing up at him.

"Well, it's a beautiful name for a beautiful girl," he said and his smile made me feel like a flower in the sun, and so we got our pizza and took it to headquarters where I ate four whole slices and immediately conked out on a cot in the coffee room.

When I woke up, a lady from social services was there to take me to somebody's house because Candy had been arrested for trying to hit me with a hammer, my mother had been arrested for the meth they found on her when she got up in the face of the cop who was trying to arrest Candy, and Sims had been arrested for violating the terms of his parole, which, because of his third-tier sexual-predator status, specifically stated that he could not reside in a domicile with any children under the age of twelve.

Two days later, when my mother was released with a court date and I was returned to her, she came home, got high, and with an unnerving burst of manic energy, packed up all of Candy's things and called one of the many Fee brothers to come and get them because, as she said while she was polishing the bathroom doorknob with the front of her T-shirt over and over and over, "I hate to do it, but she must of got hold of some *baaad* shit because she's totally out of control and I can't have her here kicking up drama all the time, especially with the cops and that nosy old Carroll bitch next door. That cat of hers better not set foot on this property or I swear to Christ she'll never see it again," she added in an ominous mutter and catching sight of herself in the mirror, scowled, abandoned the doorknob, and started raking her bitten-down nails over and over through her stringy hair. "Maybe I should go blond again. Do you think I should go blond? Maybe I should go blond. How would I look with blond hair? Like Cameron Diaz? Do you think I'd look like Cameron Diaz? I'm thin like her. It's just my hair. You could do it for me. Yeah. Go ahead. Go down to the drugstore and get me hair color."

"Mom," I said. "I have no money."

"Did I say anything about money?" she said and barked a laugh. She leaned into the mirror and picked at a sore, her once pretty face sallow and sunken. "Shit, if I'd waited till I had money to get what I wanted, I'd never of had anything." The sore started to bleed and she stopped. "Fucking bugs are killing my skin. I got to get out of here." She skimmed past me and clattered down the stairs.

I followed.

"Stay inside and don't go anywhere," she said, grabbing her battered purse. "You've got to lay low because they're watching us. Don't talk to anybody, don't answer the phone, and don't let anybody in unless you know them. Do you hear me?"

I nodded.

"Say it," she said.

"I heard you," I said.

"Good, because it's just you and me now, so don't fuck it up." She headed for the door and stopped. "Get me a beer, would you?"

And I did, feeling a small flutter of hope as I trotted back and pressed the cold can into her trembling hand, and stood waving from the doorway as she hurried out into the night.

Just her and me now.

I had finally gotten my wish, and in the days to come I certainly lived to regret it, lying awake many nights that winter huddled under my coat because we had no money, no heat, and my mother was cranked up to full throttle and heading for a spectacular crash.

And then in February, one month short of a year since Grandma Lucy died, the sheriff came and escorted us off the premises because we'd lost the blue house to foreclosure, and so we ended up out on the street.

Chapter 12

Evan wakes up screaming.

One minute I'm near drowsing next to Red in the front seat of the plow truck, watching from beneath heavy lids as the wipers swish back and forth, back and forth, and according to a glance at the battered CD case, listening to some old folkie named Jorma Kaukonen singing a quiet, kind of sad "Genesis," and the next minute Evan is thrashing and grinding out the most horrible, ragged sounds filled with pain.

Red jumps and hits the brakes, and the plow truck fishtails down the road.

I turn and scramble straight through the gap between the seats and crouch on the floor, dodging Evan's swings and somehow grabbing his arms, babbling, "It's okay, it's okay, you're all right, Evan, you have to stop, please, you're going to hurt yourself," but he doesn't, he keeps moaning and writhing until the bad knee that was lying crooked shifts from inward to outward and then he just stops and deflates, sweating, tears streaking his cheeks, and shaking, covers his eyes and turns his face away.

"What the hell was that all about?" Red says, glancing back at me.

"I think we had his knee laid out the wrong way," I say in a low voice, and am so freaked by that kind of agony, agony we might have caused by laying his leg down wrong that I feel sick. What if we'd twisted his tendons or a vein and had cut off his blood supply? What if pieces of shattered bone were sticking him or had cut into an artery and he was bleeding inside? What if—

"Sayre?" Evan whispers.

I lean close to his pale, pained face. "I'm here," I say, taking his hand and trying to smile.

"Is this the ambulance?" he says weakly.

"No," I say, and give in to the urge to stroke his poor, battered forehead. There's no reason not to—he's in pain and I'm the reason for it, and besides, once we get to the hospital we're never going to see each other again anyway—but I'm afraid of how badly I want to comfort him, and that somehow by doing it I give myself away. "It's the plow truck. It came just like we hoped it would."

We. I used that word without thinking and it's a strong one, big and obvious, like I'm joining us together in a secret hope made public.

"Good," he mumbles, his dark gaze holding mine, searching for reassurance just like a little kid. "I don't remember . . . Oh no. Shit, I'm gonna puke."

"Wait—" I say, and then he starts gagging and I have to try and lean him gently over the edge of the seat and he does throw up, down onto a pile of old coffee cups and other mud-spattered debris.

"I'm sorry," he whispers when it's over, wiping his chin on the back of his hand and turning his face away from me. "God, what a mess."

"It's all right," I say, trying to hold my breath because the smell is awful.

"Hold on." Red cracks his window and stops the truck. Opens his door, gets out, goes around to the bed of the truck for a snow shovel, and while I hold Evan up and away from the back door, Red shovels out everything on the floor, throwing it all in the back of the truck. "Poor bastard," he says, getting back in, closing the door, and cranking up the heat. "How you doing back there, buddy?"

"Like shit," Evan manages to say as I ease him back down against the door.

"Well, just hold on because we got about seven miles to go," Red says, and hands back a bottle of Snapple. "Here, let him take a slug of that. Clean out his mouth."

I open it and give it to Evan, watching as he takes a shaky drink. He hands it back and closes his eyes. Reluctantly, I climb back up front into my seat.

"Quite a night," Red says, glancing over at me. "How are you holding up?"

I shake my head, staring out into the swirling snow lit by the headlights. The winter woods are stark, barren, and offer no real shelter, no safe haven for the lost or wounded. It's a beautiful, dangerous, lonely place, and I have never been so thankful to be on my way out of it in my entire life.

"Bobcat," Red says, pointing up the road.

There, up ahead, caught in the glare of the truck's lights is a big, raggedy bobcat standing belly deep in snow at the edge of the road.

"Seen a lot of them around this year," Red says, downshifting. "Must have been a big rabbit population this summer. Too bad, because they're probably starving now."

But not all of them. Not the one by Harlow's trailer. That piece of pork I gave him might keep him going for a while and maybe, when I go back for my money and Misty, I'll bring some more food. I'll just leave it by the side of the road and he'll find it. I'll never know if it's enough to save him because bobcats are solitary, secretive, and self-sufficient; they live alone, sleep alone, and die alone, and that thought makes me even more determined to bring back food for him.

Our approach sends the big cat leaping across the snowy road and off into the night.

Red reaches into his shirt pocket and pulls out a pack of gum. Offers it to me.

"No thanks." And then I surprise myself by blurting out, "So, uh, what have you been doing since I last saw you? Are you still a youth minister down at the church?"

"Sure am," he says, glancing at me.

"I used to go to Sunday school there when I was little."

"Oh yeah? Why'd you quit?"

"Long story," I say, sorry I brought it up.

"Well, I've got the time," he says, and turns up the volume as the Beatles' "Let It Be" flows out of the CD player.

"Nice touch," I say with a wry smile.

He chuckles. "Never say God—and the Beatles—don't have great timing."

I sit mulling that over, letting the quiet grandeur of the song surround me. It's a quarter to five in the morning, the darkest hour before dawn, and the cab is warm and cozy. Evan is sleeping. My mother is in the hospital, and Beale is forever beyond my reach.

There is nothing left to stop me from talking.

I catch my breath.

There is nothing left to stop me.

What remains of my heart, curled so tight for so long, cracks open, and pain, raw and undiluted by time, unfurls with an ache that leaves me breathless.

I clear my throat and before I lose my nerve, say in a rush, "I'm sorry I never thanked you for being so nice to me back then." I don't look at him but I can feel the air in the truck's cab change. "I mean, I know it was a long time ago but it meant a lot." He remembers, I know he does, because he was there at the end, in the graveyard, his blue eyes clouded with helpless sorrow, his gentle hand holding my limp one. I will never forget how sad he looked standing by Beale, whose eyes were swollen from crying, whose whole wonderful face was drawn and devoid of life, whose hands were shaking and who burst into terrible, wracking sobs as I crept to the edge of the gravesites and laid both wild, ordinary, beautiful, sparkling-with-tears bouquets of Queen Anne's lace on the caskets.

"You're welcome, Sayre. I just wish I could have done more," he says quietly, tucking the gum back in his pocket. "I was sorry to hear that your mother and Beale had split up afterward, too. That must have been really hard for you, on top of everything else."

I nod, throat tight.

"I came out to see you after the funeral, you know," he continues, like since I'd brought up the past, it was now an open subject. "I heard that you and your mom had moved into that old cabin Candy Fee was renting outside of town, so I dropped by once to see you, thinking maybe you needed someone to talk to besides family, but you weren't home. I spoke with your mom for a couple of minutes but she had friends over and was in a hurry, so I told her I'd come back to see you another time. She said not to bother because you were doing just fine." He pauses. "I was hoping that once she told you I'd been out there, maybe you'd stop down at the church sometime, just to say hello but—"

"I never showed up," I say in a low, rusty voice. "Because she never told me." About him, or anyone else who'd cared enough about me back then to come looking. No, that information had only surfaced during our big fight over Christmas when, sick, furious, and too weak to really hurt me with her fists, she'd done something far worse, taunted me with a betrayal I hadn't even known existed, a revelation so cruel and unforgivable that it knocked my legs out from under me, dropping me to my knees in despair and leaving my mother crowing in triumph.

Red glances at me, surprised, and says, "Well, then, it's a little overdue, but tell me, Sayre, how have you been doing?"

I stare down through blurred eyes at my battered hands and the too-long sleeves of my bulky, donated sweater. "Not so good," I whisper, and start to cry.

Rock Bottom

My mother did not leave the blue house peacefully.

She yelled and fought and screamed at the bank's foreclosure guy and the sheriff's deputies about fascists and conspiracies, and while they were trying to calm her down, I ran through the house with a garbage bag, skirting the mountain of unopened mail that had accumulated in the corner of the dining room floor all these months, and throwing in whatever we had that seemed worth anything: my mother's purse and cigarettes, the few remaining family pictures, clothes and shoes off the floor, the stuff in the bathroom medicine cabinet, the file in Grandma's credenza with my birth certificate, half a bag of pretzels, the beer, the last of the afghans, and the top of my too small but much beloved Hello Kitty pajamas.

My mother's needles and all weren't lying out in the open, so I never gave them another thought, a fact that almost got me killed when we were downtown on Main Street and she finally found out.

"What do you mean you didn't go under the fucking couch? That's where I *always* keep them! Under the couch behind the tin-foil!" she shouted, grabbing me by the hair and yanking me back toward her. "What the hell is *wrong* with you? How could you be so goddamn stupid?" She released me and slapped the side of my head. "You bring *your* stuff but you leave *my* stuff behind?" The thought seemed to enrage her and her blows fell faster, making me huddle and cringe but not cry. I had learned that lesson all too well. "What're you, the only one who matters? I don't mean shit, is that it? Is it?"

"Excuse me, but you really need to stop hitting that child right now."

All of a sudden the beating stopped and I heard my mother growl, "How about you mind your own business, bitch, and take your fat ass and ugly kid out of here before—"

"If you hit her again, I'm calling the police," the woman said and I looked up in time to see my mother take three quick strides and knock the woman's cell phone right out of her hand. "Hey!" the woman said, but her voice was shocked and wobbling now because my mother was right there in her face, and she obviously hadn't been expecting that. "You're going to have to pay for—"

"Fuck you," my mother said, and gave the woman a hard shove.

The woman stumbled backward, astonished. "Stop that! Are you out of your mind? You can't touch me!"

"Oh no?" my mother said and shoved her again.

Her chubby little kid began to cry.

"Mom," I said, standing back up.

"Stop it," the woman said again, gaping at her. "You're a grown woman. What's *wrong* with you?"

"Nothing that kicking your ass won't fix," my mother said with a grim smile and, closing a fist, jabbed her hard in the arm.

"I don't believe this," the woman said, and then to her crying kid, "Run back in the store and tell Mrs. Jameson to call the police right *now.*"

"Don't move, kid, or I swear to Christ I'll make your mother bleed," my mother said.

The kid hesitated.

"Go," his mother said, flinching as my mother slapped the side of her head.

The kid took off wailing.

"Mom," I said, mortified.

"If you don't stop it I'm going to sue you for assault," the woman said, voice quavering.

My mother laughed, harsh and unpleasant. "Oh yeah? And what do you think you're gonna get? Here, I'll save you some time." She strode over and tugged the garbage bag from my hand. Dragged it to the woman and dumped it at her feet. "There you go. It's all yours. Fuck you and have a nice day. C'mon, Sayre." She walked away without looking back and I had no choice but to follow, skirting the woman with an apologetic look and scurrying down the sidewalk after my mother.

The cops caught up with us, of course, and my second time in the back of a police car was nowhere near as kindly as my first. The cop wasn't mean to me, but my mother had a lot to say about pretty much everything, her tone strident and her words insulting, and all I could do was huddle there, scared and silent and embarrassed because of all the people in Sullivan who had seen us getting arrested, and seen how crazy my mother looked, twitching, waving her arms, and running at the mouth.

Finally, the woman my mother had punched changed her mind about pressing charges and just wanted it all over. She'd left our bag of things with the cops, and so they gave it back to my mother, let her call Candy for a ride, and released us with a warning to stay out of trouble. That was fine with me but my mother did not appreciate their advice to get clean and start taking care of her business, so she told them to go screw themselves as she stalked out, with me and the garbage bag once again dragging along behind her.

We had no money and nowhere to go, so we stayed up at the big, ramshackle Fee farmhouse on the back mountain ridge for the rest of the winter, the late spring, and into the beginning of summer. I learned to move silently in the background, a dirty, neglected little kid with no voice, no wants, and who made no trouble so as not to call the wrath of the eight or so tweaking adults who lived there down on me. I drifted, faded, and became a listless, ghostlike scavenger who took what she could get. I lived mostly in my head,

and for a while actually convinced myself that I was a survivor of
one of those catastrophic earthquakes or tornados I used to see on
the Weather Channel, a dazed, bewildered, and emotionless girl
picking her way through an endless landscape of foul and stinking
rubble to try and come out on the other side.

Most of the Fees used their own meth, but they still made
money selling it, and my mother moved into Candy's brother
Bobby's bedroom with him, became his woman, so she had some
money then, too, and of course all the high she could ever need. I
was left to curl up wherever I could find a spot and so at first I tried
to sleep in the little bedroom with four of the nine other kids but
the room was a horror of stacked junk, peed-on sheets, torn window screens, cockroaches everywhere, burps, farts, kicking, pinching, and the ever-blanketing stench of the unwashed.

If it wasn't so frigid in the winter and crawling with rattlesnakes
in the summer, I would have slept in one of the old junk cars
outside. If the snarling, barrel-chested Rottweilers they kept out
front weren't so starved, vicious, and eaten up by fleas, I would
have slept in their doghouses with them. If one of the bigger,
stronger girls hadn't stolen the afghan from my bag of stuff, I
would have holed up out on the porch or on the corner of the
living room floor.

In the end, I sneaked into the room where my mother and
Bobby Fee were, crept into the closet, hollowed out a spot among
the dirty clothes, covered myself with a flannel shirt from the mess
scattered across the floor, and slept.

They knew I was there, or at least my mother did because she
was awake the next morning when I crawled out, stiff and dazed,
and she gave me a look but didn't say anything, and so I ended up
sleeping in there every night.

I caught the bus to school with the other Fees and still had
enough of my grandmother in me to be humiliated by the bus
driver's raised eyebrows when she saw me trailing on after them. I
was tired and hungry, and that bad, cat-pee smell pervaded every-

thing, so even though I washed what few clothes I had, the odor never really came out.

I remember how hot it was in that farmhouse with the wood-stove burning nonstop in the winter and how bad the place reeked in the summer. I remember the brothers counting out a big wad of cash, heading out in their pickups, and coming home with three new plasma TVs. I remember the bug strips thick and wriggling with hundreds of caught flies hanging from the kitchen ceiling, guns on every shelf, and the washroom sink littered with lighters and tinfoil, tampons and dozens of used needles, and always that terrible, throat-burning, eye-watering smell coming from the lab out back. I remember how all of the Fee toddlers were bruised and filthy, and how every so often I'd see Candy or one of her sisters-in-law put a little meth in the kids' soda so they'd stop fussing and not be hungry all the time. I remember the phones ringing nonstop, the smell of burnt coffee from a pot that was never washed, how Bobby Fee loved Kit Kat bars and how every so often he would toss me a five-dollar bill in passing.

I remember how two of the brothers plowed up the whole sunny side of the yard one day and planted dozens of tomato and pep-per plants, watermelon and bean and okra and cucumber seeds. I remember Candy's father's fiftieth birthday party, when they roasted a whole pig outside over a fire to celebrate. There was food and drink everywhere, and I remember that my mother was still kind of pretty in spite of being scrawny and gap toothed, and that she was laughing, drinking beer, wearing cut-offs and a blue halter top, and dancing in the grass with Bobby Fee to Gretchen Wilson's "Redneck Woman." Everyone was telling stories and smoking and getting along, and even the whining Rotties got more than their share of gnawed bones with meat left on them. I remember how the birthday boy, Candy's blind and burned parolee father, with his scarred sockets, and lumpy, red-and-white skin that looked like it had melted and slid down his face, slobbered when he ate the potato salad because his bottom lip was gone and so were his teeth, and his top lip was thick and mangled and flopped uselessly because the nerves were damaged.

I don't know how long we would have stayed there on the ridge, or how emotionally dead I would have been inside if that June Bobby Fee hadn't sold his product to a couple of bright-eyed, sparkly college girls who were so busy laughing at the rednecks and texting their friends on the drive back down the mountain that they took a turn too fast and wiped out half the guardrail going over the bank. One died, and the other was pretty battered and had to be Life-Flighted out to a bigger, city hospital. The state troopers found a lot of meth in the wreckage and the girls' distraught parents, all important townies, demanded someone be held accountable and so the troopers and HAZMAT geared up and raided the Fees' lab one day while half the Fee kids and I were at summer school, mostly because we all got a free lunch.

We were called down to the office, where a tired-looking woman from social services was pacing and talking into her cell phone, saying that every one of the adults at the raid was in custody, and she needed to find the lot of us emergency foster homes.

And that was how, when everything was darkest, I ended up away from the Fees and sent to stay in a cozy little house on Sunrise Road with a good-hearted lady named Miss Mo and her pretty young daughter. They gave me a hot, delicious grilled-cheese sandwich and a bowl of creamy, homemade rice pudding, a vanilla-scented bubble bath, a pair of too big pink cotton pajamas with red print hearts all over them, a feather-soft double bed all to myself in the guest room, and a view out the window to a pretty white farmhouse in the distance that would someday be both the shining nirvana and the absolute despair of my life.

Chapter 13

Red leans across the truck's cab, opens the glove box, and hands me a packet of tissues. "Sorry. I didn't mean to make things worse."

"It's not you," I manage to say, wadding a tissue up my nose to stop its leaking.

"Is it your mother?" he says as the plow truck crests the big hill and off in the distance the hospital lights shine.

Yes. No. Yes. I don't know.

Yes.

"I stopped by and sat with her for a while this past week," he says.

I drop the tissue and gape at him, shocked. "In the hospital?"

He nods, his gaze focused on the road. "The chapel there tries to provide every terminal patient with spiritual comfort, and since Reverend Marshall is over in Malaysia working with a lay ministry, I'm standing in and—"

"Wait," I say, twisting my hands in my lap. "You said t . . . terminal? For real?"

"Yes, Sayre," he says gently. "Hasn't anyone spoken to you about her illness?"

"No. I mean I know her liver's bad and we met with the transplant team and she doesn't qualify but I thought . . ." What did I think? I don't know. That despite how sick she is she'll just go on forever because she's *always* been sick and she's always gone on?

Yes. That's exactly it. My head is spinning and I can't seem to make sense of this news rushing at me. "She's really dying? I mean, *now*?"

"Yes. Her liver is irreversibly damaged by chronic alcoholism and drug abuse," he says. "Her kidneys are failing, too. I spoke to her doctors, and you're right, she's not a candidate for the transplant list. Her addiction aside, she's not even physically strong enough to withstand the medical-testing portion of the initial evaluation. I did some research after I spoke with the team and there aren't enough donated livers for everyone who needs one, so the ones they receive are precious. Quite a few people who *do* manage to pass the strenuous evaluation and make the list still die waiting for a healthy liver, so . . ." He sighs and rubs his bearded chin. "She signed a DNR—a do not resuscitate order—and said she doesn't want any type of extraordinary measures taken, so the end-of-life care staff has made her as comfortable as possible. Now it's just a matter of time."

"Wait," I say faintly. "She signed . . . I just saw her like, two weeks ago and she was bad, yeah, but she wasn't *dying* . . ." Was she? Could she have been? Had I just gotten so used to seeing her always sleeping, her body skeletal and emaciated, her face sunk in on itself, the yellow eyes and incessant trembling . . .

Was that her dying, because if it was, she'd been doing it for a long time, and right in front of me.

"Great," I say numbly, and when Evan's hand touches my sleeve for a second, his arm stretched out from the backseat and trembling with the effort, I barely acknowledge it. "Now what?"

"Well . . . now we try to find a way to help you cope with what's coming," Red says, slipping a pack of Marlboros from his jacket pocket, shaking one free, and lighting up. "I won't lie to you, Sayre. It's going to be rough, but I'll be there if you need me. You won't be alone. And if you ever want to talk, I can listen and advise you as your minister or, unofficially, as your friend. It really does help, Sayre. Sharing pain lessens the burden and sometimes it makes it more bearable."

Sharing pain? Saying it out loud? I wouldn't even know how to begin.

"That goes for old wounds, too, you know. I really wish we'd had the chance to talk before this," he says, cracking the window so the smoke can escape. "There's a Longfellow quote I have stuck on my bulletin board at the church office—'*There is no grief like the grief that does not speak*'—and it's true. I've found that keeping pain inside doesn't give it a chance to heal, but bringing it out into the light, holding it right there in your hands and trusting that you're strong enough to make it through, not hating the pain, not loving it, just seeing it for what it really is can change how you go on from there. Time alone doesn't heal emotional wounds, Sayre, and you don't want to live the rest of your life bottled up with anger and guilt and bitterness. That's how people self-destruct."

I glance down at my hands, clenched so tight they ache.

"Let me tell you," Red takes a long drag on the cigarette, and blows the smoke toward the open window, "nothing about growing up here in Sullivan prepared me for being deployed to Iraq. It was a whole different world. Brutal. I can't erase what happened there. Can't bring back the buddies I lost. I can't forget what I saw and what I did, or what they did to us. It was crazy. By the time I came home, I didn't want to feel anything anymore. Nothing. The whole thing changed me, and not for the better, or so I thought."

"My cousin's over there now," Evan says in a hoarse voice. "He says his nerves are shot."

Red glances into the rearview mirror. "How you doing back there, buddy?"

Evan grunts.

I glance over my shoulder, but his eyes are closed. I wait a couple of seconds but they don't open.

"Well, when your cousin comes home you tell him to come see me, and we'll talk," Red says, flicking his ashes out the window. "It's the best thing he could do."

"So wait, I have a question," I say, turning to Red when it becomes apparent that Evan isn't going to respond. "How did you go from coming home and not wanting to feel anything at all to becoming a minister and hanging around with dying people?"

Red smiles slightly. "Would it be a cop-out to say that God works in mysterious ways?"

I give him a look.

"All right, then, here's the abbreviated version: If you ever need a reminder to celebrate your own life, spend your time with the dying. Whatever problems you think you have, they'd trade you for in a New York minute. It's one helluva reality check."

"More reality," I mutter. "What fun."

"Seriously, it puts it all in perspective. I've learned a lot from the end-of-life patients," he says, stubbing the cigarette out in the ash-tray. "It's pretty amazing, the internal and emotional stages people go through when they know they're dying. Did you know that the first thing they usually do is deny the news of their impending death? 'What? Dying? Not me!' They struggle against it, deny it like it's a temporary setback and make big plans for the future that anyone can see are impossible. It's like they need to believe that by not acknowledging death, it won't happen."

So what else is new? My mother's been in denial her whole life.

"The second stage is anger," he continues, downshifting to slow for a sharp bend. "They feel helpless and out of control because the time has come, they're actually going to die, and there's nothing they can do to change it. It's no longer a vague, someday idea but an immediate reality."

I fold my arms across my chest and stare out at the snowy night.

"The third is the bargaining stage, where they try to make deals with God, the universe, anyone who's listening. They're willing to compromise, change their behavior, do anything for another chance." He glances over at me. "I've sat and prayed with a lot of people in the bargaining stage, Sayre. It's pretty heartrending."

"Does it ever work?" I say dully.

"No. At least not the way they want it to." He blinks his lights at the only other vehicle on the snowy road, another plow truck headed in the opposite direction. "The next stage is depression, and guilt at the pain they're causing their family."

The CD player cycles and Simon & Garfunkle's "Bridge Over Troubled Water" flows softly from the speakers.

"Oh, come on," I say, giving him a look. "Don't you ever listen to anything cheery?"

He smiles. "Ah, Sayre, we each find comfort in our own way. Your mother said as much, too. Right before I'd gotten there they'd given her a bath and the aide was very gentle, and your mother said being warm and clean and tucked into bed with a blanket made her feel safe and cared for, just like a child again."

"Yeah, unless that child was me," I mutter, scowling. "I was just SOL."

"Hmm." He gives me a considering look. "Well, she must have done something right because you turned out to be a strong, smart, brave girl—"

"That's because of my grandmother and Miss Mo and Aunt Loretta, not because of her." And then because I just want this whole conversation to be over, "So what's the last stage?"

"The last stage is acceptance. They become calm and less emotional, have little need for the outside world and turn inward, searching their souls, finding peace, and just being with themselves. Their bodies are shutting down in preparation for death and they accept that the battle is almost over. They actually become ready to die, and are all right with it."

"What about making peace with everybody they hurt?" I say. "What stage is that?"

Red hesitates. "Everyone is different, Sayre. Your mother is an addict and that's a category unto itself. I don't pretend to know what she's thinking or feeling now. I only know that she wanted to see you."

"But *why*?" I cry in frustration, spreading my hands. "That's the part I don't get! Why?"

"Maybe she just wants to say good-bye," Evan says quietly from the backseat as we top the next hill and the lit-up hospital grounds spread out before us.

Sunrise Road

Right from the beginning it was Miss Mo, my new emergency foster mother, rescuing me from the Fees, talking to me in a kind voice, making a place for me at her table, and singing a rich, haunting "You Bring Me Joy" as she cooked in the kitchen.

That first morning, with the sun streaming in through sheer white curtains.

Waffle-maker waffles with butter and syrup for breakfast.

Barn swallows diving and swooping in a brilliant blue sky.

The edge of the pasture next door outlined with billows of Queen Anne's lace.

Following Miss Mo's daughter, Mareene, out to pick rainbow zinnias from the garden.

The both of them digging through Mareene's outgrown clothes to find me a wardrobe that wasn't so shabby.

Finding out that Miss Mo and Mareene had moved up here ten years ago from Atlanta, and they *still* weren't used to the deep cold of our winters.

Being asked to help Miss Mo tuck her silky black hair up beneath the hairnet she had to wear when she served food down at the mission, and saying shyly, "It's really soft," and then listening to a story about her Muscogee Creek great-great-great-grandfather and her Creole great-great-great-grandmother who'd fallen in love and eloped, and who had almost nine feet of long, shiny black hair between them.

Getting a smile at lunch and a kiss on the forehead at bedtime, right after Miss Mo reminded me to say my prayers.

Mareene and me, sitting on the back porch in the sun drinking iced tea and watching the fawns frolic down by the wood line.

Miss Mo giving me a haircut, and Mareene fixing the bangs.

Carrying plates of fried zucchini blossoms, deviled eggs, and macaroni salad across the grassy acres between Miss Mo's little house and the sprawling Sunrise Farm to have a Sunday picnic out under the willow trees by the pond with a plump, elderly gray-haired lady they said I could call Aunt Loretta, and her tall, serious-looking grown son, Beale.

Thinking Aunt Loretta's fried chicken was the best I'd ever tasted.

Thinking Sunrise Farm, which grew and sold raspberries, black-berries, strawberries, apples, peaches, asparagus, sunflowers, and pumpkins was the most beautiful place I had ever seen.

Being quiet and wary around Beale because he was a man and the ones I knew didn't want to hear what a kid had to say, and then changing my mind when he tilted his John Deere cap back on his head and, smiling, said, "So Miss Sayre Bellavia, how about helping me with a chore?"

I said, *Um, okay,* and he told me to scrape all the meat scraps onto one paper plate and follow him to the edge of the lawn near the old cooler house. When I did, he set the plate down and in a high, silly voice sang, *Here, kitty, kitty, kitty* and like magic, a half dozen mewing, multicolored balls of fluff came tumbling out, tails high and heading straight for us. I dropped to my knees in the warm, sunny grass, enchanted, and when I looked up, laughing and surrounded by mischievous, romping kittens, he was smiling right back.

Hiding my surprise as he sat down alongside me and let the kittens crawl all over him, chuckling as Aunt Loretta called from her seat at the picnic table, "Aren't they sweet? They're to be Tabby's last litter. She's going to Doc Wendell's on Tuesday to be fixed. It's time for her to retire," and then she said something in a low voice to Miss Mo and they burst out laughing, the happy sound ringing out on the breeze like church bells.

Listening as Beale considered names for them—Stihl, Poulan, Fox, Emmett—and venturing a few suggestions of my own—Bunny, Clover, Stormy, Coconut—and kissing each of the kittens' fuzzy little heads.

Sneaking glances at Beale's strong, weathered face and calm hazel eyes, at how gentle his large, calloused hands were when they cradled a kitten, and then actually being brave enough to slip my own hand into his when he stood and reached down to help me up.

Eating two huge slabs of homemade blueberry pie with ice cream and a slice of watermelon, and having a pit-spitting competition with Beale and Mareene to see who could spit their pits the farthest. Beale won, and me and Mareene decided his prize would be to let me name one of the kittens. I chose to name the little gray Stormy and listened close when Beale started singing a song that went, "*Oh Stormy, bring back that sunny day . . .*" Standing worried and tense when Mareene threw back her head and yowled like a coyote, saying that's what he sounded like, and then exhaling in relief and joining in the laugher when I realized it was only a joke and he wasn't stomping off mad.

Beale teaching me how to play horseshoes, and then helping Miss Mo and Aunt Loretta carry the dirty dishes back into the farmhouse. Gazing at all the family pictures on the walls and the afghans on the couch, the ceramic apple-topped cookie jar and the old-fashioned claw-foot tub, at the porch swing and the crooked wooden stairs leading down to the root cellar and the extra refrigerator. Gazing at the pantry lined with jars of canned tomatoes and peaches and beets shining like jewels, the stacks of books by Aunt Loretta's reading chair, and Beale's mud-caked boots lined up by the back door.

Hating to leave, dying to hug both Beale and Aunt Loretta good-bye but being too shy to do it, waving and dragging my feet all the way back to Miss Mo's, then falling asleep right there on the stubbly tan couch in the living room, drugged by the sun and the air and the food and the bliss.

Waking up the next morning in my clean, cozy guest room bed with the sheer curtains billowing in the breeze and Mareene singing "Stormy" in the kitchen, with the mouthwatering scent of frying bacon in the air and the memory of a gentle, calloused hand closed firmly around mine, helping me stand up.

Wanting, with all my heart, to stay right there forever.

Chapter 14

"Where's my phone?" Evan says as we start down the last two-mile hill toward the hospital. "There's coverage here, right? I need to call my dad."

"Oh my God, yeah, here," I say, reaching into the backseat, tugging at my coat, still wadded behind his head, and digging in the pocket. How could I have forgotten? I hand him the phone. "Do you want me to dial it for you?"

"No, I'm okay," he says, holding it in his good hand.

I face forward again, trying to give him some privacy.

"I'll go in with you to see your mother if it would make it any easier," Red says, downshifting and taking the last winding slope at a slow crawl.

"No, but thank you," I say after considering his offer. "I feel like I should do it alone." I make a face. "I really hope Candy's not in there."

"What about Beale?" Red says. "Has anyone told him about your mom?"

"No, why should he care?" I say, avoiding his gaze. "They haven't been together in years."

"Well, he could still be a valuable support system for you," he says.

My eyes fill with tears and I shake my head, and it must be plain I don't want to talk about it because he simply nods and says, "All right, but if you want me, just tell a nurse and they'll call me immediately. I'm always available, Sayre."

"Okay," I say because the hospital is inching closer and I can hear Evan on the phone, his voice rough with exhaustion saying, *No, Dad, I swear I'm all right. My head and my knee . . . Tell Mom to stop crying . . . On my way to the hospital right now . . . Okay, but be careful, the roads are bad . . . Love you, 'bye.*

Love you, 'bye.

God, three one-syllable words and I have never heard my mother say them. Not once.

And I've never spoken them, either.

Love you, 'bye.

I can't even imagine saying them, especially naturally and without hesitation like Evan just did, as if he knows for sure, without even thinking, that they'll be welcomed and not ridiculed or ignored and left hanging there without response.

And with a pang I wonder if he has any idea how lucky he is that he can do that, say such strong words, make such a true, heartfelt declaration without even thinking of how vulnerable it makes him, how admitting it out loud opens him up to hurt and rejection, and if his parents were a different kind of people, addicts maybe, who had never wanted him in the first place, how they could use that love against him.

Who would I have been if my mother had said that to me, even only one time, and meant it? Who would I have been? Not this lost, broke, homeless girl, that's for sure. It would have given me something to hold on to . . . although . . .

My heart beats faster.

 . . . it would have been bewildering then, wondering why, if she loved me, she would always scream and hit me, ignore me and leave me behind and never care if I was cold or hungry or lonely or scared . . .

If she'd said she loved me and still did all those cruel and careless things, would my child mind have decided to accept *that* as the definition of love?

Probably.

Would I have ended up believing that love was manipulative and hurtful and full of pain, gotten used to being shoved aside, sworn at and disregarded, picked up and hugged, and then slapped around for getting in the way, starved and smiled at, neglected and cursed, told I was no good and would never amount to anything, then hefted high and proudly shown off down at the Walmart, introduced as a little pisser and a big mistake in the same breath?

Yes, I would have, because if she said she loved me and then acted that way I would have thought that was how you loved someone, and how someone should love you back.

But as it is, I *know* she doesn't love me, and while that still has the power to hurt me, in a strange, twisted way I realize I'm glad of it because now I understand that even though she is my mother and she treated me like crap, I didn't mistake it for love.

Not good love.

Love was Grandma Lucy, her wistful sighs, gentle chiding and responsible routines, Cricket the old blue parakeet, wreaths on the front door that changed with the seasons, crocheted afghans, a place at the table and ambrosia salad because she knew I liked it.

Love was Miss Mo and Mareene, not rushing me past my cautious shyness but being there when I finally reached for them, their smiles and teasing and helping hands, listening, talking, seeing brightness in every day, finding me clothes and giving prayers of thanks and happily sharing whatever they had.

Love was Aunt Loretta's reliability, her quiet firmness and sense of fairness, the way she paid attention and saw what needed to be done or heard what couldn't be said. It was her willingness to listen and to really *hear* you. It was great windswept drifts of Queen Anne's lace, rambling walks through the pastures with kittens trailing at our heels, an heirloom feather bed, oatmeal with milk and brown sugar in the morning, little Stormy tucked close beside me in winter, and picking buckets of fresh, juicy blackberries in summer.

Love was Beale, good naturedly wearing the bizarre, reindeer-antler ball cap my mother bought him as a joke for Christmas, coming in after working the fields, tired and grimy and smiling right into my eyes as if he was always glad to see me, kneeling beside me as, crying, I buried what was left of a baby possum hit by a car, helping me with my homework, sitting on the porch playing his guitar in the sultry, summer twilight, laughing and picking my mother up, twirling her around and shouting for Aunt Loretta so they could give her the good news, hugging me, providing for me, protecting me.

Love was Ellie, pure and pink and soft with her pretty hazel doe eyes and wispy brown hair, burbling and chewing on her fist in the crib. Cooing like a delighted dove when I kissed her, laughing when I blew raspberries on her stomach, grabbing fistfuls of my hair and chortling when I dressed her in her little pink onesie.

Sweet Ellie, as beloved and enchanting as the sun, splashing in her bathwater, making nonsense noises, and lighting up like all the stars in the universe when she saw me. Ellie, who was never afraid to show her heart, who trusted me enough to fall asleep in my arms and who I loved more than anything.

And who loved me, too.

I would have been such a good big sister.

My cheeks are wet and I can feel Evan's hand on my arm and Red looking at me, but I don't have enough in me to respond.

Love you, 'bye.

In my world, it means something totally different.

Paradise Lost

When I first saw Mareene and Beale together at the picnic I thought they liked each other and would be boyfriend and girlfriend, even though Beale, at thirty-five, was much older than her, but when I sidled up to Miss Mo the next day while she was sorting laundry, I found out I was wrong, and Beale and Mareene had never been anything but friends.

Mareene, it turned out, was dating a guy from the other side of Sullivan, and even though Miss Mo didn't come right out and say she didn't like him, I could see by the flash of fire in her dark eyes and the way she starting flinging the clothes into separate piles, whites away from reds, towels away from jeans, underwear away from everything else, that she just wasn't happy about it.

"For two whole years that girl has put up with his nonsense," she said, stuffing a whole set of yellow-flowered sheets in the washer. "Him running around on her, never calling, showing up late, coming here drunk and high and mixed up in God only knows what kind of business . . ." Frowning, she snatched up the detergent bottle and dumped some in. "That boy . . . no, that *man* has disrespected her in every possible way, but does she use the backbone the good lord gave her and tell him it's over? No, she does not. *But, Mom, I love him,* is what she says every single time I try and talk some sense into her."

"Hmmph," I said because I'd learned that if I stayed quiet and listened, most times adults would forget who they were talking to and just keep giving air to whatever was on their minds.

She heaved a hearty sigh, shut the lid on the washer, and turned it on. Leaned an ample hip against it and blotted her damp forehead with her sleeve. "So I've given up. I'm not going to argue against him anymore because every time I do, she rushes to defend him. *But, Mom, he's one of God's children, too. But, Mom, he didn't have a good upbringing like you gave me, and I feel I can help him. But, Mom, it's his medication that makes him act mean like that.* You know what I told her? What do you want with all of that 'give me your wretched, your messed-up, and your cheater' stuff? You're not the Statue of Liberty!" She snorted and shook her head like she just couldn't figure it out. "I don't know what kind of hold he has over her, but you just watch how that child loses all the good sense God gave her the next time he shows up. But I'm not saying a word, oh no. Not anymore. Now I'm just going to try to remember that yes, even Harlow Maltese is one of God's children, and sometimes the hardest folks to love are the ones who need it the most." She picked up the empty laundry basket. "In the meantime, I'm going to pray for God to give her the strength to break free of him."

"Okay, I will, too." Even though I'd only been there for six days, I already loved Miss Mo and Mareene, and didn't want trouble anywhere around them.

Mareene went on seeing her no-good, cheating boyfriend and two weeks into the praying, we got word that the prosecutor's office had charged the Fees but that thanks to Bobby Fee's gallant insistence that my mother, Candy, and the sisters-in-law were only users and not dealers, they were mandated to an assortment of residential rehab facilities and counseling instead of being sent to prison with the rest of the family.

Forty-five days.

That's how long I had left on Sunrise Road.

One short month, and two weeks.

It seemed like no time at all, especially now that when Miss Mo was home from her mission work she was teaching me how to make squash pancakes and homemade dill pickles from scratch, and Mareene was finally getting just a little tired of her bad boyfriend's behavior (although she hadn't quite given up on him yet) and talking about either going to college or taking one of those Carnival cruises she was always seeing on TV. Aunt Loretta had a fresh pitcher of iced tea ready every day at six when Beale quit working and we would all sit out on the steps and talk about chickens and horoscopes and honeybees and whatever struck our fancy, while Aunt Loretta embroidered and Beale had a cigarette and I guzzled iced tea and chewed the ice cubes, making everyone shudder, and the kittens pounced on each other in the grass.

Only forty-five days until it would all be over and I would be back with my mother.

Rehab.

It meant she would be quitting drinking and drugs.

It was impossible to imagine. I had no idea who she was without them, what she would look like, how she would act, whether she would treat me any different . . .

I just didn't know, and the questions swirled in my head, making it hard to sleep at night. Would she want me with her? Why? Where? We didn't have anywhere to live. Would she let me stay here instead, now that she was sober? And wouldn't it be the great irony of my life if that, when she was stoned, she didn't care where I was and so I could have stayed here forever without a worry, but now that she was going to be sober, she wanted me with her?

I fretted about it for two weeks and finally went as far as to ask Miss Mo if I could live here with her even after my mother got out. I shouldn't have done that because she was preoccupied with Mareene, who was depressed because her boyfriend had cheated on her again and was trying to decide if she had finally had enough, and it was the only time Miss Mo was impatient with me, saying it was very brave of my mother to go to rehab, to try and do the right thing, and how terrible she would feel if, after all of that work, her own daughter didn't even want to try and work things out.

She must have seen my stricken expression because she sighed and gathered me close, stroking my hair as I buried my face in her ample waist and saying, "Baby, baby, do you know how many people would give everything they own to see their mother or father or brother or sister make it through rehab and step into the world clear-eyed again? Trust me, I see them every day down at the mission, drifting in like zombies with some kind of hurt so bad and so deep they'd rather numb themselves to all the glory in the world than face one day of the pain of it. You're one of the lucky ones, Sayre. You're gonna get to see your mother as sober as God intended rather than as man has made her. Now isn't that something to be excited about?"

I shook my head, keeping my arms locked tight around her. "I don't want to go with her. I want to stay here with you." I wanted to tell her I loved her, too, but those words had never passed my lips and they didn't this time, either.

"Oh, baby," she said softly, "I know you're scared, and I know you had some tough times but—"

"She doesn't even like me," I mumbled.

Miss Mo's arms tightened around me and we were quiet a moment, gently rocking back and forth.

"Will you do something for me, honey?" she said finally, sliding a finger under my chin and tilting it up so she could see my face. "Will you give your mother a chance to show you she's changed? What if all this time it's been nothing but the drugs and alcohol making her so unhappy around you?"

"What if without them she doesn't want to be around me at all?" I said brokenly because I was losing and I knew it. Miss Mo didn't know the whole story and so she didn't understand, and she wasn't going to keep me. I was going to have to go back to my mother and it would be just as bad as it had always been. "Then can I stay here?"

"No, baby," she said, holding my gaze. "I've raised my daughter and I'm too old to take on a young child. I keep my door open for emergency fostering and that's all I can handle. You have to give your mother a chance, Sayre. She's making a fresh start and she's gonna need all the love and support you got in you. Will you do that for me?"

I could have kept begging, could have sworn I wouldn't be any trouble or even threatened to run away, but it was Miss Mo and I loved her and she was already worried about her real daughter, Mareene. I couldn't make her worry about her foster daughter, too. So what could I have said but, "All right, I'll try."

And once I said that, it was like I'd already left. I felt myself pulling away from them, receding, watching them as if from a distance and tucking away each kind word and smile to relive again later, when I was back with my mother.

I didn't cry when I told Aunt Loretta and Beale over iced tea on the porch that I would be leaving soon, but I wanted to, especially when Beale tilted his cap back on his head and gave me a long, considering look from those steady hazel eyes. "Well," he said finally, with a slow, thoughtful nod, "it isn't going to be the same around here without you, that's for sure. You've grown on me, Miss Sayre Bellavia, and I'm gonna miss you." And then he slid a sturdy arm around my shoulders and hugged me hard and quick. "And don't you worry; me and Ma will keep an eye on that kitten of yours, okay?"

"Okay," I whispered. "Will you sing that Stormy song for me one more time, please? The one about bringing back the sunny day?"

"Sure, but you know what? I don't think I ever sang it for you from the beginning," he said, and looking out over the pink-and-gold sunset across the field, sang softly, "'You are the sunshine, baby, whenever you smile . . .'"

I drew my knees up to my chin and my eyes blurred, stared

down at my bare, grass-stained feet. The song wasn't as happy as I'd thought but that was okay because I didn't feel happy at all. I felt like breaking down and bawling the way I did when Grandma Lucy died and suddenly the pain of it was too much. I couldn't sit there with them anymore knowing it was done, so I just pushed myself off the step and took off across the grass, running blind with tears, back toward Miss Mo's, and I heard both of them call from behind me, "Sayre? What's wrong? Are you all right?" and no, I wasn't, but in three days I'd be gone and—

"Hey," Beale said, running up along beside me and catching hold of my arm. "What's going on? Are you okay?" He slowed, and I slowed, and stopped. "Aw, honey, are you crying?"

I couldn't answer, just stood there staring at the ground as tears, more than I knew I had in me, ran down my cheeks and splashed onto my T-shirt.

"Don't tell me my singing's *that* bad," he joked gently. "Come on now. What is it?"

"I don't want to go," I sobbed, holding myself. "I want to stay here forever. This is the best home I ever had and it's not fair that I have to go and you guys get to stay. I want to stay, too. Please?" I was blubbering now, caught up in the fierce pain of longing. "Please, Beale? I'll be good, I promise. I could help with the chores and I won't be any trouble—"

"Aw, Sayre." He sighed, and crouched in front of me. Took one of my damp hands and cradled it between both of his big, strong, steady ones. "I wish you could stay, too, but you have to go back to your mother and—"

"No," I cried angrily, pulling my hand free and swiping my hair from my eyes. "I don't want to! I hate her!" The words rang out huge and harsh and ragged, shocking us both into silence.

"*Hate*'s a strong word," he said quietly.

And that was it. The end. I gave up because it was all there in his tone, including the regretful good-bye.

"Come on now, it's not like you're moving out of state or

anything," he said, rising. "We'll see you around town, you know that."

"Mm-hmm," I said, sniffling because I knew otherwise. Sullivan was small, but my mother and Beale did not inhabit the same universe, not even close, and I knew that when I was back with her, I wouldn't, either. "I have to go now."

"Hey," he said, tugging a lock of my damp, lank hair. "We'll always be friends."

I nodded, unable to speak past the lump in my throat, and walked away, knowing that he was still standing there watching me go, knowing that I would probably never see him again in my whole, entire life.

It was the hardest thing I'd ever done, and by the time I reached Miss Mo's house I couldn't take it anymore, so I turned, praying he was still there watching and he was. I stood up on tiptoe and waved and waved, and he and Aunt Loretta, who had joined him on the lawn, waved and waved back.

And finally, exhausted, I stopped, and trudged inside.

I didn't sleep at all that night, or the next.

Hardly ate.

I didn't talk much, either.

What was there to say?

The day before my mother was released from rehab, Mareene's boyfriend got pulled over for another DUI and called Mareene to come down and bail him out. What the police said when she got there was that he'd had a woman in the car with him, also drunk, who claimed she was a stripper down at a club in Scranton and that he still owed her twenty dollars for a lap dance.

Instead of bailing him out, Mareene had coolly thanked the officers and come straight home again, not only leaving him there but leaving a message on his voice mail telling him it was over for good, and not to call or come around again, *ever*.

Miss Mo sat on the couch and commiserated with her, patting her back when she cried and being sympathetic when she ranted about all the times he'd hurt her, but she couldn't quite hide the hallelujah sparkle in her eyes, and I was glad for them.

It was good that at least some of the prayers around here had been answered.

And the next afternoon when the social services lady pulled into the driveway to get me, my knapsack was packed and I was calm, quiet, and unemotional again.

I was ready to go.

Chapter 15

"Run in and tell them we have a car accident victim out here with injuries and we need a stretcher pronto," Red says, pulling the plow truck up in front of the emergency room entrance.

"Okay," I say, piling out as soon as the truck stops moving and bursting into the hospital waiting room. It's stiflingly hot and my eyes go blurry for a moment.

"Can I help you?" a woman says from the desk in front of me.

"Yes," I say and blurt out what Red told me to, adding that it was a head injury and a knee injury and it happened at least three hours ago and—

The nurse makes the call and within minutes they're rushing a stretcher out the door to the plow truck. I turn to follow but the desk nurse stops me.

"What about you? Were you in the vehicle?"

"Yes," I say and then, "no, I mean I wasn't in the truck, I just saw it happen." I tell her Evan's name, and that his parents are on their way, and my name, and then, "And . . . my mother's in here, too, but I don't know what room."

"What's her name?" she says, hitting a key on the computer's keyboard.

I hesitate because if I tell her, this will be it. I will know where my mother is and I'll have to go up there and see her dying and once I see that I can never un-see it, and it will become real even though I already know it is, I do, but—

"Sayre . . ."

I turn and see them wheeling Evan through. His head wound looks terrible in the light, jagged and swollen and crusted with dried blood. I can see the pain contorting his face, the way he lifts his head and half-reaches in my direction as he passes and says through clenched teeth, "Hey, look, we made it . . . ," and I try to smile and reach back and just manage to brush his outstretched fingers and say, "Yeah, we did," as he's whooshing by and he's still talking, and all I catch before the doors close behind him is ". . . see me after you see your mom."

"I'm sorry, your mother's name?" the desk nurse says, giving me an expectant look.

It's so quiet now. The waiting room is empty, and the clock up on the wall says 5:13. It isn't dawn yet, but it isn't nighttime anymore, either.

I meet the nurse's gaze and say, "Dianne Huff."

She taps the keyboard, staring at the screen, and when she looks back up at me, her gaze is soft with compassion.

And that's when I know that my mother really is dying.

My Mother After Rehab

When the social services woman and I walked into the office waiting room, a slim, brown-haired woman sitting in a turquoise plastic chair glanced up, set down her magazine, rose, and clearing her throat, said, "Hey, Sayre."

I fell back a step and stared.

My mother was still too skinny and I could see the white scars on her bare arms where the sores used to be but her eyes were wide open and focused, her hair was clean and cut shorter and sleeker, and she was wearing a magenta-flowered sundress and white sandals.

I had never seen my mother in a regular dress.

Never.

"Well, aren't you even going to say hello?" she said with a nervous laugh. "I mean, c'mon, I can't be *that* different."

And it was the underlying rasp in her voice, that hint of sandpaper impatience that grated whenever she had to talk to me that I recognized, and gave me the courage I needed. I took a deep breath and said, "Hi. You look a lot different."

"Yeah, well, the good ladies down at the Methodist church got together with the Mission of Mercy people and voilà, one new outfit," she said, looking down at the dress and shrugging. "It's not really me, but—"

"It looks pretty," I said, and after a discreet nudge from the social services woman, plodded across the waiting room. I knew I was supposed to give my mother a hug but I didn't want to and besides, I didn't know how. She wasn't soft and squeezable and brimming with welcome like Miss Mo. She was stiff and hard and—

"You got bigger while I was gone," she said, reaching out and stopping me before I could touch her, ruffling my bangs, keeping her gaze focused on my hair and not my face. "Got a new haircut, too. Hmmph. I guess the foster family thought it was a good idea."

"I like it," I said, and saw something flash in her eyes.

"Well, that's good," she said with a thin smile, "because you're the one who has to live with it. So," she hoisted a big tote bag and turned to the social services woman, "are we done here or what?"

All of my wondering had been answered and I knew the way things were going to be now, so I tuned the two of them out and wandered around the waiting room dragging my knapsack and killing time, humming the little bit of "Stormy" that I knew and wishing I'd learned the rest of it, feeling really tired and hollow, flopping a limp wave at the social services lady when my mother finally said it was time to go, and following her out.

"Hungry?" she said, pausing out on the sidewalk and looking around as if she'd never seen this town before.

I shook my head and traced the crack in the sidewalk with the toe of my sneaker.

"Well, I'm supposed to eat three healthy meals a day, so come on," she said and started down the street toward the diner.

I automatically followed, trudging along behind her until she stopped and glanced back. "Why are you always so slow?"

I shrugged and she waited until I caught up, then paced herself to walk beside me.

"So, they found us a room over at the motor court near the mission, and I have what's left of my checks from before rehab, and if we don't go crazy spending, it should last until I start work down at the factory," she said and smiled slightly at my startled look. "Yeah, you heard right. They're putting me to work. Funny, huh?"

"No, that's good," I said, and then added tentatively, "Mom."

The waitress gave us a booth and I discovered I really was hungry, so I had a California cheeseburger with fries and a Coke, and she had fettuccine alfredo with a salad and coffee. I had no idea what to say so I stayed quiet for most of the meal, sneaking peeks at her until she finally set down her fork and said, "This is weird, huh?"

I nodded.

"Yeah." She stared past me out the big plate-glass window. "Was that gas station always over there?"

I followed her gaze. "Yeah."

"No kidding," she said musingly, and twirled up another forkful of fettuccine. "I never noticed it before."

We finished the meal in silence, and neither one of us wanted dessert. She got a coffee to go and I waited outside while she paid, struck by the fact that this was the first time my mother had ever taken me out to dinner.

"Well, I guess we'll go back to the room now," she said, gazing down the street at the Colonial Pub for a long moment, and then shaking her head and starting off in the opposite direction. "I haven't been there yet, so I hope it has cable and a kitchen, you know? We can save money by making some of our own food."

"I know how to make squash pancakes," I offered, trotting along beside her.

"Oh yeah?" she said, glancing at me. "Where'd you learn that?"

"At Miss Mo's," I said. "Her and Mareene and Beale and Aunt Loretta taught me all kinds of things, like . . ." I thought hard for a moment. "Um, how to play horseshoes and Aunt Loretta showed me how to get eggs out from under chickens without getting pecked. Beale is really good at spitting watermelon pits and he sang me a song called 'Stormy' and gave me a kitten, too. Miss Mo told me all about her ancestors, and . . ." I paused because we had just rounded the corner to the mission and Miss Mo's car was there in the lot, so she must have been volunteering. I turned to my mother, excited, and said, "Look, that's her car, the little white one! Come on, we could go and say hi and—"

"Slow down." My mother held up a hand. "You're running on high and I'm running on fumes, and all I want to do is get into that room and try to figure out what the *fuck* I'm going to do with the rest of my life, okay?" She wiped her sweaty forehead and hoisted the tote-bag strap higher onto her shoulder. "I mean, do you think this whole stupid sobriety thing is easy? Because let me tell you, it isn't. Not even a little, but I'm trying, so do you think you could not give me a hard time for like, the next *year* or so?"

My eyes filled with tears.

"Oh, for . . ." She stared at me a moment, her face a study of anger, exasperation, and frustration. "Don't do this to me now. I'm serious. I'm barely hanging on as it is. Just stop, Sayre. Isn't it time you outgrew that shit, already?"

I didn't mean to cry. I forgot how much it annoyed her.

"All right, just . . . let's just get to the motor court so I can drink my coffee and wish I was dead," my mother said, and we walked fast past the mission and across the grimy, pothole-studded street to the motor court where the sign hung crooked and the garish pink paint was chipped. Crushed cigarette butts littered the ground and tall weeds grew through the cracks in the pavement.

Small knots of people were gathered in the parking lot, fat women in stretch shorts and stained tank tops showing their bra straps; little kids in sagging diapers; and sweaty men with potbellies, T-shirts, and beers, leaning against an assortment of junky old cars and watching us approach.

"Oh great," my mother muttered. "What is this, a friggin' welfare motel?"

I moved closer, accidentally bumping into her. "Sorry."

"Jesus, do you have to be right on top of me?" she snapped.

"*I'd* like to be right on top of you," one of the guys drawled, lifting his beer in salute and smirking at my mother.

Another guy laughed, two whistled, and a few of the women shot her dirty looks.

Face burning, I stared straight ahead and just kept trotting beside her.

"That's all right, mama, you go take care of your business," beer guy called after us. "When you're finished, you come on back. I'll be right here, waiting for you."

My mother never turned, never broke stride, only shot her hand into the air, middle finger held high, and kept moving toward that motel office.

And only I saw the effort it cost her, saw the yearning for that beer in her eyes, the pretty pink flush his crude flirting had brought to her cheeks, and the determined grit of her jaw as she struggled to move forward in a place so easy to fall backward.

Chapter 16

My mother is on the sixth floor, in the End-of-Life Care Wing, room 622.

The last room at the end of the hall.

At least this is what the night nurse tells me when I step out of the elevator and lurch over to the reception desk. The place is deserted, strung with holiday decorations and a garland and a fake Christmas tree and a big HAPPY NEW YEAR banner hanging slanted from the ceiling. I'm exhausted, haven't slept in days, and the weight of where I am, the scents and sounds and reason is crushing me.

"Thank you," I mumble and turn completely around where I'm standing because there are four hallways off this desk, and my eyes just won't focus long enough to make out the room numbers on the wall plaques. "Um, which one again?"

She points, and that's the way I go.

The floors are polished, shiny, and the overhead lights are on in the hallway. I pass room after room sunk in shadows, hear the restless thrashings, the moaning, snoring, and mumbling of those close to letting go.

The end of the hall is in sight.

There is only one room left.

My steps falter and for a moment everything but that doorway blurs. Fear rises inside me, raising chills across my skin despite the suffocating heat and drawing me down, pulling the strength from my knees and turning my feet to lead, rooting me to the floor only four steps from her room.

I can't do it.

I thought I could but I can't.

My heart pounds in my ears.

I have followed after her most of my life, and now I have to do it again and I don't want to. I don't want to go where she's taking me.

I'm out of here.

Good. Go.

And I did go, but now I'm back and oh, I don't want to be like Harlow's dog who gets kicked and cursed and slapped around, and who bellies back every time, whimpering, groveling, and grateful for any careless scrap of kindness.

I don't want to be, but I'm afraid I am because I don't know any other way.

I'm afraid the year we were happy seeded something deep inside me, something that rooted and survived even the meanest ground, something that still hangs on despite neglect and all efforts to kill it, despite being despised and trampled on and—

I'm afraid that I love her, and I don't think I can bear finding out if it's true.

"Oh, hi," an aide says, coming out of another room. "Do you need some help?"

I blink, and the doorway pulls back into focus. "No, that's okay, thanks."

I take a deep, shaky breath and walk into my mother's room.

Two Steps Forward, One Step Back

The motel room was dingy and shabby, the bedspread had suspicious stains on it, and the kitchenette consisted of a coffeepot, a little fridge, and a hot plate with a banged-up frying pan, a fork, and three butter knives. It had two double beds, a view to an abandoned warehouse, a toilet that never stopped running, and was right next door to a couple with a baby who never stopped crying.

My mother did all right the first week. We went food shopping and got Styrofoam bowls and plates and plastic silverware, and some easy stuff like cereal and lunch meat and bread. She didn't have a car, so she talked to the ladies at the church and arranged for a ride to work with one of them when her factory job started. She notified the school of my new address and showed me where my bus stop would be when school started again. We went to the laundromat and washed our clothes. We went to the library and I picked out books and she paged through magazines, waiting for me to finish. She bought a disposable cell phone. She drank coffee, watched talk shows, and paced.

She didn't call Candy or any of the other Fees. She didn't go out after dark or linger in the parking lot talking to the guy with the beer. She snored and ground her teeth at night, tossed and turned, twitched, and sometimes groaned. She hacked and spit in the morning, and sat out on the curb in the sun at noon, trying to get some color in her face and arms.

We still didn't talk much, not about anything important, only things like *Don't leave your underwear on the floor* or *God, I wish they'd just take that goddamn baby to the clinic to see what's wrong with it, already. Nobody can cry for seven straight days and not be really sick, don't you think?* or *I have to find a better room somewhere. This place is a hellhole.*

That surprised me because this place was like heaven compared to the Fees or that weekend we stayed in some guy's shack by the river or even Grandma Lucy's house at the end. Then I realized that what she saw when she was high were not the same things I'd seen, and now that she was sober she was seeing them, too.

I never knew that before, and it made me feel a little softer toward her.

Seeing real life didn't make her feel better, though. Not at all.

"Bleak, disgusting, miserable," she would say every time we walked into the room. "How the mighty have fallen. Great. Welcome to my new life. Jesus, if this is straight, I'll take stoned any day of the week." And then she would shake her head and say, "Kidding, kidding. I'm still here, aren't I?"

But it worried me.

When we ran out of cereal, I talked her into going over to the mission because they served a free hot breakfast and I was able to see Miss Mo again. I wanted to run around that long serving counter and hug her and tell her how much I missed her but I was self-conscious and embarrassed now, being on the receiving end of it, and so I just stood there in line with the others, waiting my turn.

She was surprised to see me that first morning, and when I introduced her to my mother, she gave her a big smile and said, "Ms. Huff, you have a wonderful daughter there and it was a real pleasure having her stay with us."

My mother glanced at me, eyebrows raised, and said, "Well, I'm glad you two got along so well. Now, can I get rye toast with my eggs instead of white?"

I looked back at Miss Mo as we got our food and moved on, and she was watching me with such softness in her eyes that I knew she saw how it was, and was maybe even a little sorry she had let me go so easily.

We ran out of food and were running low on money, so instead of buying more groceries we started eating all our meals at the mission for free. My mother hated being there—she called it Loserville—so she would get her food and eat it as fast as she could, almost always finishing way before me and then getting cranky because she had to wait.

That's exactly what happened on the day the junkie next to me in line freaked and hit me with his elbow. My mother was way off at a back table eating and didn't notice a thing, while Miss Mo soothed him and sent him on his way. She held up the line to make sure I was all right, smiled at me like she really cared, and put an extra-big serving of Tator Tots on my plate.

That was the last time I would ever see her alive.

Chapter 17

The hospital room is spotless, dimly lit by a small fluorescent light, and has only one bed in it, only one slight, skeletal woman lying on her side under a white cotton blanket draped over her swollen, fluid-filled belly and with a loose fist curled like a child's under her chin. Her eyes are closed, her mouth open, and her breathing slow and labored. Her hair, liberally streaked with the gray that began when Ellie died, is pressed flat against her head, as if she'd been laying on it and had just rolled over. Her skin is dull and blotchy, cast with a yellow tint, and sagging off her cheekbones, neck, and arms as if dying has drained every drop of moisture inside her and left a loose, wrinkled husk over the bones.

I pad to the edge of the bed. Her muscles twitch in her sleep and her eyes rest in sunken, gray hollows. Trembling, I grope behind me for the armchair and sink into it before my knees give out. I have no strength left in my body and slowly, as if caving in, I lean forward and rest my head against the cool aluminum guardrail on the side of the bed. Her fetid breath puffs out, hot and sweet like rotting meat, and the smell is nauseating but I don't turn away because at least she is still breathing. Death is here, waiting in this room, as calm and patient as only a sure thing can be but I've been waiting, too, and surely that counts for something.

"Sayre?" someone whispers from behind me.

I sit up and turn to see Red standing in the doorway with my coat, my purse, the canvas tote bag, and the ruby velvet blazer.

"I'm sorry to intrude but you left your things in the truck and I thought you might need them," he says in a low voice, tiptoeing in and setting them down next to my chair. He straightens, looks at my mother, then back at me. Puts a warm hand on my shoulder. "Are you all right? Would you like me to stay for a while?"

No, I don't, but I don't want him to leave, either.

I don't know what I want.

Yes, I do.

I motion for Red to pull over a chair, and when he does, I shift to face him and say in a low, fierce voice, "Do you know how many times I tried to get her to a doctor but she wouldn't go? She said all they wanted was her money, and all she needed was her stupid, *stupid* pills. And now look." I motion blindly toward the huddled figure on the bed. "That's my *mother* and she's dying and there's nothing I can do. There's no way to get her well again. Look, there are no heart monitors or catheters or IVs or anything in here. They're not even trying."

"That's what end-of-life care is, Sayre. They do what they can to make the patient comfortable when there is absolutely no chance of recovery. So in that way no, they aren't trying." He takes my hand, cradling it in his. "She can't live without a liver, Sayre, and hers is so damaged it's ceased functioning. She's not eligible for a transplant. There is no other answer. I'm sorry."

"Well, wait. What if I give her some of my liver?" I say slowly, sitting up straight. "Why didn't I think of this before? Mine is healthy. Why can't *I* be the donor?" I look around, feeling a wild surge of hope. "Who can we talk to? What do I have to do? C'mon, Red, we have to go find someone fast because—"

"Sayre, wait. Look at her," he says softly, holding tight to my hand as if to pull me back to earth. "She's so weak she'd never live through the operation."

"You don't know that," I say.

"She has to be lucid enough to initiate the evaluation and be able to get to the transplant hospital of her own accord," he says, holding my despairing gaze. "She has to be awake and physically strong enough to survive the evaluation, and it's invasive. They do a series of tests: blood, a heart catheterization, X-rays, ultrasounds, a liver biopsy, and more. She has to have been sober for a minimum of six consecutive months."

"But she's *dying*," I say, because he just doesn't get it. "And maybe I can—"

"You're a minor, and her daughter, and it's a clinically hopeless situation. They wouldn't even *talk* to you about donating under those circumstances, not to mention the psychological trauma and guilt you'd suffer if you changed your mind and said no, which is always your right. It's a very serious surgery, Sayre, for both you and your mother."

I stare at him, silent.

"Part of your liver rests beneath your ribs, so they make a Y incision and spread your ribs for access. They take out your gallbladder to get to your liver. They take out part of a vein in your leg, too. You'd be on the operating table for six or more hours and that's providing there are no complications. You could hemorrhage. Get infected. The liver could be rejected. Insurance companies don't always pay for transplants. They cost hundreds of thousands of dollars. And Sayre"—his voice is very soft and solemn now—"even if you somehow overcame all of those ob-stacles, what about the hepatic encephalopathy? The ammonia that's been built up in her brain all of this time? It's hit a level she can't recover from. Do you understand what I'm saying? It's toxic, and it does damage. Irreversible damage. *Brain* damage. Even if a miracle occurred and she somehow survived the surgery, her mind wouldn't be—"

"Stop!" I cry, repulsed, and yank my hand from his to clutch the bed railing, head spinning. "All right, I get it, Red. Just stop."

"I'm sorry," he says wearily, rubbing the side of his face. "I was just trying to help you understand—"

"I *do* understand, okay? I understand. You're saying I'm just supposed to sit here and let her die."

"No, Sayre, I'm saying you can't save her. No one can, now."

"But she's only *thirty-three*." Frustrated, I look at my mother's pale, sunken, yellowish face, at the skeletal hands curled under her chin, and want to scream and rage, bang my head and pound my fists on the walls until they bleed, until death gives way to one more chance, but it won't, I see the miserable, unacceptable truth of it right in front of me and so instead I just sit there breathing hard, stomach sick and fingers locked like iron around the bed rail.

"I know," Red says quietly, settling back in his chair. "We're the same age. We had the same homeroom in sophomore year of high school until she dropped out."

"Which was when she got pregnant with me," I say dully.

"Her father passed away right around then, too," he says, like he's trying to shift that legacy off me. "When I was here visiting, she told me she's been an addict for seventeen years, and for the last seven or so has been drinking anywhere between a quart and a gallon of vodka a day, depending on what she had access to. And taking those painkillers that started with her back injury, of course."

"Oxycontin. Vicodin." I watch my mother but she doesn't stir. The smell of her breath is terrible, thick and sweet with decay, surrounding me, choking me, and suddenly I can't stand it. I let go of the bed rail and lean back, just to be able to breathe. "When I was little it was meth and drinking. Then, after Ellie . . . after she hurt her back, she's been taking anywhere between twenty-eight and forty-three Vicodins a day. And yeah, still drinking."

"My God, the acetaminophen alone . . ." Red shudders and rises, goes over to my mother's tray and pours two cups of water from her pitcher. "She said after the funeral . . . uh, after what happened to the baby, she just didn't care anymore. She went as far as to say that she doesn't think she ever got over the death of her father, either. The guilt, I mean, but she wouldn't discuss it with me any further."

"Did she say anything else about Ellie?" I ask, accepting the cup he hands me and draining it.

"No," he says, sitting back down beside me.

"Beale?"

"No."

"Me?"

He sighs and shakes his head. "I'm sorry, Sayre."

"But she still wanted to see me," I say, at a loss.

"Perhaps because you're her only daughter?" he says gently.

"Oh God*damn* it, and whose fault is that?" I snap, and any lingering sadness is buried beneath a landslide of pent-up, molten anger. "I'm serious. Whose fault is that?" Oh, I am raging now and the low fury in my voice scares me. "It's not *my* fault and it's not Beale's fault, it's *her* fault, only just like everything else, she didn't want to deal with it so now what, she's just gonna die because life was too hard? Because if she had a new liver then she couldn't party anymore and if she can't party then she has nothing to live for?" The words fly and I don't even try to stop them. "What about me? I'm her *daughter.* Aren't I something to live for? No, don't even try to answer because I already know, okay? The answer is NO, I am not something for her to live for and I never have been."

"I know you two have a lot of unresolved issues and she hasn't always been the best mother—"

"Try *any* kind of mother," I mutter, staring down at the empty paper cup in my hands.

"Well, she can't change that now even if she wanted to, but what we *can* do is go forward in a way that will help you cope with what's coming."

Oh, I didn't like the sound of that at all. "If you're saying I'm supposed to forgive her just because she's dying, forget it," I say, shocked by the cold fury in my voice. "No offense, but you don't know anything about my life, Red. You have *no idea,* and you don't know what she's really like, either. *I do.*"

"Sayre," he says, but the dam has burst and there's no stopping it now.

"All you see is some tragic, pathetic girl you probably had a crush on back in high school who fed you all her *Oh, poor me, I had such a hard life* bullshit stories and you're sitting there holding her hand and feeling bad and suddenly she's a saint just because she's thirty-three and dying, but you know what? She did it to herself. She *chose* it, just like she chose to hate me for being born."

"Not hate, Sayre," he protests.

"You don't know," I say with a sharp, dismissive gesture. "I do, but somehow it doesn't seem to matter because she's finally managed to kill herself and now I'm supposed to be the bigger person"—my voice is rising—"and forgive her for making sure I knew—in *every possible way*—that I was a mistake and she wished she'd never had me. That's not the kind of stuff you tell someone you love, especially a little kid, unless you *want* to hurt them. And it worked, because you know what that does to me, even just saying it?" I grab the front of my shirt in a fist. "It tears me up. Do you hear what I'm saying? I'll never forget that. *Ever.*"

"Sayre, I—," Red begins, glancing at my mother's slight form. Her feet are twitching and her eyelids are fluttering, and he looks like he's going to shush me and if he does, if he tries to stop me from finally saying what I feel then I'm going to lose it, I am, and the crazy he saw in Iraq will be peanuts compared to the crazy I'll let loose in here.

"I mean if your own mother doesn't want you, who will? And she didn't, Red, right from the beginning and that never changed." It takes effort but I manage to lower my voice slightly. "She never took care of me. We had no food, but she *always* had meth. Or vodka. Or pills. She sold everything we had to get high. She stole from people who were good to her. She left me with strangers.

Tweakers. Jesus, Red, a *murderer.* Her best friend tried to kill me with a hammer. Doesn't that matter?"

"Of course," he says, and is about to say more but I cut him off.

"*She's* the mother. The *adult.* The one who's supposed to be loving and caring and who shows me how to live, and how to be a good person. She *chose* to have me and isn't that choice supposed to mean that I'm wanted? Isn't it supposed to mean that I'm *worth* something to her?" I've never said these things out loud before, never dragged my pain out into the middle of the room and left it there for everyone to see. "I'm the *daughter,* Red. The kid. The one who was supposed to be wanted. So what the hell happened?" I sit back in my seat, feeling raw and miserable and totally humiliated.

The huge silence stretches, broken only by the hum of the fluorescent light and the sound of my mother breathing.

"You're right, Sayre. I owe you an apology. I *don't* know what you've been through," he says finally, rising and pacing the room. "I'd heard some talk, of course, about her drug arrests and being banned from the stores downtown for shoplifting and I thought I saw her once down by the mission, but she turned away, so I was never actually sure it was her . . ." He stops and looks at me. "I never imagined it was anywhere near as bad as you've said. I admit it was quite a shock, walking in here and seeing a girl who used to be so pretty and lively and always seemed so . . . limitless, I guess, end up like this, and not being able to offer anything other than comfort, but . . ." He turns and stares out the window a moment, watching the snow peppering the glass, then turns back to me. "No buts. I was wrong, and I'm sorry. I never should have believed her assurance that you were fine. I should have followed through. I just never imagined . . ."

"It's okay. You didn't know. Nobody does." I give a weak snort. "Well, until now."

"Really?" he said, and turns back to me in concern. "What about Beale? Did he know how badly you were treated?"

"No." I rest my elbows on my knees and lower my head into my hands. Close my eyes and feel a tear run down and drip off the end of my nose. I am exhausted, aching inside and out. "I don't know. *I* never told him. I mean, he knew things weren't great between us but . . . no. I don't think he had any idea of how it was before we got to him. Or after. He c . . . c . . . couldn't have imagined it, Red, b . . . because he had such a g . . . g . . . good heart." I wipe my face on my sleeve. "I'm not t . . . trying to be mean, but could you g . . . go now? I . . . I just really need to be alone."

"Of course. I understand." He gives my shoulder a brief squeeze and turns to leave. "I'll be here for a while longer, so if you want me, the nurses know how to reach me." He nods, his blue eyes soft with sympathy, and disappears out the door.

I take a tissue from the box on the table tray. Blot my face and blow my nose. Sit in the quiet and stare at the shrunken ruin of my mother. Part of me—the part that still shouts *She doesn't get to be forgiven just because she's dying!*—wants up and out of here because staying is surrendering, giving her all the comfort and tenderness she never gave me, and that side of me balks hard at letting her have it.

The warring sides twist me up. What am I doing here? What's wrong with me? What if she dies and never gives me anything at all, not a look or a smile or a word or ANYTHING?

No. There has to be something.

There has to be.

That hand, tucked under her chin, so cozy.

Does that mean she's at peace?

I'm not.

Not at all.

I want to know what she's thinking, want to know what's going through her mind right now because she feels so far away. I want to know if she's remembering her life, if that's what Red meant when he said the dying turn inside themselves, and have no need for the outer world anymore. That annoys me briefly, because *I'm* in the outer world. I want to know if she's searching her soul and making peace, or if her life is flashing and tumbling before her in a kaleidoscope of brilliant, broken fragments with no order and no end. Is there panic, knowing tomorrow's slipping through her grasp, is the spark struggling to stay burning, or is she simply done, tired and ready to go?

If I lean closer and talk to her, will she hear me?

The Tragedy That Birthed a Miracle

When my mother and I walked to the mission the next morning for breakfast, there was a big pile of flowers and teddy bears and candles placed near the front door, but it wasn't until we got closer that I could see the familiar, smiling face staring out of the framed picture at the heart of the tribute.

"That's Miss Mo," I exclaimed, stopping in front of it and staring up at my mother. For a moment my brain refused to process what this meant, and translated the little Madonna statues and sympathy balloons into birthday tributes. "We didn't bring her a present!"

My mother looked at me funny, pulled the door open, and said, "Come on, let's go see what's up."

I followed her, not really getting what she meant—or maybe I did, but just couldn't bear to acknowledge it—although once inside with the people talking, crying, and praying all around us, everything became clear.

Miss Mo had been murdered last night in her carport.

Stabbed by Mareene's ex-boyfriend.

Mareene had found her.

The cops had arrested Harlow Maltese, who was splattered with Miss Mo's blood and still had the knife on him.

Mareene was a basket case, and her father was flying in from Georgia to stay with her.

The wake would be in two days, the funeral service out of Holy Mercy Baptist Church, and the burial at Holy Mercy cemetery.

Somehow my bewildered brain let me hear it and make sense of it all, but not feel it. Miss Mo was dead, but that fact hung somewhere out ahead of me like a distant, neon sign and it stayed that way until the other volunteer ladies went back behind the counter to begin serving breakfast. We all got in line, but when I got to Miss Mo's spot it was empty and the pan that she always gave me scrambled eggs from was empty and her fun, red-striped apron hung limp on the hook and all of a sudden I wasn't hungry anymore so I got out of line, and dizzy, with knees like water, walked out the door to the tribute and sat down on the sidewalk in front of her picture, just sat and stared into her wonderful eyes until my mother finally came out and found me.

"Did you eat?" she said.

"No," I said, pushing myself up off the ground and dusting my hands on my jeans. "We have to go to the wake."

And she must have seen something in my face because she didn't argue, only said, "It starts Wednesday afternoon," and walked quietly beside me all the way back to the motor court.

We went down to the Methodist church on Tuesday because they'd had a clothing drive for the needy and my mother found me a pair of navy blue pants and a plain white top with crocheted lace around the edge of the sleeves, and a black pin-striped pants suit and a cream-colored V-neck blouse for herself. She found black high heels, too, and I got a pair of decent running shoes. The church ladies suggested I pick out a few more things and so I did, because school would be starting soon and I didn't have much.

My mother was quiet all day Wednesday, not mad quiet but almost like thoughtful quiet. When she put on her suit, she stood looking at herself in the mirror for a long time, first, I think, like studying how different she looked and second, gazing straight into her own eyes, like she was trying to figure herself out.

"So this is what I would have looked like if I'd gone to law school like I was supposed to," she said finally, straightening the front of the jacket. "Pretty bizarre, huh?"

I didn't know what to say because she didn't look bizarre, she looked a little like Katie Bingo's mother who always smiled and kissed her good-bye when she dropped her off at school in the morning before she went to work, who drove a shiny red car and gave Katie lunch money and took her to Disney over the Christmas holiday. If my mother's side tooth wasn't missing and her hair was swingy and shiny and she had rings and earrings and more makeup than just that rose-colored lipstick, then she would look just as good, if not better, than Mrs. Bingo.

"That bad?" my mother cracked, looking at me in the mirror.

"No, not at all," I said, coming to stand beside her. "You look nice, Mom."

She gazed back at me. "So do you, kiddo." And just as my shy smile began to bloom, she cocked her head and added, "God, you know, you really do look like your father. Well, from what I remember, I mean, which isn't much, but you don't look *anything* like me, so . . ." She shrugged and busied herself buttoning and unbuttoning the jacket, seeing which way she liked it, while I stood there stricken, staring at myself in the mirror. "He was tall and had big, dark puppy dog eyes with all those long black lashes, just like you do." Her mouth twisted into a wry smile. "Funny, the stuff that comes back to haunt you, right?"

I bit my bottom lip, then with a burst of courage blurted out, "Was Bellavia his last name, too?"

In an instant her smile died and a flash of something—embarrassment?—crossed her face, then dissolved into anger. "Goddamnit, Sayre, why do you do that? Can't you just take what you get and be satisfied? Do you always have to have more? Just . . . stop, all right? Don't ask me any more stupid questions." She stalked across the room and grabbed her purse. "Now let's go before I change my mind."

And so we walked to the funeral home in the center of town, with me always just a few steps behind and struggling to keep up, and it was mobbed. Crowds of people were standing outside smoking and looking tragic, parting for the new arrivals and then closing ranks again. The carpet in the foyer was plush and the walls were dark, gleaming wood. We got in line behind a sad-looking guy with saggy pants who I recognized from the mission, and little by little we inched forward into the room where the wake actually was. There were folding chairs set up in rows and every seat was taken. It was hot and the air was heavy with perfume and BO.

"What, did she know everyone in town?" my mother muttered, pushing her damp hair back off her forehead. "This place is packed." Her mouth twisted again in that weird, wry smile. "Well, you won't have to worry about standing room only at my wake. You and Candy will be about it, and Candy's so pissed off that I won't go out partying with her that she probably won't show up, either, just to spite me."

"I didn't know you still talked to Candy." I stood on tiptoe and tried to see the front of the room where Miss Mo was supposed to be, but it was impossible.

My mother gave me a defensive look. "Well, what am I supposed to do, block her calls? She's my best friend. Just because we're not hanging out doesn't mean I can't talk to her, you know. God, what're you, my parole officer?"

"Okay, okay," I said because she wasn't whispering anymore and I could feel my cheeks getting hot. "Look, there's one of the ladies from the church."

It took us a full twenty-five minutes to get to the front and when we did, I wished we hadn't. Mareene couldn't stop crying, sobbing and hugging me when she saw me, radiating pain from every pore and drenching me with her tears, telling me how her mother had loved me, and how empty the house was when I left, and on and on.

My mother, already tired of waiting, poked my arm and gestured to herself, made a cigarette motion and pointed out the door. She passed Miss Mo's casket without pause, and disappeared into the crowd.

"Come on, honey, I'll go up with you," Mareene said, sliding a trembling arm around my shoulders. "I know she would've wanted to see you again."

And so we walked up to the edge of the casket and it was so hot and there were white lilies everywhere. My head was spinning and my heart was aching, and I looked at this lifeless Miss Mo dressed in her light pink church suit with her silky hair all neat and curled wrong, and too much face makeup and no smile, not even a little one, and that big, vibrant bouquet of rainbow zinnias that I knew were from the garden, and Mareene was standing beside me saying, *Doesn't she look good? I had to put the flowers over her hands, though, because of all the cut wounds on them,* and then her crying, crying, crying until an older man who must have been her father came and led her away. Someone put a hand on my shoulder and said quietly, *Hey, Sayre* and I looked up into Beale's dear, solemn face, and that's when I cracked.

He gave me a tissue and waited while I clasped my hands tight in front of me and whispered, *Dear God, please love this lady. She's very kind and generous and she loves you more than anyone but Mareene, so if she can't be here with us then I hope she's in heaven with you. Amen,* and then he ushered me through the crowd to the back of the room.

"Is Aunt Loretta here?" I asked, craning my neck to scan the ever-increasing crowd.

"No, she wanted to come, but she's down with the flu," he said. "She's going to try to make it to the funeral, though. Losing Mo just broke her heart." He shook his head. "You're not here by yourself?"

"No, my mom came—ow!" I said, yelping as someone stepped hard on my foot.

"Come on," Beale said, and taking my hand, led me out of the wake into the foyer. "Where's your mom?"

"Outside smoking," I said.

"Sounds like a plan," he said, edging us past a gaggle of church ladies squeezing in the door, down the steps and over toward the lawn.

"No, this way," I said, leading him over to my mom, who was standing alone under a maple tree. The brilliant rays of sunset cast a golden sheen over everything and I saw my mother, wearing her pin-striped suit and high heels, glance up at us, her face glowing in the light, and go still, her eyes widening slightly but not fixed on me. When I turned to see what she was staring at, I realized it was Beale, and he was staring right back at her with the same kind of dazed and shimmering look.

I never saw the arc of lightning pass between them, but I felt the air shiver when Beale cleared his throat, introduced himself, and shook her hand. My mother felt it, too, I'm sure, because her eyes turned to great soft, black pools and her cheeks went pink and she was smiling, closemouthed to hide her missing tooth. Beale was smiling, too, only his was wide and beaming and I stood there between them as this whole immense thing was happening, unbelieving yet at the same time lit with dawning hope, hardly daring to breathe lest I interrupt and ruin everything because they were talking and laughing quietly, shifting back and forth on the grass in a weird kind of dance that brought them closer with every step.

Somehow, Beale ended up taking us out to the Applebee's on the highway for supper and while I sat there eating fish and chips and watching them, scarcely believing the miracle that was unfolding right in front of me, my mother and Beale talked and laughed and she didn't yell or swear and he didn't drink. Her face was shining and pretty, and Beale never took his eyes off her.

It wasn't until the waitress came and joked about how I'd eaten every last thing on my plate that Beale started and kind of woke up, looked at me with real distress, and said, "Sayre, I'm sorry. I can't believe I haven't even asked you how you've been," and then he brought me right into the conversation and ended up telling my mother about my little Stormy kitten and how Aunt Loretta had grown so fond of me and what a help I was and on, and on.

"So *you're* the one who taught her how to spit watermelon pits," my mother teased, and to my amazement, Beale actually blushed and ducked his head, which made my mother and I laugh and then it hit me, the lilting music of our mingled happiness, and I almost cried because it was such a good sound.

That night, the night of Miss Mo's wake, was the beginning of something I'd never even dared to dream of, and I always knew that it was Miss Mo who'd caused it, watching out for me from heaven, smiling her wonderful, soft smile and saying *You keep your heart open to miracles, Sayre, because I'm sending you one right now.*

No Rain

The miracle of my mother and Beale didn't end like I was afraid it would, but only intensified as the days passed. We became an astonishing threesome and I got to see my mother straight, not high, in love and warily happy, hanging back sometimes, awkward and shy, as if she couldn't believe it, either, and was just waiting for the ax to fall.

But not Beale.

He came to us every day as strong and bright and reliable as the sun, making us smile, taking us out to eat, to the park, back to his house on Sunrise Road where Aunt Loretta embraced my mother like she wasn't a recovering addict scared to death at all the good things suddenly coming her way, but like she was the woman who was making her son sing all the time now, and that was good enough for her.

"And you," she said, laughing and hugging me, "are my beautiful bonus prize! Oh, Sayre, it's so good to see you again. Come on, would you like to go see Stormy?"

It made me breathless, made my heart actually hurt sometimes at how happy I was just sitting at the kitchen table or helping Aunt Loretta cook, and listening to my mother and Beale sitting out on the front porch talking.

I learned that even though Beale had gone over and cleaned out the carport after Miss Mo's death, hosing it down so that every last drop of her blood was gone, Mareene still couldn't bear to live in her house anymore, and so she'd put it up for sale and gone back to Georgia with her father. I wandered over there alone one afternoon while it stood empty, a little scared, a lot sad, but once I got to the carport I felt the hair on my arms rise. It was quiet but it was an eerie quiet, an unnatural one, like residual violence still hung heavy in the air, and it made my skin crawl, so I didn't go any closer, only ran around to the garden, picked zinnias, and then took them back and threw them hard into the carport as some kind of antidote or exorcism, I guess.

It didn't feel like enough so I said a speedy Lord's Prayer and then followed the edge of the field back to Beale's, pausing every few feet and grabbing bunches of Queen Anne's lace because they felt clean and pure and safe. Their tough, wiry stems fought me but I fought back, pinching them off with my fingernails because they felt like hope, and I wanted my hands full of it.

I gave them to my mother, shocking her speechless, and I think Aunt Loretta was the only one who realized she didn't know what to do with them or what to say to me, so she offered to put them in water. My mother seemed relieved to surrender them.

I didn't mind. I would have endured almost anything to keep us here, and happy.

And then my mother finally started her job at the factory and I started school. We only saw Beale at night and on the weekends, when he would take us out to the farm on Friday and bring us back Sunday night. He called the motor court a roach motel and hated that we lived there, said he'd never seen a place this bad in his life, but my mother told him it was all we could afford right now and no matter how much he grumbled, there was no changing it.

It was kind of thrilling, watching him cast dark looks at all the guys hanging out in the parking lot, leaning against their pickups or sitting on the curb drinking beer. He was my mother's boyfriend, he knew about her past addiction and how she was trying so hard to keep clean, and it worried him that this was the environment we called home.

It made me feel proud to have him care about us like that.

Like we were worth protecting.

I dug in and started bringing home A+ papers from school. Last fall, when we'd been staying at the Fees, my grades had been terrible, but this year I not only had food and a bed and a mother who, while she wasn't fawning all over me, at least wasn't telling me to get the fuck out of her way as she staggered over to smoke some meth.

It made a difference.

Beale helped me with my homework, too, and I studied hard because I wanted to make him proud. And I suppose I wanted to show my mother what I could do, thinking maybe if she didn't like what I looked like then maybe she'd be happy with my brains, but mostly I loved the way the slow, delighted smile would break out over Beale's face when he saw the big red A+ at the top of the page, and the way he would give me that brief, strong, one-armed hug and say, "I've said it before and I'll say it again, Miss Sayre Bellavia: You're a keeper."

My mother wasn't quite as impressed, and the first fight I ever heard them have was over one of the papers I did for English. The teacher had written *Wonderful! Vivid scenes, excellent language skills! You're a natural-born writer!* Beale made a big fuss over it, and my mother, tired from working and having her period, watching from the little counter in our room where she was making coffee for the two of them, snapped, "Jesus, Beale, will you give it a rest already? It's only a school paper. It's not like she found a cure for cancer or anything. God."

My laughter died, and Beale, who had just gotten me in a congratulatory headlock and was giving me a gentle noogie stopped cold, and released me. "Oh, come on now, Dianne. You can't stand there and tell me you're not a proud mama while our girl here gets genius grades."

"Stop telling her stuff like that," my mother said, scowling and dumping milk in the Styrofoam coffee cups. "You keep filling her mind with big ideas and all you're doing is creating false hope. This is Sullivan, Beale. Dug County. Last time I looked there weren't any Einsteins hanging around down at the Colonial Pub."

Beale stared at her for a long moment, which made her scowl even harder and busy herself sugaring the coffees. "Sayre, would you mind stepping outside for a couple of minutes? Your mom and I have something we need to discuss."

"Okay," I whispered because his face was strange, it gave nothing away, and he must have heard the tremor in my voice because he gave me a reassuring smile and it was enough to steady my knees and get me out the door.

Happily, although the curtains were drawn the window was cracked open, and so I loitered close enough to hear what they were saying.

"Why do you do that to her, Di?" Beale said. "She was happy and proud and she should have been. She's doing really well now, and I hope she keeps it up. Grades like that will get her scholarships someday and maybe even into a decent college."

"Not if she gets pregnant in sophomore year and fucks up her life," my mother said.

It was silent a moment.

"Why would you even want to say that?"

"Because guess what, it happens. I was supposed to go to law school and be some big important attorney rolling in dough, you know, but I had *her* instead and if *I* had to give up everything to do it, why should she be any different? I don't get why you think she should have more. More than what? More than me? Why can't she just take what she gets? I had to."

"But she's not you, Di," Beale said carefully. "She's a completely different person and she gets to build her own future. You don't want her to go through what you went through. Christ, even the little bit you told me about the drinking alone . . . nobody wants their kid to live a life like that. I mean she's only what, ten years old? Think about what she's already been exposed to."

"It wasn't that bad," my mother said defensively. "And she was a kid, she didn't know what was going on."

Beale remained silent.

"Well, she didn't," my mother said, angry again. "What? Why are you looking at me like that?"

"It was her *childhood,* Di, and somehow she managed to survive it without being all messed up. You've got one smart, strong kid there and it's like you don't even get how lucky you are," Beale said. "She could be really screwed up, out drinking or getting high or messing with boys, but she's not. She's got a good head on her shoulders and that's worth something. I mean, I know you had a hard time, but so has she, and as a mom, you have to want more for her than this kind of life."

"So you're saying this life is good enough for me but not for her?"

"No, I'm saying she's a smart kid—"

"Oh, wait, I thought she was a genius," my mother said in a mocking voice.

"Stop, Dianne. You know what I mean," he said quietly. "She works hard, trying to please you. Why don't you ever congratulate her or hug her or something? You see the way she looks at you: She's like a pup chained up just out of reach, hungry for affection and—"

"Excuse me, but I don't remember asking you how to raise my daughter," my mother said in an icy tone.

I bit my lip, anxious, scared, and almost wishing I'd never even gotten the stupid A+.

"Look," he said finally and his voice was farther away now, so he must have gotten up and gone over to her. "I don't want to fight and I'm not trying to tell you how to raise Sayre. I'm just saying there's no harm in praising her when she earns it."

"Fine, whatever," my mother said after a moment. "Do what

you want. Tell her she's a goddamn fucking princess and the whole world is her oyster for all I care. Fill her full of bullshit fairy tales that'll never come true. I won't stop you."

"Good, because I think she *should* have high hopes and expectations, and not just settle in life. There's been too much of that already." His voice was strange, like he wanted to say more but was holding back. "So . . . are we okay again?"

"I don't know what you mean," my mother said, and it sounded like she was sulking.

"Oh yes you do," Beale said and then his voice dropped to a murmur. After a while I heard my mother laugh softly and then there was silence again, but this time it was a good silence, so I sat on the curb while the kids played, the ladies gossiped, and the men drank and talked trash in the parking lot, and stared up at the sky thinking about all the nice things Beale had said about me and being glad that I had a good head on my shoulders. I sat there thinking and thinking until my mother called me back in, which was only about ten minutes later but still long enough for me to find the North Star and make a fervent, heartfelt wish.

I wished Beale was my father.

Chapter 18

A nurse whisks into my mother's room and stops when she spots me sitting beside the bed. "Oh."

"Hi." I tuck my hair behind my ear. "I'm her daughter. Is this okay?"

"Oh," she says again, as if even more surprised. "I'm sorry. I didn't know she had a daughter. The only one I've ever seen her with is that other woman . . . uh . . . ?"

"Candy," I say, trying to keep my voice low so as not to disturb my mother, but it doesn't seem to matter. She isn't sleeping so much as sinking, disappearing into herself.

"That's it," the nurse says, nodding. "She never said Dianne had any family."

"Yeah, well, me and Candy don't really get along," I say, and then, gazing down at my mother, "She's not doing too good, is she?"

"Well, we're keeping her comfortable and she's not in any pain but no, her ability to function and respond to outside stimuli has rapidly decreased since last night," the nurse says quietly. "You came just in time."

I look up at her, my eyes filled with tears. "Do you think she knows I'm here?"

The nurse hesitates, and says, "I think we'd all be surprised by what they hear and feel and know. I've seen terminally ill patients in comas not respond to any stimuli, until someone they love comes in and then . . ." She gives me a sympathetic smile. "I'll leave you alone with her. If you need anything, just press the button, all right?" She turns to leave, and pauses. "If that woman Candy returns, I can tell her you'd like some private time with your mother for a while."

"Yes, thank you," I say, watching as she pads out, and then pull my chair closer to the bed and whisper, "All right. I don't know if you can hear me, but I'm here, Mom. I'm back. You're not alone."

Her feet twitch in her sleep but that's all and the longer I sit there, the harder it hits me that this isn't going to get better, and that what we have right now is all there's ever going to be. The things we never talked about will never *be* talked about, the wrongs will never be righted, and if there's anything I want her to know, I had better hurry up and find a way to say it.

Another New Bus Stop

"No," Beale said, shaking his head. "It's impossible. I'll never be able to see you, and what about Sayre? She can't stay alone in this crack-infested dump all night. You can't work the night shift. Forget it. You're just going to have to tell them you can't do it."

"Easy for you to say," my mother said, giving him a look. "You're not the one who's living hand to mouth, here. I don't want to work nights but I need this job, Beale. Nobody volunteered and I've got the least seniority, so I'm it."

We were at the diner having supper and I was the only one eating because I was trying to act like I wasn't listening. We were supposed to go to the laundromat after this, an activity we all hated because the place always had at least one yowling, snuffling baby and lots of sneezing, snotty-nosed kids running berserk and at least two people shouting into their cell phones to be heard over the washers and dryers, and the whole thing just gave Beale a hideous headache, which always amused my mother and made me putter like a mother hen, patting his arm and offering him sips of my grape soda.

"But what are you going to do about Sayre?" he said, taking off his cap and running a hand through his hair. "You're not just going to leave her there alone all night?"

I stabbed up a pile of French fries and stuffed them in my

mouth, because yes, she *was* going to leave me there. She hadn't said it yet, but I knew it was true because she'd left me in far worse places before, even if she had been high when she did it.

"Well, actually," she said hesitantly, peering up at him from beneath her hair, "that's where I was kind of hoping you'd come in. I thought maybe Sayre could come and stay with you and your mom on the nights I have to work. It's four days a week, so it wouldn't be every night and I could give you money toward her food and all . . ." She half-shrugged and, avoiding his gaze, toyed with an empty coffee creamer. "I know it's a lot to ask, but I really don't know what else to do. I don't know anybody down at the motel well enough to ask them to babysit—"

"Ew, I don't want to stay with any of *them*," I said, which is something I never would have done if Beale wasn't sitting there, and it still earned me a sharp look but I couldn't help it. I *didn't* want to stay with them.

"All right, I have a much better solution to this problem," Beale said, giving my mother a slight, mischievous smile and putting his hand over hers. "Come and live at the farm."

OKAY, I said immediately, but only in my mind as I was so excited I couldn't even speak, could only sit there, heart pounding, holding my breath and waiting for my slack-jawed mother to say yes.

"I . . . I don't know what you're saying," my mother said finally, looking dazed.

"Yeah, you do," Beale murmured, leaning over and dropping a kiss on her lips. "I love you, and I'm asking you and Sayre to come live with me. I've been thinking about it for a while now and my mother's all for it, too, so . . ." He smiled. "What do you think?"

Oh my God, I was quivering so hard the top of my head was about to rattle off. Say yes, Mom. YES YES YES. Say it. SAY IT.

"I would have to pay you rent," my mother said slowly, but there was a light dawning in her eyes that didn't match her cautious tone. "I pay two hundred and fifty dollars a month at the motor court. I could pay you a little more than that but it would have to include meals because I have to start saving for a car."

"Sure, hell, why not, pay all the rent you want," he said expansively, his smile broadening. "I love an independent woman."

"And Sayre gets her own room?" she said.

"I wouldn't have it any other way," he said, giving me a grin.

Come on, Mom, say yes, I begged silently, curling my hands so tight that my fingernails dug into my palms. COME ON.

"And your mother's all right with this?" she said, giving him a searching look. "I mean, two women in the same house . . . I don't want to cause any hard feelings."

"We're willing to risk it," he said.

"How am I going to get to work?" she said.

"I'll drive you, or you can use the truck, and if I need to, I'll use my mother's car," he said, leaning back in his seat. "Come on, what else? Give me your best shot. I can take it."

"Does the school bus pick up out there?" she said.

"Ahhh!" I clutched my throat, flung myself back in my seat, and slid down, boneless, until nothing but my head was above the table line. "Who *cares* about the stupid school bus!" And then, because Beale was snickering and my mother didn't look mad, just good-naturedly peeved, added, "Say yes or I'm going down for the last time," and when she didn't speak, I closed my eyes and, squeaking, "Say yes and save me Mom, save me!" disappeared below the table.

"Dear God," my mother said weakly. "Is this what I have to look forward to?"

"This and more," Beale murmured, making it sound like a promise. "So?"

"All right," my mother said as I scrambled back up. "I can't believe I'm actually doing this, but . . . okay. Yes. Oh my God." She turned and leaned against Beale's chest, burying her face in the front of his shirt and saying in a muffled voice, "I can't believe you're doing this in the middle of the diner."

"Hey, a man's gotta do what a man's gotta do," he said, grinning.

"This is not a joke," my mother said, peering up at him. "It's huge, Beale. I'm too happy. I don't know if I can take it. This is all new. I . . . I hope I don't disappoint you."

"Never happen," he said tenderly, and kissed the top of her head. He glanced over at me and with his heart in his eyes, smiled, and said, "Hey, Miss Sayre Bellavia, what do you think, huh? We're finally going home."

Chapter 19

"Mom," I whisper, leaning over the bed rail.

She doesn't stir.

"Mom," I say, putting my mouth closer to her ear. "I know you can hear me." That's a lie because I *don't* know it, can't stop thinking about what Red said about hepatic encephalopathy and the ammonia levels getting higher and higher in her brain. . . .

Brain damage.

My mother's brain is flooded with ammonia, her thoughts, her dreams, her memories are all drowning, and even if she *does* hear me, she still might not recognize my voice anymore.

"Mom?" I wait, but her breathing doesn't change, nothing changes, and for one hot, shocking moment I just want to seize her terrible, bony arm and shake her until she wakes up, disturb her peace and force her back, make her stay to deal with me and the mess she's leaving behind, shake her until all the hurt and rage and sadness, all the lost moments and careless cruelties and yearning fall away, until she opens her eyes and sees me, *really* sees me and not the ghost of my hated father.

"Just one time," I whisper, holding tight to the bed rail and blinking back tears.

Please.

My Cup Runneth Over

My mother and I moved into the farmhouse up on Sunrise Road with Beale and Aunt Loretta on Halloween, and less than a month later, on Thanksgiving morning, my mother got sick and threw up. She stayed in her room all day because she thought she'd gotten the stomach flu from people at work, and just the smell of all that food was making her nauseous.

Not me, though.

Maybe it sounds mean, but the day was still wonderful, even without my mother. Mostly because she *wasn't* there, and I had Beale and Aunt Loretta all to myself, and there was nobody giving me censorious looks when I voiced an opinion or got giggly and food stupid from eating too much, nobody who looked at me like I was a suck-up when I helped baste the turkey or put the brown sugar and butter in the sweet potatoes or whipped the cream for the pumpkin pies. Nobody who raised an eyebrow and drawled in a low, sarcastic voice so only I would hear, as I went on humming "Stormy" and setting the table for dinner, "My, my, who knew you'd turn into such a little homemaker?" or gave me an irritated look when I filled my plate for the second time with a taste of everything, wanting to savor it all, even the cranberry sauce, or said, "God, Sayre, do you always have to have more? Aren't you ever satisfied?"

And nobody was critical when I got all choked up as we went

around the table, just the three of us and said what we were thankful for, although Aunt Loretta did give me a questioning look over her glasses when I stammered out, *I'm thankful for living here with Beale and Aunt Loretta and Stormy and the other cats, and for getting all As on my homework and for my new pants and I guess even for my new sweater only it itches sometimes, and I hope I can stay here forever and . . . that's everything. Amen.*

And then I reached for my fork and noticed Aunt Loretta's curious look and like a bolt of lightning I realized what I'd forgotten and so I quick said, *And I'm thankful that my mother and Beale are in love and happy. Amen again.*

That cracked them both up and we went to work on that big, beautiful table full of food and every so often beneath the chatter I'd hear the bedroom door open upstairs and my mother lurch to the bathroom. Maybe I was a bad person to talk louder and faster when it happened so that nobody else would hear it, too, and leave the table to go up and check on her because if that happened it would change the mood of us, change the happy rhythm and the way we were together, which was kind of like it was back in the beginning when I first stayed with Miss Mo, and they just liked me for me.

I knew I was only living here because of Beale and my mother, but sometimes I could make myself forget that and Thanksgiving was one of those days.

My mother made it to work that night, though, armed with a plain turkey sandwich in her lunch bag. She came downstairs pale and a little shaky but drank some ginger ale and ate a piece of butter bread and felt better, so Beale drove her in saying that if she felt sick, to call him no matter what time it was and he'd go back and get her.

She'd been paying him rent, a hundred dollars a week for the two of us, and was very proud of never having missed a payment. Beale called her Miss Moneybags and she would swat him when he said it but her eyes would sparkle and I could tell she liked that.

She was different in other ways since we'd been out here at the farm, too. Beale kept her laughing, and Aunt Loretta was helpful but still went about her own life, and so slowly, my mother relaxed. Aunt Loretta was a really good cook, with her cinnamon rolls, peach conserves, and raspberry pastries winning ribbons at the county fair, and my mother gained enough weight to fill out her jeans. She came home from the factory with stories of her coworkers and lingered in the kitchen after supper, making coffee and telling us all the latest gossip. She knew, before we did, that Miss Mo's little house had been sold to a young couple from York who'd been transferred up by the factory, and she knew when it went on the market again because the couple had left, homesick.

She was still wary, though, sometimes and would go quiet and withdraw, like she couldn't afford to completely believe. I knew how she felt because I would catch myself being almost *too* happy, and would hurriedly try to make it smaller and less noticeable so it wouldn't be snatched away.

But on December third, right before supper, we threw caution to the wind and let joy get the better of us all.

Chapter 20

She breathes so slowly.

Inhale . . .

Silence.

Exhale.

I wait.

And wait.

Inhale.

I get up and go to the bathroom. Flush the toilet and wince as the whooshing roar echoes in the silence. Stick my head out the door, but the hallway is deserted. Sit back down in my chair by the bed. My mother is lying exactly as I left her. I pick up the nurse's call button, a TV remote-shaped lifeline to help, and hold on to it. It's comforting to know that if I call, someone will come.

Exhale.

The hush in the room settles around me, magnifies the sudden rasp of my mother's feet twitching beneath the sheet, and the slight puffing sound she makes at the end of each slow breath. The longer I listen, the more unnerving it gets because they go on and on, these slight, measured breaths that don't change or gain strength, don't show any sign of her rising to consciousness, don't do anything but continue, automatic, and nothing more than the basic functions of struggling organs in a failing body. These stale, foul breaths are not what made my mother who she was, the woman I followed, feared, hated, and waited for, the woman I need so much to talk to. No, that person is trapped in a sea of ammonia, and she's the one I want, but . . .

She's really leaving, and this time I can't follow.

Inhale.

"Mom," I whisper. "You're scaring me."

Exhale.

She's leaving, and I'm not even eighteen. What am I supposed to do? How am I supposed to live? Who'll know my life besides me? Who'll know my family stories, or Grandma's parakeet's name, or that I look just like my father?

No one.

Only me, and if I forget, then my history disappears forever.

Inhale.

"Mom, you can't do this." The words hang in the silence. "You can't. You have to wake up. I mean it. This isn't funny anymore, do you hear me? Come on, you have to wake up. We have to go home right now." I push myself out of the chair, knees trembling, and set the call button back on the bed. "Come on, give me your hand, it's time to go."

Exhale.

"You don't understand," I say when she doesn't move. "If you stay here, bad things will happen. Don't you see? You have to get up, Mom. You do. Right now. *Please* . . . " My voice breaks and years of tears begin to fall. "*Please* wake up, Mom. Please." I can't stop crying now, because she isn't moving, she won't listen, she's *never* listened, and although that means she's still in there somewhere, that she *is* still herself, it also means what it's always meant, that nothing's changed and I can't stop her, can't save her, can't even make her *hear* me . . .

Oh.

But where there's life, there's hope, isn't that what Grandma Lucy used to say? and so even though I can almost see death stirring in the corner, moving to sit beside her on the bed and settling itself between us, my mother and I are not done yet.

I am going to talk to her, to tell her things, lots of things, some old and overdue, some newly discovered. And she's going to listen because there was something else Grandma Lucy used to say, something my mother absolutely loathed and thought weak and stupid, but it wasn't. It was strong in a way my mother never understood, for she equated kindness with weakness, caring with powerlessness, and love with terrifying vulnerability.

And maybe love *is* terrifying. I'm terrified now, but not in the way she would think.

I'm terrified because I hate who she is and what she's done, I do, and yet there is *still* something strong and powerful between us, some kind of deep, primal bond that won't end, won't snap or break or change, it just remains there inside me, as solid and factual as my blood and bones—she is my mother, I am her daughter—and I don't know what to call it because it doesn't feel like love, not the good kind I felt for Ellie, with all my heart, but instead an instinctual pull that's been there from the beginning, drawing me back to her again and again, this woman who has hurt me like no one else ever could, and now she's dying and the bond is still here, inside me, and I won't call it love or hate because emotion has nothing to do with the fact that she is my mother and I am her daughter, and we will be connected in that way forever.

Inhale.

Every family needs a peacemaker.

All right.

I will make peace, if not for her, than for me.

I lean over and pick up the ruby velvet blazer. Rise, walk around the far side of the bed and with a hitched breath, ease down onto the blanket beside my mother. Wait as she shifts but doesn't turn over, doesn't wake up, and when she is still again I stretch out, tucking myself close to her, spread the embroidered ruby blazer across the two of us, wrap my arm around her fragile frame, rest my head on her pillow, and with a soft, quivering sigh, close my eyes.

Exhale.

Silver Bells

It was December third, a late Wednesday afternoon. Aunt Loretta was in the kitchen listening to Christmas carols and making pork chops and scalloped potatoes for supper, my mother was upstairs getting ready for work, and Beale was due in from the barn any second. I had already set the table and was on the floor in the living room, painting my toenails red and green and teaching Stormy how to fetch a fuzzy mouse cat toy.

"Sayre," my mother said in a loud whisper, beckoning me from the top of the stairs.

"What?" I said, glancing over but not getting up.

"Come here."

"I'm busy," I said, carefully putting the last green stripe on my big toe. "What do you want?"

She made an impatient noise. "Would you just come here? I want to talk to you."

I sighed loudly, and pushed myself up. She'd been acting weird for a whole week now, being angry and impatient and obnoxious, watching us with wary eyes, hanging back like she was trying to put distance between us all but then falling all over Beale in sudden fits of ferocious affection, eating nothing and then eating everything, and once even saying really loud, like it was an announcement in an argument no one was having, about loving her job more than anything, loving that she was earning her own money and paying her own way, what a great feeling of satisfaction it gave and how she never wanted to quit for anyone at any time because there were no guarantees in life and things changed and you never knew what was coming.

We all just sat there at the dinner table, forks poised and listening in astonishment until she finally saw our puzzled looks, got embarrassed and then defensive, and ate the rest of her supper in silence despite our efforts to draw her back out.

"What?" I said, going to the bottom of the stairs and hanging on the banister.

"Come *here.*" She gave me the laser eyeball, wheeled, and went into her's and Beale's room.

I followed her and plopped down on the edge of the bed. I wasn't allowed in here much and never alone, and it seemed a very exotic, masculine place. Even though my mother had brought all she owned, and her makeup and stuff was spread out on the bureau, the room was still primarily Beale's. It smelled of his deep, woodsy aftershave, was decorated in navy and brown and forest green, and his furniture was all real wood, dark and sturdy, solid and antique, like it had been passed down in his family. "What?"

My mother paced the room once, then stopped in front of a pile of clean laundry and started folding it. "We've been in some pretty shitty situations, haven't we?" she said without looking at me.

I stared at her, bewildered. "Huh?"

"The way we've lived," she said impatiently. "It's been pretty bad."

"Well . . . yeah," I said cautiously because this was something that had never happened before.

She was quiet a moment, righting the sleeves of one of Beale's work shirts that had gone inside out. "Those bonds everyone says that kids are supposed to have with their mothers; I didn't get you till you were what, almost eight? What chance did that really give us? You were already a person by then."

I had no idea what to say.

"I mean I wasn't a *bad* mother," she said hurriedly, filling the silence. "I held you when you were little . . . I don't know if you remember. I know I wasn't perfect but . . ." She fights with the shirtsleeve, gives up, shoves it over a hanger and into the closet. "I had a lot going on back then."

"I remember," I said.

She flashed me a look that spoke volumes, like she had just realized I was alive and had eyes and thoughts of my own about how she'd made me grow up, that I had borne witness to the last ten years, that she wasn't the only one who knew what she had done and how she'd been, and that I might actually remember more than she did, seeing as how she'd been drunk and high, and I'd been straight the whole time. It was a look that said *Oh, no* and *Oh, really?*

And *Oh, you'd better not,* all at the same time.

"So you do blame me," she said, turning back to the laundry.

"You blame me, too," I said, staring down at my hands, clasped in my lap.

The silence stretched, and I don't know how it would have ended if we hadn't heard Beale come in and call out, "I'm home. Hey, where's my good-looking welcoming committee?"

My mother's face changed then, and she dropped the laundry and went straight to the mirror, smoothing her hair and telling me, "Go down, Sayre. I'll be there in a minute."

And so I ran down the stairs, pushing aside the strange conversation with my mother because Beale was home, and when I reached the foyer he was taking off his coat and I was just about to say, "Guess what we're having for supper?" which is what I said every night, when my mother came down the stairs and said, "Beale?"

"Hey, sweetheart," he said, hanging his coat over the hook and smiling at her. "Where's my kiss?" He reached for her and she stopped him, put a flat hand against his chest, and then took a deep breath, and said, "I'm pregnant."

Chapter 21

My mother twitches in her sleep.

I lift my head from the pillow and gaze down at her. She's still lying on her side, facing away from me, and the rich velvet blazer with its delicate embroidery serves as a stark contrast to the thin cotton of her baggy, faded, green-print hospital gown.

Her fingertips flutter and the motion is delicate, graceful.

Gentle.

"Are you dreaming about Ellie, Mom?" Saying that beautiful, forbidden name aloud still feels like a violation, but I'm determined to make peace, speak all the unspoken, and I'm about to go on but the yearning rises so fast and fierce that it cracks me wide open. I bury my face in my hands until the wail that has been waiting inside me all this time is once again muted and when I can speak, I whisper, "Are we all together again?"

Sing Me to Sleep

"I'm pregnant," my mother repeated, lifting her chin. "About five weeks. Think Halloween." The words were clipped, rushed, as if each passing heartbeat mattered, as if time hadn't stopped and shock hadn't sucked the oxygen from the room.

Pregnant.

My mother.

And Beale.

Beale.

I caught my breath.

Beale stared down at her, all the glory of the dawn in his face, and said huskily, "Are you sure?"

"Yes," my mother said, searching his expression.

It was the whoop that dropped me, the exultant cry that exploded from him like fireworks on the Fourth of July. It zapped the last of the strength from my knees and sent me sinking to the steps right as he swooped my mother up in an exuberant bear hug and, laughing, swung her around, legs flying and nearly kicking me in the head, kissing her and calling, "Ma! Hey, Ma, come here! Dianne and I have something to tell you!" and my mother, limp and teary eyed, laughing, and Aunt Loretta bustling in, drying her hands on her apron and taking one look at her beaming son and my blushing, glowing mother and bursting into tears, hugging them, hugging me, and saying, "Oh, Sayre, come July you're going to be a big sister! Isn't it wonderful?"

And that centered me again, pulled me back down to earth and made me sit up straighter because I hadn't thought of that.

I was going to be a big sister.

Me.

Sayre Bellavia.

I looked up at them, all laughing and chattering, at my mother smiling and wiping her eyes, at Beale, shining like the noonday sun, at Aunt Loretta, who kept looking from my mother to Beale, and back again, and in one hot, shocking sweep I realized that this baby would not be me. It would not start out unwanted, hated, cursed, and left behind. No, this baby would have a father who not only adored it but who would claim and protect it, and a mother who would hold it and dress it and feed it, rock it and smile at it. This baby would have a last name that meant something, that had roots and was connected to someone instead of a random phrase that couldn't be matched to anyone anywhere, which left it floating alone in the world. It would have a beautiful home and a real family, a grandmother and love and care.

It would never be left in a field or have to go to bed hungry or huddle in a closet with its hands over its ears because its mother and Bobby Fee were going at it on the bed. It would never watch its mother shoot up or be covered in bruises or eat from a Dumpster or be told it should never have been born.

This baby's five-week-old life was already different from mine.

Better than mine.

Because this baby would have Beale for a father, a *real* father, and when my mother looked at that baby she would see Beale, who she loved, and not the old memory of a guy who had gotten her pregnant and left without a backward look.

And Beale would look at that baby and see his own kin, his blood, and not have to settle for me anymore, who just loved him.

"It isn't fair," I whispered, and the words were lost in the chatter but I guess my old habit of patting myself on the arm was not, because Aunt Loretta detached herself, reached out a hand to me, and said, "Well, somebody has to go check on the pork chops, so I guess it'll be me and my best helper. Come on, sweetie. Let's go make our magic."

I rose, feeling heavy and sick, and when I went to slip past Beale he hugged me hard, squishing my face into his stomach and said, "This kid's gonna have the best big sister out there and if it ever gives you a hard time, Miss Sayre Bellavia, you just come and tell me and I'll give that little weezer what for, you hear me?" He kissed the top of my head and, releasing me, said, "Anybody messes with my number one girl, they answer to me."

And just like that, I could smile again.

Chapter 22

The snow is lessening and the sky outside the window is a lighter shade of gray.

My mother's legs move restlessly, twitching and jerking without direction.

The room is stifling but her skin is cool.

I have talked and talked. Whispered her name. Tapped her. Even shaken her arm a little.

No response.

I'm so tired.

Bone tired.

I get what that means now.

But I'm not done talking yet.

I—

There's a rising commotion outside in the hall, furious whispers, and hustling, squeaking shoes.

I lift my head from the pillow and see Candy standing in the doorway. She looks terrible, drawn and manic, with big dark circles under her pale eyes, scabs on her cheeks, and that thin, ratty, orangish hair flying everywhere.

The nurse appears beside her. "I'm sorry, I tried to stop her," she says to me, giving Candy a really pissed look. "Security is on the way up."

"You got some balls, kicking me out of this room when you're the little fucker who walked out on her," Candy says, scowling.

"You need to leave," I say but don't lie back down because Candy's simmering and only a fool ignores that kind of warning.

Her eyebrows go up. "*You're* telling *me* what I need to do? Oh, that'll be the day." She plops into the armchair next to the bed. "I been with her for her whole fucking life and now you think you're gonna tell me to leave." She snorts. "Right."

"Keep your voice down," the nurse says. "There are other patients on this floor."

"Yeah, yeah," Candy says, waving an irritated hand.

I stare at her, too exhausted to do battle over who has more of a right to sit with my mother's emaciated shell. I'm her daughter, her blood and next of kin, but Candy has always been her chosen one, confidante and partner in crime. . . .

Her lifelong friend who shared everything, good and bad.

All the whys, wheres, and whens. All the how comes.

All the reasons.

And possibly the answer to the question my mother is no longer capable of answering.

I hate to do it, hate to ask Candy anything because that will only give her more power over me, knowing she has something I want but—

"Why is my last name Bellavia?" I hear myself say suddenly. "Where did that come from, anyway?"

Candy glances at me, surprised, then snorts again, this time in amusement. "God, I haven't thought about that in years." Smirking, she leans back in the chair, stretches out her legs, and cracks her knuckles. "What do you want to know for?"

I give her a look.

"Hey." She shrugs, enjoying herself. "I don't care either way."

"Was it my father's last name?" I make myself say, hating her more than I ever thought possible.

She must see it in my face because her amusement dies, her face grows cold, and she says, "That asshole? No. Who knows *what* his last name was. You got Bellavia the day Mrs. Marinelli, the language arts teacher, caught us smoking out in the parking lot at school. Your mother was like eight months' pregnant and feeling pretty crappy and I guess Mrs. M. was trying to spin it into something to be happy about—good luck on *that* score—and she said, *A baby is something to celebrate, Dianne. We women are blessed to be able to bring new life to this world. So joyful. Bella via, such a beautiful way,* and your mother was like, *Yeah, it's really joyful being fat, and having stretch marks, and giant hemorrhoids, and I can't wait to go into labor. That's gonna be a real beautiful way.* I don't even remember. Anyhow, it was such a stupid thing to say that we couldn't resist, so . . ." Her mouth curves into a mean little smile. "Happy now?"

And I thought I couldn't feel any worse.

"So all this time it didn't mean anything," I say finally, heartsick, staring down at the unconscious woman lying beside me, and wondering how she could have done it.

"Nope," Candy says triumphantly. "Joke's on you, huh?"

The nurse glances out the door. "Security's here." She gives me a questioning look.

I gaze at Candy, my mother's best friend, the one who's loved her and been there for her since the fourth grade, the one who had no sisters of her own and made my mother the sister of her heart, the one who fought for her, claimed her, laughed with her, cried with her, got high and got straight with her, then high again. The one who put her up when she had nowhere to go, who held back her hair when she puked, who came to her baby shower sloppy drunk and alternated between telling my mother she loved her and crying because the old days were gone.

Candy, who wants more than anything to stay with my mother until the end.

Who will be lost without her.

I look at the nurse waiting with the security guard and say calmly, "I'd like to be alone with my mother, please."

And when a second security guard arrives and Candy is finally physically removed and her sobbing, threats, and curses are a dim and distant echo, I lie back down, pull the ruby velvet blazer over me, and close my eyes.

Perhaps I am my mother's daughter after all.

The Wait

After the baby announcement time seemed to fly, and I don't know whether that was because my mother was pregnant and the focus in the farmhouse shifted to getting ready for the baby, or if it was because Christmas was zooming toward us and there was so much to do, or because my time of being an only child was running out.

I kept flip-flopping at the thought, excited one day about being a big sister, and sulky the next at having to share Beale and Aunt Loretta with my mother, who had become the center of attention and was milking it for all it was worth. Whenever she spoke, someone listened. Whenever her stomach gurgled, there were offers of food or Pepto-Bismol or belly rubs. When she watched TV, she got to snuggle under my favorite afghan while I had to take the scratchy orange one. Aunt Loretta started cooking really healthy foods so the baby would be strong, and we had to have stupid fruit for dessert instead of German chocolate cake or peanut butter pie. And worst of all, my mother said my kitten made her nose itchy, so little Stormy was gently but firmly relegated to the barn, which made me really mad, but it didn't matter because now, being pregnant, my mother came first.

It burned me that she didn't seem to care that *I* had been here first, not her, and sometimes I would look at her sitting there, all petted and pampered, and wish she was gone. Not dead, just out of the picture so it was only me, Beale, and Aunt Loretta, happy together in the farmhouse. I wished my mother still lived with Candy or out on the back ridge with the Fees, or anywhere but here, and that fantasy was the most fulfilling when she was away at work and the rest of us were home, getting along just fine without her.

I was also mad at her for being so happy this time, for resting her hand protectively over her belly even though she wasn't showing yet, for going to the doctors and taking vitamins and eating right, and deciding to give this baby Beale's last name.

That part hurt the most.

The baby would belong to this family and the world would know it, while I, who not only loved them dearly but who had also brought my mother and Beale together, was stuck with a last name that kept me separate, unattached and unclaimed.

It wasn't fair, and if I thought about it too much it would make my stomach hurt so I tried not to, instead getting all caught up in the excitement of the holidays, and relishing the hours when my mother was at work and it was just the three of us again.

One cold, gray Saturday morning before Christmas when the air was heavy with the promise of snow and my mother was sleeping after working the night shift, Aunt Loretta went into town for groceries and I went outside to help Beale refill the bird feeders and bring in wood for the stove.

"So, Miss Sayre Bellavia," he said, capping the last feeder and leading me over to the woodpile. "What do you think about this whole new baby thing?"

"I wish it was me," I said without thinking, hefting a piece of split wood that must have weighed ten pounds and staggering over to dump it in the wagon behind the quad. It fell with a hearty thud and when I turned to get another one, I found Beale looking at me in alarm.

"Uh, don't you think it's too soon to be thinking about having a baby?" he said, tilting up the brim of his cap and rubbing his forehead. "You're not even eleven yet and you've got your whole life ahead of you. You want to go to high school and have fun, graduate and maybe even go to college, get out there and see the world, meet a good guy who'll do right by you and fall in love with him, get married, and *then* maybe think about starting a family. Not now. Jesus." And then he looked even more alarmed. "Wait a minute. You haven't . . . those boys in school better not have messed with you because if they have, I swear to God I'll—"

He was talking too fast and his voice was getting louder and I didn't want him to wake up my mother, and so even though it was mortifying, I had to tell him what I'd really meant. "No, that's not what I meant. I don't wish I was *having* a baby. Ew. I wish . . ." Face flaming, I bent down for another piece of wood so I wouldn't have to look at him and said in a rush, "I wish *I* was being born now. I mean, that this baby was me instead of . . ." My throat tightened and it was all I could do to speak. "If I was born now then you would be my real father instead of . . . nobody and I would be your real kid." I dropped the chunk of wood in the wagon and grabbed another. "That's what I meant."

I stood there for what felt like a thousand years, embarrassed by admitting my deepest desire and kind of scared that he would tell my mother what I'd said, and so all I could do was stare down at the piece of wood, my face hot and huge, my fingers picking at a piece of bark stuck to the otherwise smooth log.

"Whew. You had me scared there for a minute," Beale said finally, and came over and gave me one of his quick, solid, one-armed hugs. "I'm not ready to be a grandfather yet, Bellavia. Maybe in another twenty years." He gazed down at me and his smile grew thoughtful. "You know what's so great about tomorrow, Sayre? There's not a mark on it. You can get out there and be anyone, go anywhere, do anything. The sky's the limit. The only thing that ever really holds you back is yourself, and what you're afraid of. . . ." He paused, staring out toward the frozen field. "I don't think I ever told you this but when I graduated high school I figured I'd just work on the farm with my father, but he wouldn't let me."

"Really?" I said, glancing up at him.

"Really." His mouth curved into a reminiscent smile. "God, he was stubborn. He told me he'd been setting aside money for me ever since I was born so I could go to college and learn about something I was interested in, get out of Dug County and live on my own for a while, meet different kinds of people and see other parts of the country and then, after all of that, if I still wanted to come back and work the farm at least I'd be doing it of my own free will, instead of just doing it because I didn't know any better or didn't think I had any other options."

"So did you do it?" I asked. "Go away, I mean."

"Oh yeah," he said, nodding and smiling slightly, still lost in the past. "My father didn't give me a lot of money, just enough to get going, so I had to go to school and work at the same time, but yeah, it was great. A real eye-opener. I did more and learned more than I ever thought I could. And I met a lot of great people, too." He refocused on me. "The point is that my father wanted more for me than he'd had, a better life, and I want that for you, too. That's what all parents want for their kids."

"But I'm not really your kid," I said, staring up at him.

"Well, maybe not in the normal way, but I couldn't be prouder than if you were my own daughter." And when I didn't answer, just lowered my head and let my hair swing forward around my face, he teased, "Oh, c'mon, you don't think you're like a daughter to me? Who else sits next to me at breakfast every morning, hogging the maple syrup, and gets to help me load all this backbreaking wood—"

"Big deal," I mumbled, trying not to smile.

"And who sneaks her cat in from the barn to sleep with her at night—"

I shot him a surprised look.

"Oh yeah, your old man knows more than you think," he said,

giving me a stern look and then ruining it by waggling his eyebrows. "Who else in this family gets nothing but As and Bs and gets to pick her own dessert every marking period, hmm? Not me, that's for sure. Who else is getting a big surprise for Christmas—"

"Who?" I demanded, breaking into excited giggles at his guilty look. "Me, Beale? Me? I'm getting a surprise? What is it?"

"Time to zip the lip," he said, making the motion.

"Tell me," I said, tugging on his arm. "Please? I promise I'll act surprised."

"No, you'll *be* surprised because that's all I'm saying. Now come on, let's get this wood done so we can get out of this cold. Brr." He glanced up at the silvery-gray sky, and launched into a hearty "It's Beginning to Look a Lot Like Christmas."

I didn't know all the words but I chimed in when I could, and by the time we finished moving wood Aunt Loretta was home, it was snowing, and the warmth from the fiery woodstove was second to the warmth glowing inside me.

That security and newfound confidence must have come through somehow because before Christmas, Trey, one of the boys in my class, invited me to his birthday party out at the bowling alley and so I went, eaten up with shivery anticipation, wearing new jeans and a new red shirt, with my hair French-braided by Aunt Loretta, and despite my mother's snide comment that I would look trashy, my newly pierced ears decorated with tiny little gold hoop earrings, compliments of Beale.

Beale drove me into town and dropped me off at the bowling alley. Before I got out of the car he gave me ten dollars and said, "I'll be back for you at five, right here out front. If you want to come home earlier, call, okay?"

"Okay, 'bye," I said absently, scrambling out of the truck and watching some of the other kids in my class go inside. I didn't have any real friends in school, but yesterday Jillian Jergenmeier had offered me a piece of gum and said she'd see me at the party, and that had sounded almost like a promise.

It was hard to go in alone but I did it. I didn't even know how to bowl but to my delight neither did Jillian and another girl, so we grouped together and decided to go eat French fries at the snack bar instead.

"So you live with the Galens up on Sunrise Road," Jillian said when the other girl got up and went to the bathroom. "My mother said she was in the same class as your mother. She said your mom was really pretty but a total bitch and then she got pregnant, dropped out, and turned all skanky from drugs." She leaned over, dipped one of her fries in my ketchup and ate it, watching me. "She said she saw your mom in the grocery store two weeks ago and she looked really good again. She said if your mom was still a drug addict, though, I couldn't be friends with you. So," she cocked her head, "is she?"

I sat there silent and staring down at my full plate of fries, humiliated.

"I didn't say it to make you feel bad," she said, salting the last fry on her plate and eating it. "I'm just telling you what my mom said. She didn't really tell me to ask you that. She was just talking to her best friend, Monique, on the phone—they gossip *all* the time, that's why they're so fat, because they don't do anything but eat and drink wine and gossip, at least that's what my dad says and my mom gets *so mad*—and I heard her say it, so I figured I'd ask." She plucked a fry off my plate. "You don't have to answer if you don't want to. We could be friends anyway. I don't care what your mom does."

"She doesn't do that anymore," I said after a moment, and pushed the plate of fries closer to her. "Actually, her and Beale are gonna have a baby." I shouldn't have said that and I knew it, but nobody had come right out and said it was a secret, only that they wanted to hold off announcing it until after the holidays, and besides, I was proud to have good news. "In July. We don't know whether it's a boy or a girl yet."

"Cool," she said, and went on talking about how her little brothers annoyed her while she polished off all of my fries and half of the other girl's, whose name I don't even remember, only that she got mad and stalked off and Jillian just looked at me and shrugged. We both started laughing and then I ate some of those fries, too, and they were cold but still tasted really good.

Chapter 23

I'm lying here next to my mother, warm, drowsy, exhausted, whispering the story of our past, confessing, finally without fear of punishment or rejection, the way I remember our time up on Sunrise Road with Ellie, Aunt Loretta, and Beale. It feels good to resurrect them, the people I loved so much, to say their names aloud over and over, to gather them close again instead of burying and banishing them every time those memories begin to rise.

The more I say, the easier it becomes, and the longer I lie there beside her, tucked close, the more natural it seems, and so I'm drifting along on memories of the coming of Ellie and how good she felt in my arms, slow tears dampening my half of the pillow, when my mother makes a noise that is more than a moan, but less than a word.

"Mom?" I quick push myself up onto my elbow and peer at her. "Are you awake?"

Her eyes dart and roll under the lids.

"Mom, it's Sayre," I say again, leaning closer. "Can you hear me?"

Her eye cracks open, only a sliver of half-moon white showing beneath her lid, but her arms start moving and she gives a slight, feeble rock backward, toward me.

"Do you want to turn over? Okay, here." I slide farther over in the bed, my heart pounding with sudden hope. "Come on,

I'll help you." I put my hand on her bony shoulder and ease her onto her back. "Is that good? Is that what you wanted?" I wait, anxious, but she just lies there twitching, hands and feet in continuous shaky spasms, eyes closed, and once again gone somewhere out of reach.

But it's all right because I'm not done talking to her yet.

Christmas

I'd never had a Christmas like the one up on Sunrise Road before and the laughter and hugs, presents and cookies, sparkling lights and carols were so overwhelming that I cried three times that day.

The first was when I opened my surprise gift from Beale, my mother, and Aunt Loretta, which was a laptop of my very own.

I took one look at it and burst into tears.

"Uh-oh," Beale said, glancing at his mother.

"No, I'm just happy," I blubbered and it sounded so funny that I started laughing through my tears. Someone handed me a tissue and when I could breathe again I fumbled the box open and slid out the beautiful, brand-new laptop. "*Wow.*"

"Look at the stars in her eyes," Aunt Loretta said to Beale, nudging him and smiling in my direction. "Do you like it, Sayre?"

"I *love* it," I said, running a light hand across its sleek top. I'd never had a computer of my own before, I'd always had to use the ones at the library and at school. "And it's silver, my favorite color!"

My mother glanced at Beale. "You were right," she said, and then to me, "So what do you say, Sayre?"

I knew what to say, I always did, because manners had been really important to Grandma Lucy, and my mother's premature nudge annoyed me, but the laptop was so cool that I just said, "I know," and scrambled up to hug and kiss Beale and Aunt Loretta, and called, "Thanks, Mom," because she had gotten up and gone to the bathroom before I could get to her.

The second crying jag happened when my mother opened Aunt Loretta's gift to her, which was the rich, plush, embroidered ruby velvet blazer.

"Well," my mother said, lifting it slowly up out of the box and watching it unfold. "This is amazing, Loretta. Feel how soft. And look at these flowers stitched onto the lapel. I never saw anything like this."

"And you won't, because I did the embroidery myself," Aunt Loretta said, leaning over around Beale and patting my mother's hand. "I hope you won't think it's silly, but in the language of flowers, Queen Anne's lace represents sanctuary, and that's what I hope you and Beale and Sayre always find in each other, Dianne. This is a one-of-a-kind piece now, and when Sayre grows up you can hand it down to her, and then she can wear it, too. That's how family heirlooms begin."

Family heirlooms.

My family.

We finally had something beautiful worth passing down.

The thought made me tear up all over again, and I quick grabbed my stocking and rummaged back through it like I was searching for something, but really, I just wanted to keep the feeling to myself because I knew I could never explain it.

The third time I cried there was no way I could hide it and I didn't even try.

"This is a gift from Santa to all of us," Aunt Loretta said near the end, picking up a thin, rectangular box wrapped in silver paper and pausing a moment, as if wondering who to hand it to. Her gaze fell on me and she smiled. "Let's let Sayre open it."

"Okay," I said eagerly, pulling off the bow and sticking it on the front of my shirt with all the others. I pried up the tape on each end—I was a slow unwrapper, always wanting to make things last—and opened the paper. "Oh, how pretty!" It was a piece of needlepoint in a wooden frame, like a little poem, with all kinds of holly leaves and berries embroidered around it. "Did you make this, Aunt Loretta?"

"*Santa* brought it," she said, lips twitching. "What does it say? Read it aloud."

"Okay," I said, and taking a deep breath, read:

> "'*The best of all gifts around any Christmas tree:*
> *the presence of a happy family*
> *all wrapped up in each other.*
> —*Burton Hillis*
>
> *Our First Family Christmas*
> *Loretta Galen, Beale Galen, Dianne Huff, Sayre Bellavia*
> *And our beloved Baby-in-Waiting.*'"

By the time I got to the end my voice was wobbling and my nose running and I couldn't see the needlepoint anymore, so I thrust it at Beale, threw my arms around Aunt Loretta and, hugging her, whispered, "Thank you."

"Merry Christmas, honey," she whispered back and held and rocked me while my mother opened Beale's surprise gift to her, which was a pretty amethyst promise ring that had been passed down in his family for ages. Beale slid it on her finger, and when she stared at it, dazed, he told her it was a Galen family tradition that this amethyst ring stood in the place of a real engagement ring until the diamond was picked out.

They were going to be married.

Winter Becomes Spring

It snowed and snowed.

The bus almost slid off the road three times.

Beale started driving my mother to and from work, and sometimes when the roads were really icy, she'd just call and tell them she couldn't get in. She fretted on those nights, worried about her money because she still insisted on paying rent and no matter what Beale said to try and soothe her, she just brushed it aside and kept worrying.

Jillian and I weren't in the same classes but we had lunch together every day. Sometimes we had spitball fights with Trey and his friends, sometimes we thought they were gross and didn't even want to look at them. We didn't hang out much after school because she lived all the way across Sullivan and her mother didn't like to drive in the snow, and Beale was usually too busy working or driving my mother around to haul me all the way down the mountain to town for a few short hours.

Beale gave my mother chocolates on Valentine's Day but they couldn't go out to dinner because it was snowing really hard and the wind was whipping, and the roads got treacherous, so Aunt Loretta and I put candles on the dining room table and made them a romantic dinner of stuffed flounder and baked potatoes. She tied one of her aprons around me and I became the waitress serving them.

"Oh, you can't be serious," my mother said when Beale ushered her in and pulled out her chair. She looked at the lit candles, the good china, the low lights, and me at the other side of the room trying to get the soft music going from the little stereo. Smiling, she shook her head and let him help seat her. "Did you do this?" she asked when Beale sat down across the table.

"Not me," he said, grinning and sitting back as I hustled over and filled his water glass. "Talk to your daughter."

She cocked her head and glanced sideways at me from under her hair. "Was this your idea?"

I gave her a look, pulled a pad and pen from my pocket, and cleared my throat. "Hello. Happy Valentine's Day. My name is Sayre and I'll be your server this evening."

"Hello, Sayre," my mother said, lips twitching.

"I highly recommend our special tonight," I said, looking at Beale, who was clearly enjoying himself. "We have a delicious stuffed flounder with a salad, baked potato, peas and . . . uh . . . oh, fresh rolls and butter." I beamed at him, pleased I'd remembered.

"Dianne?" Beale asked.

"That sounds good," my mother said.

"Make that two," Beale said, and then with a mischievous look, picked up his fork and examined it. "Um, waitress? Can I get another fork? This one is spotty."

"It is not!" I exclaimed, indignant. "I polished the silverware myself. It's fine."

"Okay," he said meekly, giving my mother a laughing look. "Oh, and, waitress? Don't tell the cook I said that. I don't want her spitting in my food."

My jaw dropped. "Beale! Aunt Loretta wouldn't—"

He and my mother cracked up and then I got it, so giggling and calling out, "I'm telling!" I ran back to the kitchen to tell her exactly what Beale had said.

"Wretched boy," she said, chuckling and wiping her hands on a dish towel. "I've got a good mind to stick a sock in his flounder."

She handed me the basket of rolls. "Ah well, tonight's their first Valentine's Day together so I guess I'll let it pass. Now here, take those in and come back for the salads."

It was a fun holiday, and so was Easter when it finally came. The snow had mostly melted and we went to church in the morning. My mother went, too, because her morning sickness had stopped and she was showing some now, and besides having a bad case of cabin fever from holing up in the farmhouse half the winter with nothing big to do, I'd finally told her what Jillian Jergenmeier's mother had said all those months ago. . . .

"*Who* called me a skank?" my mother said, turning from the mirror where she was in the middle of examining a pimple and staring at me in outrage.

"Jillian Jergenmeier's mother," I said matter-of-factly, winding a Band-Aid around my pinkie where Stormy had scratched me.

"Jillian Jerg . . . who? Jesus Christ, Sayre, that doesn't tell me anything! What's her mother's name?"

I thought a minute, and said brightly, "Mrs. Jergenmeier?"

"Oh, for— Wait a minute." My mother grew thoughtful. "Let me think. She said we were in the same class at school? And her best friend was Monique? Wait . . . oh God, who the hell was that skinny girl with the thick ankles who always wore those stupid denim capris and ugly flat sandals? She was really short, like a pygmy, but she walked around like she was hot shit . . . Candy shoved her off the blenchers once, just for being annoying." Her face lit up. "Karrie Troik! *That's* it. Yeah, come to think of it, I remember hearing that she married some military guy with a funky last name but that was years ago. . . ." Her expression blackened into a scowl. "*She* called *me* a skank? Oh, that'll be the day."

I tried to tell her that Jillian's mother had said she was only a skank when she was on drugs, not now, but she wasn't listening. Instead, she got all dressed up, determined to walk into that church and really give Jillian's mother something to talk about.

The best part of Easter, besides the ham, was standing in the

pew between Aunt Loretta and Beale singing "Christ the Lord Is
Risen Today," seeing the sun glowing through the stained-glass
windows and the amethyst promise ring on my mother's hand
sparkling.

After the service, while Aunt Loretta was introducing me and
Beale to the new youth minister, Reverend Ganzler, who had a
fuzzy red beard and would be teaching our Sunday school classes in
September, I saw Jillian's mother lumber over to my mother, who
was standing on the sidewalk a little ways apart from us. Mrs. Jergenmeier's smile was fake, her face makeup heavy, and I could hear
the tortured swish of her panty hose rubbing as she passed. Her
hair was short, dyed blond and poufy, and the wind kept catching it, lifting up whole sheaves of tight, sprayed layers and then
lowering them again, which I thought looked pretty funny but my
mother just stood there with an eyebrow cocked, a slight smile, and
a calm, vaguely disinterested air as Jillian's mother gushed on and
on.

It wasn't until later, on the car ride home, that my mother
glanced over at Beale and said, "I can't believe you went out with
her."

"Who?" Beale said, glancing at her, puzzled, and then, "Oh.
Yeah, that was a long time ago. Back when I was young and stupid."

"How long were you guys together?" she asked, shifting in the
seat to face him.

He shrugged and signaled to take the scenic route out of town.
"I don't know."

"A week? A month? A year?"

"I don't know," he said, rubbing his forehead. "A couple of
months. Why?"

"Just wondering," she said lightly. "She talked like she'd practi-
cally lived up at the farm while you two were together."

"Well, yeah, she kind of did," Beale said, tightening his fingers
on the wheel and keeping his eyes on the road. "That was the

summer she graduated high school and her parents were splitting up. Ma, you and Dad took the RV out to New Mexico, remember?" He caught my mother's raised-eyebrow look and, sealing his doom, added, "She was upset about the split, and just out to have a killer summer and forget everything for a while, you know?" Silence. "She was different back then, I mean, funny and cute and up for pretty much anything, just some wild, skinny little grunge chick—"

Instantly, the air in the car was electrified.

"Really? That's nice," my mother cooed, although her expression said the exact opposite.

Beale must have heard something in her voice because he glanced over and visibly started.

"So where did she sleep while she lived up here?" my mother said in a pleasant tone, like she was asking the price of lettuce. "In your room with you?"

"Well . . . yeah, I guess, I mean not always. We did some camping out in the woods and . . . God, I don't know, it was a long time ago," he said, gazing desperately out the side window at a wide-open field. "Hey, you guys keep your eyes open for wild turkeys. They should be moving around today."

"Sleeping out under the stars together," my mother mused, refusing to be diverted. "How romantic. Did you share a sleeping bag? Was it fun? We haven't done it yet, so *I* wouldn't know."

I glanced at Aunt Loretta, who was sitting next to me in the backseat.

She shook her head, and remained silent.

"We will," he said hurriedly, glancing over at my mother. "Maybe later, after the baby comes. You'll love it, I promise. There's a great spot up on the ridge near a waterfall—"

"Is that where you two camped, way back when?" my mother said.

Beale opened his mouth, then shut it again.

"Oh, so it already has good memories," my mother said with

real ice in her voice. "You know, I think I'll pass on that, Beale. I wouldn't want a fat, ex-pregnant chick to screw up the great memories you made there with a cute, skinny little grunge chick, you know?"

"Why are you doing this?" Beale said. "I mean, c'mon, Di, you're not fat—"

And at the same time, I couldn't take it anymore and blurted out, "You're not fat, Mom. You're really pretty."

"That's not the point! How do you think I felt standing there listening to her lay out all this fake-sweet bullshit about what a great guy you are and how fabulous the farm is, like the hayloft and the meadow and isn't that antique furniture in your bedroom just to die for?" my mother whipped back, ignoring me. "Why didn't you tell me you went out with her, Beale? I mean, I stood there smiling like a fool, totally humiliated, and she knew it because she just kept going, with stuff like *Do they still have that great tire swing by the pond? Oh, that was so much fun! That water is so cold, even skinny-dipping in the summer and oh my God, he threw me in once and I screamed so loud he thought I was hurt and it was so funny because he jumped in to save me and then of course it turned into something else . . . oh, maybe I shouldn't have said that. I know you two are together now and I don't want to cause any trouble . . .*"

"Christ," he said weakly.

"So how did you guys end?" my mother said, her gaze riveted on the side of his face.

"What do you mean?" he said.

"Who broke up with who?"

His answer, when it came, was defeated. "She, uh, broke up with me."

"Great," my mother said, sitting back in her seat and staring straight ahead. "Just . . . great."

We drove in silence for a moment, and then he pulled over to the side of the deserted road and stopped the car.

"Look, I'm sorry I didn't tell you, but I swear I never even thought about it," he said, unbuckling his seat belt and turning to face my mother. "It ended a long time ago, and I'm glad because she was bitchy back then, too." He reached over, pried one of my mother's tightly locked hands from the other, and cradled it between his own. "I don't want *her,* Di, I want you. I love *you.* I think you're beautiful. The prettiest girl in Dug County. Karrie was a long time ago. Come on, Di, we both have pasts. Someday I'm going to run into one of your old boyfriends somewhere and yeah, I'm going to hate it, and if he gets mouthy I'll probably end up decking him—"

"You don't know how close I came," my mother muttered, but the tension in her shoulders eased some.

"Well, no matter what, I love you and only you, okay?" Beale murmured, gazing straight into her eyes.

"Okay," my mother said grudgingly.

I exhaled as they exchanged a quick kiss, and I think Aunt Loretta did, too, and from then on I never told Jillian anything about my mother and Beale unless it was something really good because I knew she would run right home and pass it on.

Well, except for when I told her that Beale had totally forgotten he'd gone out with her mother because she was such a fat, nosy old bitch now that he hardly even recognized her, which got us in an ignoring fight for three days and then we made up, although her mother called and told Aunt Loretta what I'd said, the big tattletale, and so I kind of got into trouble.

"But she *is* one," I said when Aunt Loretta sat me down at the kitchen table. "Beale said so."

"No, that's *not* what he said, and even if it was, that discussion was our own private business and not for you to repeat, especially since you did it just to hurt her feelings," she said after a moment, sighing and looking at me like I should have known better.

"So what," I mumbled, scowling down at the sugar bowl. "She made my mother feel bad, so that was wrong, too. Fat thing."

"Sayre!" Aunt Loretta snapped in a voice I rarely heard. "There are worse things in life to be than fat, and one of them is ignorant. Another is prejudiced. Another is deliberately cruel. Jillian's mother was deliberately cruel and that's what I fault her for. Her weight is her business, not mine to judge, and not yours, either. Do you understand what I'm saying?"

And in a flash I did. "Hate the behavior, not the individual, right?" I said, sitting up straight in the chair because my grandma used to say that all the time but I never really got what it meant before.

"Exactly. I'm glad you understand, Sayre, but you're still not allowed to use your computer for anything but schoolwork for three days," Aunt Loretta said briskly, rising. "Now what do you say we take a couple of walking sticks and stroll around the meadow, and see if any of the wildflowers are up yet? I'm in the mood for a spring bouquet."

And so we did and it was such a nice day that I forgot all about being punished and just had fun watching for snakes, baby rabbits, and wildflowers. It was still too early in the year for most of the flowers, including Queen Anne's lace, but in another month it was easy to bring home big bouquets of yellow and orange butter-and-eggs, hawkweed, violets, wild purple phlox, and orange daylilies.

And later in May, when I turned eleven, I had a wonderful, exhausting shopping spree at the mall with Jillian followed by a birthday picnic down by the pond. We had hamburgers and hot dogs on the grill, and when dusk fell, Beale sat on the porch steps and played "Stormy" on his guitar. My mother sat rocking in the porch swing, one hand on her seventh-month belly, and the other taking *my* hand and holding it there, too, so I could feel the baby kick. Her face was soft in the rising moonlight, as soft as I'd ever seen it, and I didn't know which was more shocking, her holding my hand to her belly or the feel of the baby kicking against it. I wanted to ask if that hurt, if she was excited, if she wanted a boy or a girl, but I didn't want to seem greedy and ask for more again, and make her mad, so I just smiled back and kept quiet.

When Beale finished playing I went down the steps and sat next to him. "Guess what? I just felt the baby kicking."

He smiled down at me and said, "Pretty cool, huh?"

"Yeah," I said, then tugged his head down and whispered in his ear, "Beale, do you think the baby will like me?"

He leaned back, gazing at me with a strange expression, and said in a gruff voice, "This baby is going to love you, Sayre."

"Good," I whispered, ducking my head with happiness.

And then Aunt Loretta brought out lemon sherbet and called me the birthday girl, and with all of the contentment in the world running warm and sweet throughout me, I had no idea this bliss would not last and that eleven would turn out to be the darkest, most agonizing year of my life.

Chapter 24

I whisper these memories to my mother, pressing my lips close to her ear and hoping she can hear me, hoping what's left of her mind can grab one of them and hold on to it. I want her to remember, I need her to know how I felt, how I *still* feel, and I'm not holding anything back because honest is the only way it will come out. She couldn't stop me now if she rolled right over and opened her eyes, looked straight at me, and said, "Jesus Christ, will you shut the fuck up already, Sayre? You see I'm trying to sleep, here."

And who knows, maybe that's *exactly* why I'm doing it. Maybe my way of making peace is to disturb hers. Maybe she shouldn't be allowed to just drift away from me so calm and tranquil, leaving me with a legacy of unacknowledged chaos, pain, and disregard. Maybe I *want* to break her heart, to make her feel what I feel, to realize exactly what she threw away and exactly how she got here. Maybe I'm pushing her on purpose, charting a path so big and obvious that she *has* to remember, has to see the wreckage, has to open her eyes and tell me to stop. . . .

Because she's going, and this time she won't be back.

This truth leaves me weak, hollow, and so I rest my head on the pillow, close my burning eyes and keep talking, although my words are slow and stumbling now. Exhaustion is winning, and the closer I get to remembering Ellie the heavier my words become, the more grief spreads its thick, gray cloak over me, draining my body and pulling me down like gravity into yesterday. . . .

And Then There Were Five

My mother worked up until the third week of June, then reluctantly took a leave of absence and came back to the farm to finish the baby's room and be surprised that Sunday with a baby shower in the local grange hall.

Aunt Loretta and I had gone over Saturday and decorated it with a wishing well and blue, pink, green, and yellow streamers because my mother and Beale had decided not to find out if the baby was a girl or a boy. We got a beautiful white sheet cake from the bakery with pink and blue rosettes all over it and hired the church ladies to do the catering, since it would have been impossible for Aunt Loretta to do it at home with my mother underfoot.

The only worrisome thing, for me, was the guest list.

For the past three weeks, every time Jillian's mother saw me, she had hinted for an invitation. Horrified, I'd never mentioned it to Aunt Loretta, hoping Mrs. Jergenmeier would just get the hint, but no such luck. She actually called one night to ask about it—thank God my mother was in the bathtub at the time—and I answered the phone. When she asked to talk to Beale I held the phone out to him, bugging my eyes and vehemently shaking my head while whispering, "It's Mrs. Jergenmeier and she wants to know if she can come to Mom's shower." I finished my show of opposition by mouthing *No, no, no* and making violent slashing motions across my throat just in case he still didn't get it.

"She *what*? Oh, for . . ." Beale said, scowling and taking the phone. "Hello?"

I couldn't hear the whole conversation, only Beale's side, and although my mother never found out about Mrs. Jergenmeier's call, she would have been proud of Beale's no-nonsense response: "I'm fine. Now, what's this about?" Silence. "No, Karrie. Sorry." Silence. Snort. "I think 'friend of the family' is a pretty big exaggeration." Silence. "Well, you didn't have to get the baby anything but thank you. Dianne and I appreciate it." Silence. "Send it to school with your daughter before Friday and Sayre will bring it home with her." He caught my alarmed gaze and made a "wait" motion with his hand. "No. No. Look, I'm in the middle of something, so . . . Sure. Thanks again. 'Bye." He hung up, and looked at me, boggled. "What the hell was that?"

"A really close call," I muttered, as upstairs the bathroom door squeaked open and I heard my mother's footsteps trudge down the hall to the bedroom. "I can't bring that present here, Beale. Mom will have a fit!"

"Yeah, I know, but what was I going to say? We don't want your stinkin' present? You can't say that." He sighed and rubbed his forehead. "Maybe we could just change the card to something like 'Jillian and Family'? That would be better than anything Karrie's going to write."

Yes, it would, but that still wasn't good enough. "You know, if the card fell off before the shower, then the present would be anonymous," I said casually, with a very innocent shrug. "Stuff like that happens all the time, right?"

Beale stared at me for a few seconds, then grinned. "Well, Miss Sayre Bellavia, now why didn't I think of that?"

Unfortunately, the Jergenmeier dilemma wasn't my only worry.

While my mother and Candy hadn't hung out together since they'd completed rehab, mostly because my mother had gone on and built herself a brand-new sober life, and Candy hadn't, they still talked on the phone every once in a while, and so occasionally her name would pop up. Aunt Loretta and Beale had heard of the Fees, of course—who hadn't?—but since the Galens inhabited such a completely different world they'd never actually met Candy, had only heard a few of the laughing, carefully edited stories my mother told over the dinner table. I'd never said much to Beale about the old days, my mother's addictions, how we'd lost Grandma Lucy's house, or the way we used to live. I never said much about Candy, either, because if I did, I'd have to tell him how scummy she was, and from there it was only a short hop to confessing that we'd been scummy, too, and I couldn't bear to do that. I never wanted to see that realization dim the light in his eyes.

So, since Candy was my mother's best and only friend, and without knowing how awful she was, Aunt Loretta had gone ahead and invited her to the shower.

My lone shred of hope was that Candy never RSVP'd, and so every day, right up to the shower, I sent out a fervent wish that she'd never gotten the invite and didn't even know the shower was happening, or that she had lost the invitation, or was in jail, or if all else failed, she would get really stoned that morning and forget all about it.

The funny part was that Mrs. Jergenmeier turned out to be the forgetful one, as I waited till Friday and Jillian never brought that baby present from her mother to school. I never asked about it, either, and Jillian, who had always passed on news the second she got it, never said a word.

Personally, I think Mrs. Jergenmeier lied about that present just to get invited.

When the big day finally dawned, Aunt Loretta and I got all dressed up, and on the way out we told my mother we were going to a church event because we knew she wouldn't ask any questions. Aunt Loretta had curled her hair and put on lipstick, her pearl earrings, peach-colored slacks, and a peach-and-white flowered blouse. I wore my new blue skirt and a really cool blue-

and-white fleur-de-lis print tank top that Aunt Loretta had given me for my birthday.

I was beside myself with excitement when I walked into that grange hall and set my gifts up on the front table. I had gone to the mall and blown my entire allowance on a stuffed-animal cat that looked like Stormy, a cuddly blanket with lambs on it, and best of all, I'd had a little white baby T-shirt made that said SAYRE'S MY BIG SISTER on the front.

My mother was so shocked when Beale brought her into the hall and we all called, *Surprise!* that she had to be led to the decorated chair up at the front of the room. She was big now, ripe, Beale called it, and pretty. Her face had lost all its hollows and her skin had cleared up and glowed a healthy tan. She felt ugly a lot, though; I knew that because I'd heard Beale comforting her at night, but that was private and I didn't share it with anyone.

And just when everything seemed perfect, Candy came in, already half drunk and *I* was the one shocked speechless because I had forgotten that dull, haggard, alcoholic look, the thick skin and puffy, bloated face, the slurred words and stupid, slack smile. I had forgotten—maybe on purpose—that my mother used to look like this, too, and was really glad when Aunt Loretta bustled over and found her a seat at a table full of Beale's out-of-town cousins.

She stood back up though, waving at my mother, and although my mother waved back I think she was kind of embarrassed because Candy kept calling, "Open mine, open mine!" when we started on the presents.

The baby got a lot of nice things: diapers, blankets, a rocking chair, a baby swing, toys, onesies and booties, and one of those snuggly baby carrier slings that my mother could strap on and wear the baby in the front of her so they could be together all day.

"Well, we know who this is from," my mother said when she held up the T-shirt I'd had made, and I got all embarrassed when everybody laughed and clapped, and Aunt Loretta hugged me.

"Open mine, Di," Candy called again, and so my mother opened the first one, which was an infant set in a blotchy green-and-brown camouflage print, with a hat and bib and blanket and romper, and the sight of it made Aunt Loretta mutter something under her breath. My mother opened the second smaller package, which was another bib that said MY MOMMY'S TATTOOS ARE BETTER THAN YOUR MOMMY'S and when she held it up, smiling and shaking her head, Candy called out, "Remember that night, Di? Man, we were really fucked up. I—"

"Let's take a break, everyone, and have some punch!" Aunt Loretta called, clapping her hands, and like magic, the women rose and chattered and bustled about.

My mother went over to Candy, who hugged her and started blubbering and saying she missed her and loved her and wanted to know why they never hung out anymore, and she was loud and sloppy and everyone was pretending not to listen but they really were. My mother kept trying to calm Candy down and looking more and more desperate, until finally she snapped and dragged her outside, and in a voice I hadn't heard since we'd moved to the farm, said, "Jesus Christ, Candy, what the hell are you doing? This is a baby shower! You don't need to come here all fucked up, and if you can't keep it together, I hate to say it because you're my oldest friend, but you're gonna have to leave. I'm not kidding. Do you hear me?"

Candy gazed at her a moment, eyes bloodshot and sagging like an old hound dog, and then sniffled, lifted her chin, and said, "Fuck you. I don't even know who you are anymore, but if the real, fun Dianne ever comes back, *she* can give me a call. You I don't give one shit about."

And then she turned and walked with the exaggerated dignity of the drunk back to her car, got in, and drove away.

My mother stood there a moment in the sunshine, shoulders slumped and staring after her, then drew a deep breath, smoothed her hair, and turned back to the grange hall. Spotting me by the door, she said, "Why did you even invite her?" and swept past me before I could say that I hadn't, Aunt Loretta had because my mother had told her that Candy had gone through rehab, too, but not that she'd relapsed.

The rest of the shower went fine, and later, when we were home and done with putting away all the new baby stuff, I lingered in the baby's room, sitting in the new rocker that had been a gift from Aunt Loretta, sniffing the scent of the powder and baby lotion all lined up and ready to go, staring up at the puppy and kitten mobile hanging over the crib, and making a solemn vow to never let Candy anywhere near this baby.

Ten days later and four days earlier than expected, one clear, sparkling, early July morning while I was out floating down the river on an all-day tubing trip with Jillian and her family, my mother went into labor and by the time we finally landed on shore at dusk and I got all the voice-mail messages, my baby sister, Ellie Joy Galen, had been born.

Ellie, Ellie

Something happened to my mother after Ellie was born.

While Aunt Loretta and Beale were over the moon and I was absolutely enchanted with this little pink, fist-waving, soft and silky new baby sister, and spent hours sitting with her, talking, playing with her fingers and toes, and calling *Ellie, Ellie* in a gentle singsong that she soon came to recognize, my mother was . . . removed. She was quiet and touchy and didn't sleep much, didn't want to eat or fuss over the baby, and got irritable when people gave her funny looks about that. She fed Ellie and changed her but she didn't cuddle or talk to her, and actually seemed relieved when me or Beale or Aunt Loretta held out our arms for our baby girl.

And she started talking about going back to work.

"But this is only the second week and you have another six weeks off," Beale said, cutting up his lasagna. "I say take them and enjoy. Stop worrying about the money and relax with the baby for a while. You've earned it."

"Your poor body needs time to heal," Aunt Loretta added, handing Beale the grated Parmesan.

"I know," my mother said dully, toying with her salad. "I'm just getting a little stir-crazy, I guess. I mean I was pregnant for nine months and I ate right and did everything I was supposed to do and now I . . . I don't know, I just feel like doing something for me.

Alone." She dropped her fork and pushed away from the table. "I don't feel good. I think I'm going to go lie down."

Beale looked at his mother. "What was that all about?"

"It's a big change for her," Aunt Loretta said, leaning back in her chair and pressing her fingertips to her temple. "Darn this headache. Sayre, will you get me an aspirin, please?" She smiled her thanks as I handed her the bottle, swallowed two with a sip of iced tea, and returned to the subject of my mother. "Think about all she's been through, Beale. You two didn't have that much time together before she got pregnant and it sounds like she's feeling overwhelmed and needs a little time to herself to go out and have some fun, and feel young and pretty again. Trust me," she said, giving him a look over her glasses, "it's hard to feel attractive when you haven't slept in a week and there's spit up all over your shirt."

I didn't say anything at all, just watched them and wondered if anyone else had seen the flat unhappiness in my mother's eyes, or if I'd just imagined it.

We all sat out on the porch later that night, my mother and Beale on the steps while he idly strummed his guitar and she fidgeted, Aunt Loretta on the swing, and me in the wicker rocker, holding Ellie. She was asleep, her little pink cheeks glowing like the moon, and every couple of minutes I would kiss her forehead or her nose or one of her little fists. I couldn't help it. She was the most beautiful, unspoiled thing I'd ever seen, and my heart grew so big it actually hurt my ribs every time I looked at her.

"I have a sister and she's you," I whispered into her ear. "And you have a sister, and she's me, Ellie, Ellie."

"So, Di, I was thinking that if you wanted to take a ride into town and go shopping, or go to lunch or something, I'm sure my mom and Sayre could babysit Ellie for the day," Beale said casually, leaning back against the porch post and stretching out his legs. "How's that sound?"

"I don't know," she said listlessly, shifting on the wooden step. "I still have all this baby weight, so there's no point in buying clothes, and if I go to lunch I'm just going to gain even more weight and then I'll never fit into anything, so."

"Hey, c'mon," Beale said, setting down his guitar, sliding over, and putting his arm around her. "What's the matter, hon?"

My mother shrugged and lowered her head, staring down at the ground.

"Di," he said, pulling her closer to lean against him. "Don't be so hard on yourself. Don't worry, okay? We've got a good life ahead of us. We've got a great family and we're all healthy and I'm saving for your ring—no, I haven't forgotten—and as soon as that's on your finger we can start planning our wedding." He waited and when she didn't respond, said, "Did I tell you I've got a couple of new restaurants in Scranton interested in letting us supply them with all of their raspberries, and maybe peaches, too? If that works out we can triple our canes next year. And there's a livestock auction coming up in September, and I've been thinking about going because . . ." He noticed her disinterest, stopped, and cleared his throat. "The point is that this place is making money, and okay, it's not a huge amount, but we're doing fine." He stroked her hair. "And look at that sky. Have you ever seen so many stars?"

"No," she said without raising her head.

"Oh, c'mon, you didn't even look," he chided with a smile.

And something about that made her lift her head and say coldly, "Do you really think I haven't sat out here and looked at the stars before? Jesus Christ, all we ever *do* is sit outside in our little nightly committee meeting and watch the bats fly around and the deer wander by and look at those goddamn stars like they're some kind of friggin' miracles when they're not, Beale, they're just big balls of gas."

"Shh," I said as Ellie stirred in my arms. "Mom, you're gonna wake up the baby."

"Oh, excuse me," she snapped. "You're right, of course, because you're our local genius and you know everything now, don't you?"

"Hey," Beale said, dropping his arm from around my mother

and leaning away to look into her face. "What's gotten into you tonight?"

"Tonight?" my mother said wildly. "You think it's just tonight?"

And that's when Aunt Loretta rose from the swing and, opening the screen door, motioned me and Ellie in behind her to give them some privacy.

It didn't matter, though, because except for the jangling chorus of peeper frogs, the creeks flowing, and the wind in the trees, the country is very quiet at night, and voices easily carried.

Not that my mother was trying to keep her voice down.

"I mean, are we always going to live like this?" she asked.

"Like what?" he said, sounding bewildered.

"Oh my God, like *this*! Like work and kids and TV and food and maybe having sex once a week if we're lucky and just sitting out here every fucking night watching the seasons go by and doing the exact same things the exact same way over and over and *over* again."

"Take the baby upstairs," Aunt Loretta said in a low voice and headed for the kitchen. "I'll be up in a minute."

Holding Ellie close, I turned and padded up to her bedroom. She was still asleep, but I sat down in the rocker anyway, rocking and soothing her, patting her little arm and whispering, "Don't worry, baby. I'm here and everything's going to be fine."

"Well, what do you *want* to do, Dianne?" Beale said, sounding both frustrated and a little angry. "God, you just had a baby, I thought you'd be happy having time off—"

"Why, to sit here and look at the stars?" my mother cried. "Or no, wait, maybe I should be in there pumping this stupid milk out of me like a goddamn cow or running up and down those rotten cellar steps to wash load after load of baby clothes, or do dishes or cut the grass or any one of a thousand other chores that are killing me just thinking about them. Do you know that? I think about doing the same thing day after day for the rest of my life and I just want to . . . I don't know. Scream. Run."

Ellie sighed in her sleep.

I kissed her forehead.

"I don't know what to say," Beale said finally, in a weary voice. "I love you, Dianne, and you're not going to like it when I say this, but I love our life. I love the farm, the way it's always changing and growing, and the peace and knowing that when I walk in that door after work Sayre's going to be there with Ellie and my mother, and you're gonna come down those stairs with that smile . . . It's ordinary stuff, but it makes me really happy. It's all I ever wanted."

Crickets chirped and the breeze rippled through the little lamb-print curtains.

"I know," my mother said and she sounded exhausted. "I'm sorry, I am. I'm just so tired and . . . I think I've got a bad case of the baby blues or something. I don't know. I do love you and I didn't mean that the way it came out. I just . . . never expected it to be like this. So constant and overwhelming."

"You know, you're going back to the doctor's for a checkup soon. Why don't you tell her how you're feeling?" Beale said quietly. "I mean, if it's the baby blues, maybe you two can talk about it or she can give you something for it."

I stopped rocking.

"Yeah," my mother said after a moment, sounding a little more upbeat. "That's a good idea. I really want to feel good again and enjoy Ellie and sitting here with you—"

"Looking at the stars?" Beale said dryly.

"Just being with you," my mother said.

They didn't speak again and I gazed down at Ellie, so tiny and vulnerable sleeping in my arms, so pure and perfect, with no hurts or disappointments or betrayals yet, and I thought about my mother being sad and restless and maybe it was normal but it set off distant warning bells inside me.

It made me want to take my sister and run.

I couldn't do that, though, so instead, for the rest of the summer me and Ellie became almost inseparable. My mother had gone to the doctor and gotten a prescription for her postpartum depression, so Ellie was being bottle-fed now instead of breast-fed, which freed up my mother and gave me even more time with my sister.

She was a happy girl, with big hazel doe eyes and a little rosebud mouth, a drooler and a laugher, an arm waver and a screecher, just for the fun of it. She would chatter like a little monkey whenever she saw me, kick her legs and flap her arms and pitch a fit of baby temper when I tickled her nose with my hair or tried to change her diaper.

I was bad at diapers, the dead belly button thing was nasty, and the sour spit up grossed me out, but Aunt Loretta was good at that stuff, swift, gentle, and efficient, and so she had plenty of Ellie time, too. So did Beale, who loved laying on the blanket on the floor with her after work as she pushed herself up on her wobbly arms and burbled and spit and cooed, and then fell asleep on his chest.

Somehow our whole family began to revolve around my sister, like she was the sun that lit up our planets. Even my mother, her mood better on antidepressants and smiling occasionally, had taken to wearing Ellie around the front of her in the baby sling while she went grocery shopping or folded laundry or strolled around the yard.

Once I even caught her dancing out at the edge of the field under the willow tree with Ellie in her arms, moving to music only she could hear, smiling and kissing my sister's cheeks, telling her she was beautiful and adorable and that Mommy loved her.

Can a person feel two violent emotions at the same time? Can a person ache with love and seethe with jealousy, be both happy and miserable with longing, because that's how I felt standing there watching them.

That's exactly how I felt.

My mother wasn't like that all the time, though. Sometimes she was snappy, irritable, and lonely, I think, because the farm and the mountain could be a lonely place. She wasn't back to work yet and had taken to leaving the baby home in the afternoons and head-

ing down into town to visit a woman she'd met in Lamaze class, a
transferee to Dug County whose husband was in management at
the factory and who lived in a big new house and had money and
jewelry and went to the spa and had parties all the time and had
been to Greece, and Italy, and Paris twice.

When my mother told us these stories, the envy in her voice
was right out there, undisguised, and she would gaze at us with a
mixture of accusation and dislike, as if we were the reason she had
never been to Paris.

She never came home from those visits happy, only more and
more dissatisfied. She started mocking her amethyst ring, calling it
"quaint," and would stare at herself in the mirror like she was trying to drill holes into her own soul.

"Maybe you shouldn't go down there anymore," I offered, hanging around in the bedroom doorway and watching her actively
despise her hair.

"Oh really? Then tell me, where am I supposed to go to get out
of here, Sayre? Come on, you're so full of answers these days. Tell
me. I don't *have* a lot of friends. I have one. Her. What am I supposed to do?" she said, glaring at me in the mirror.

"I don't know," I said, shrugging and running an idle finger up
and down the wooden door trim. "But friends aren't supposed to
make you feel bad about yourself, Mom. They're supposed to make
you feel *good*."

She held my gaze for a long moment, and something in her face
changed.

"You know, you're right," she said, walking across the room and
perching on the edge of the bed, near the night table. She picked
up the phone, and without looking at me, said, "Close the door on
your way out."

Sixth Grade

School was starting the day after tomorrow and I was worried about leaving Ellie.

I mean, I'd been with her every single day since she'd been born; how could I just up and leave? She wouldn't understand why I wasn't there in the morning playing a goofy game of peek-a-boo or blowing raspberries on her stomach after her bath. What if she forgot me, or worse, what if she thought I had abandoned her?

"Don't worry, I swear I'll say your name at least twenty times a day, all right?" my mother said with good-natured irritation when I whined my concerns one night at supper.

"Really? How are you going to . . . ?" I stopped, blinked, and shoved a whole piece of butter bread in my mouth to prevent myself from finishing that sentence because ever since that day we'd talked about friends, my mother had been leaving the farm early in the morning and coming home around four, breezing in, strapping on the baby sling with little Ellie in it, and bustling around with more energy than she'd had in the last six months combined, helping with dinner, toting laundry down from upstairs and then down again into the cellar to do the wash, vacuuming and sweeping the summer grit off the front porch. She hummed as she worked, her eyes bright, her movements quick. She was losing the baby weight, too, and came out of the bedroom crowing with triumph when she fit back into her skinny jeans.

The only thing was, I was afraid she was using meth, or at least drinking again. I'd seen her stagger once, and trip over nothing while wearing her flip-flops, spotted some sloppy hand gestures, and smelled it on her twice after she'd gotten home, the familiar vodka scent buried beneath layers of mint gum and toothpaste, perfume, and even garlic. We'd been alone with Ellie at the time, so I'd taken a second, louder sniff and looked at her funny. She'd ignored it but wouldn't meet my gaze and that made me suspicious enough to check the calls received on her cell phone and sure enough, Candy's number was there at least once a day.

She was still on the antidepression medication and I knew from reading the bottle that she wasn't supposed to drink or take other drugs at the same time.

It worried me, but the family was happy again, and I was reluctant to wreck it.

"How am I going to do what?" my mother said curiously. "Say your name? Well, first I'm going to form the letter Essss . . ."

"Ha ha," I mumbled and just kept on eating and watching her talk and laugh and pick at her food, and then hustle around clearing the table, shooing Aunt Loretta, Beale, and Ellie into the living room to relax.

"Thanks, honey, for being so nice to my mom," Beale said, lingering in the doorway, catching my mother's arm as she swept by, and giving her a quick kiss. "She's been really wiped out these last couple of days. I don't know if it's the heat or just her refusing to take it easy for a while, but she really needed a break tonight. You're the best."

"Ah, that's what they all say," my mother teased, giving him a look from under her lashes. "You go relax, too. Me and Sayre will get this."

"But I wanted to play with Ellie," I said, sulking. "I don't have hardly any time left to be with her, Mom."

"You go ahead, Sayre. I'll help your mom," Beale said, giving my mother a mischievous look and a light slap on the butt. "Come on, woman. Let's get it on."

I slid out of my chair and ran into the living room, laid the white cotton sheet out on the floor, and eased Ellie out of Aunt Loretta's tired arms. For the next hour me and my sister lay on that rug and played blinky-eyes staring games that made her dissolve in laughter, and tickling games that made her cackle and kick her feet, and near the end, when she was yawning and her eyelids were drooping, she caught hold of my finger in her little fist and, keeping her soft, hazel gaze on my face as if learning it by heart, listened to me croon, *It's sleepy time, baby girl. The moon is out and the stars are shining. Sweet dreams. I love you so much, Ellie, Ellie. Good night, sleep tight.*

And when she fell asleep and I drew away from her, I looked up and saw that Aunt Loretta had fallen asleep, too. I was glad because she'd been having headaches and dizziness for the last couple of days, and had even gotten nauseous for no good reason last night. She said it was nothing but the unrelenting heat and all she needed to do was go lie down in a dark room with the ceiling fan on, but I'd seen how hard she worked all day, usually right up to bedtime, both indoor and outdoor chores, and taking care of Ellie, too, didn't help matters any.

I lay back down next to Ellie on the sheet. "Only one day left for us. I wish I didn't have to go to school." I snuggled closer, turning on my side so she was tucked into my body, and up against my heart. I kissed the top of her head and her wispy, brown baby hair. Closed my eyes and lay there drowsing until somewhere in my hazy subconscious I heard a murmured voice that sounded like Beale, and then someone took Ellie from me and the rush of air that followed was cool with loss. I frowned in my sleep and Beale whispered, "Sayre? Come on, sweetheart, you can't stay here like this all night," and then he lifted me into his arms and carried me up to bed.

I never forgot that. What it felt like to have the father I never had tuck me safely into bed, kiss my forehead just like I'd kissed Ellie's, and whisper, "Sleep tight, Miss Sayre Bellavia."

Chapter 25

I fall silent, lingering in the residual happiness of that memory, but my mother is suddenly restless, agitated, her legs trembling and feet twitching, her palsied fingers plucking at the sheet, her head moving back and forth on the pillow. Her eyes roll wildly beneath the lids and she's breathing faster now, in short, hitched puffs that sound as if something is happening inside her, as if she's somehow struggling, and in a burst of panic I lean over her and fumble for the call button, have it right in my hand, thumb poised to descend when her body relaxes and her breathing slows to normal again.

"Mom, what is it?" I whisper, shaking, and after a while, when she doesn't answer, only keeps on breathing, I set the call button back on the bed, rest my head on the edge of her pillow and heart pounding, speak to her of Ellie.

Ashes, Ashes

It was weird that first morning, having to leave the house so early and stand out in the hot, baking driveway waiting for the school bus. I kept looking back at the farmhouse where the rest of my family was—Beale packing his gear and getting ready to head upstate to the livestock auction, my mother barely awake and looking a little hungover to me, although no one else seemed to notice it, Ellie still sleeping, and Aunt Loretta in the kitchen making breakfast without me—and wishing hard that I could be in there, too.

But then the bus came and I got on and three girls liked my new shirt and I got all caught up in the whole first-day-of-school thing, getting my seat in homeroom and liking my new teacher, seeing Jillian in the hall and having lunch together, getting my schedule and then hopping the bus home again.

It was a good day and I chattered like crazy during supper, hogging the conversation, making Beale laugh and poor Aunt Loretta, who still didn't feel good, try to smile. Finally, my mother told me to stop talking and start eating because if I wasn't done by the time the table was cleared, I wasn't getting any dessert and there was butterscotch pudding.

So I did, and the talk turned to Aunt Loretta. Beale made her promise to call the doctor tomorrow and make an appointment because her headaches hurt so bad sometimes that her vision got blurry, and he was worried and annoyed that she hadn't done it yet. "I mean, c'mon, Ma, what're you waiting for?"

"I know," Aunt Loretta said, removing her glasses and rubbing the red mark on the bridge of her nose. "I was hoping the weather would cool down once September got here and maybe that would help but . . . I guess I have to. I've been wondering if they're migraines but I've never had one before so I don't really know."

"That's because you're not a doctor," Beale said with good-natured impatience. "Swear you'll call Doc Goodwin tomorrow and make an appointment? I don't want to come home from the auction and find you all laid out because of some stupid heart attack or something."

And they joked a little more about it, but it wasn't a heart attack, it was a brain stem stroke, and he wasn't the one who came home and found her.

I was.

We All Fall Down

The second day of school was as good as the first, except this time I got off the bus with homework in my backpack. The weather was still scorching, and my shorts were stuck to me from sitting on the sweaty, vinyl bus seat. All I wanted to do was get inside and eat a grape Popsicle, but when I started walking up the driveway I could hear Ellie crying from inside the house, the thin, forlorn sound echoing out in the still air and the closer I got the funnier it sounded, different than usual, hopeless and raspy and exhausted, like she'd been crying for a long time . . .

I started walking faster.

Beale's truck was gone because he'd left for the auction and Aunt Loretta's car was gone but my mom usually took that when she went to town or to Candy's and there wasn't any real reason why my heart should be pounding so hard and my blood thrumming in my ears—

I took the front-porch steps two at a time and the front door was closed.

And locked.

That's when I knew something was wrong.

Aunt Loretta always kept the front door open from morning till night in good weather so the cross breeze could sweep through the screen door and cool the house.

I knocked hard on that door but ran back down the steps, not waiting for an answer. I could hear Ellie wailing upstairs, and that scared me even more because Ellie always napped downstairs in the afternoon where it was cooler, so why was she upstairs where it was so hot, and why was she crying and crying and no one was soothing her?

I raced around the house, shrugging off my backpack as I went and dumping it on the grass. The back screen door was unlocked and I yanked it open and went inside, calling, "Aunt Loretta? I'm home. Aunt Loretta?"

The kitchen was silent, deserted, and the dirty breakfast dishes still sat on the table.

"Aunt Loretta?" I yelled again, backing slowly out of the kitchen and into the hallway, my gaze glued to the remains of that ominous meal left lying there for what, almost nine hours now? No, no. Something was desperately wrong. Even the *air* was wrong, flat and still and empty. "Aunt Loretta?"

Ellie must have heard me, because her crying turned to screaming.

"I'm coming," I called, and whirling, grabbed the banister and flew up the stairs. My legs were shaking, my knees like water. "I'm coming, Ellie! Aunt Loretta? Where are you? Aunt Loretta?"

I bounced off the walls running down that hallway and into Ellie's room. She was lying in her crib, her face scarlet and her hair plastered to her forehead, wearing a diaper that reeked and the little teddy bear pajama top she'd been put to sleep in the night before. "Oh, baby, come on, baby, come on," I babbled, picking her up and gagging at the smeary mess on the sheet and up her back. She was hot and crying with no tears, and her head looked weird, like the soft spot was kind of sunk in, and she stared up at me with such solemn, tragic eyes that I ran then, I took her and ran down those stairs and into the kitchen, shaking so hard I almost fell.

I wet paper towels and put them on her forehead, put water in a bottle and gave her a little and then a little more and called, crying now, "Aunt Loretta? Where are you? What happened? Where

ARE you?" and then I couldn't take it, so I picked up Ellie and the water bottle and went through every room looking for her, and was about to go down into the cellar when Ellie threw the water up all over me. I started crying even harder and was running back to the kitchen to call someone, my mother or Beale, when a car door slammed outside and I heard my mother's rubber flip-flops slapping and scraping an uneven, stumbling tattoo across the sidewalk and up the wooden porch steps.

I flung open the door, Ellie crying in my arms, and my mother, in the middle of opening the screen door, reared back in surprise. "What the hell?"

"I can't find Aunt Loretta," I sobbed, catching a gust of alcohol in her exhale and too upset to care. "I came home and Ellie was upstairs all alone and she's still wearing her pajamas from last night and I yelled and looked everywhere but she's gone—"

"Let me see that baby," my mother snapped and plucked Ellie, still screaming, from my arms. "Jesus Christ, look at her. Move, Sayre." She swept in past me and headed straight for the kitchen. "Are you sure Loretta isn't here? Did she leave a note or anything?"

"No," I said, hiccupping and wiping my face on my arm. "The front door was closed and locked and look, Mom, look at the dishes on the table . . ." I started crying all over again. "She wouldn't go away and leave Ellie all alone. She *wouldn't*."

"Shh, Ellie, shh," my mother said, peeling the damp paper towel off her forehead and picking up the baby bottle. "God, she looks dehydrated. What's in here, Sayre?"

"Water, and I only gave her a little at a time, but she threw it back up," I said, wringing my hands.

"Water? That's no good. Why didn't you give her Pedialyte?" my mother asked, her voice sharp and rising.

"Because I don't know where it is," I cried, now really scared that I'd hurt my sister.

"Downstairs in the fridge. Go get it. Hurry." My mother opened the water bottle and dumped it into the sink. "Hurry, Sayre. We might have to go to the hospital."

Sobbing, I flicked on the light and ran down those steep, wooden stairs to the fridge. Whipped it open, and pushed aside all the juice and extra milk and eggs until I found the bottle of Pedialyte. Grabbed it, shut the fridge, and turned to go back upstairs.

And saw a foot.

Two feet in slippers, lying on the cold, hard, cement floor.

Two pale feet in *Aunt Loretta's* slippers, lying over by the washing machine hidden behind the chimney.

The Pedialyte slipped from my hands. The plastic bottle hit the floor and rolled under the steps.

A small, quiet moan escaped me. *No,* I thought, rooted in place and unable to stop staring. *No, no, no.* Dimly, in the back of my stunned and bewildered mind, I knew I should go over there and see if she was alive or call to my mother or shout or do *something* but all I could do was stand there palsied and mute, staring at those bare ankles and the feet tucked into those slippers—

"Well? Did you find it?" my mother called impatiently from the top of the stairs, Ellie squalling in her arms. "Sayre? Come on, goddamnit, this is not a joke! This baby needs fluids! What the hell are you doing?"

My mouth opened but nothing came out.

"Sayre?"

I turned back to the steps, wanting to tell her, wanting to say, "I found her," or "Help!" or even just "Mommy," but before I could make myself form the words she said, "I don't know what the hell you're doing down there but I swear to God if anything happens to this baby . . . Goddamnit, Sayre. Do I have to do everything myself?"

And then she started down the stairs, fast and furious, rubber flip-flops flapping, my whimpering sister in her arms, and in one frozen heartbeat I saw it happen, saw her stub her toe and the other flip-flop come down too far over the edge of the step, saw her foot tip and skid forward through the front of it, snapping the T, saw her knees buckle and her free hand, the one not clutching my sister, fumble desperately for the railing, but she missed, she missed, and my hands reached out but I was too far away so I missed, too, and she pitched down through the air and hit the ground hard, hit the cement floor hard, hard on her face, she hit and Ellie hit and the sound of them hitting that floor, first Ellie and then my mother as she landed on top of her, the sound of the air bursting from their lungs and then the silence, the silence everywhere, in front of me, behind me, inside me . . .

The silence.

And then my mother twitched and I drew in a searing breath and ran for the phone.

Blur

Babbling into the phone to the 911 dispatcher.

Calling back because I'd forgotten to tell them about Aunt Loretta.

Grabbing Ellie's empty water bottle on the way back downstairs so she could have Pedialyte and feel better.

Whimpering, being afraid to touch the two of them and watching as my mother, forehead bleeding, teeth gritted and groaning in pain, pushed herself up off my sister and somehow balanced there. Crouching beside her, sobbing and frantically patting her arm, and her gasping, "I can't. My back. Ellie . . . Don't move her. Go call . . ."

"I did," I cried.

"Beale," she finished. "Oh God, oh God, oh, Ellie . . ."

I rose and backed away, frantic because her body was crooked and twisted and she *did* smell like alcohol and it was bad, really bad and there was so much blood and suddenly my mind was filled with black terror because Ellie wasn't crying and she should be crying, no, she should be *screaming* . . .

Calling Beale, losing it when he answered and said cheerfully, "Ha, missing me already? How are all my girls?" and not even being able to tell him if Ellie and Aunt Loretta were alive, hearing a tone in his voice I'd never heard before and realizing it was the same kind of terror I had, and wishing he wasn't three and a half hours away but here, right now. . . .

Sirens growling closer, getting louder, screaming into the driveway and people piling out, following me in and flowing past me down those stairs and into the cellar, saying things I didn't understand, asking me if there was anyone I could call to come stay with me and me saying *I'm going with my mother* over and over.

Sitting alone in the living room, holding Ellie's little stuffed cat as they left with her in the ambulance.

The paramedics, all volunteers from Sullivan, loading my agonized mother into the second ambulance, her eyes huge and stricken, her hands lying frozen, upturned and empty.

Riding to the hospital with her, and neither one of us saying a word.

Being taken into the waiting room and the blast of chilly air that hit me when the doors opened and the paramedic ushered me in.

Telling the nurses my mother's name and Aunt Loretta's and Ellie's, and answering their other questions as best as I could, trying to think, telling what had happened from the minute I stepped off the school bus, telling everything I heard and saw, except . . .

My mother's drinking.

I said everything but that.

It seemed to take forever but finally Beale came striding into the emergency waiting room and when he saw me he came right over, picked me up, and hugged me hard, really hard, and said, "Thank God you're all right," and I started to cry all over again and let out an exhale I'd been holding for hours.

And then Beale took over, talking to the nurses and asking for answers, and within moments one of the emergency room doctors came out and led us to a small, private room with a table and chairs in it.

Beale held my hand the entire time the doctor spoke, and at one point, when he told us Aunt Loretta was gone and they thought the cause of death had been a stroke, Beale squeezed my hand so hard I felt the bones grind and I blubbered, "Ow." Beale loosened his grip but didn't let go, just sat there listening to the doctor, his expression stunned and drawn, tears slipping unheeded and unnoticed down his face.

My mother had a concussion, stitches, bruises, and contusions from striking the floor. She had injured her back, severely, and was headed up to Radiology for additional X-rays.

"And my daughter Ellie?" Beale choked out. "How is she?"

I wiped my eyes in time to see the doctor shake his head and give Beale a very grave look, and a terrible humming, like a thousand angry hornets, filled my ears, and a shimmering wave of silver speckles washed across my vision. I made a noise, a sick-sounding noise and suddenly Beale had my chair pulled back and was bending my head down toward my knees, and I held on to him like I was drowning until I could see again.

Ellie was in critical condition.

She was dehydrated.

Her ribs and her pelvis were broken from the fall.

She had a very severe head injury.

She was unresponsive.

Her skull . . .

Barring car accidents, it was the worst he'd ever seen in an infant.

"I want to see her," Beale said, holding my hand even tighter. "We need to see her." His voice hitched. "She'll be scared all alone in that crib without us. We're a family, you see, and Ellie's used to having all of us . . ." A sob escaped, harsh and raw, and then he let go of my hand and buried his face in his arms and cried.

I sat beside him patting his arm, and when he stopped, we got up and went to see Ellie.

The Darkest Hour

Ellie lived for two days after the fall, and I was with her almost every second of them.

Beale was a zombie, splitting his time between Ellie, my mother, trying to make arrangements for Aunt Loretta's funeral, and running back and forth home to feed the animals.

But not me.

I stayed with my sister who never once opened her eyes to look at me, who never once wrapped her strong, tiny fingers around one of mine or cooed or burbled, laughed, cried, ate, or drank. She had tubes running into her, huge black-and-blue bruises from the fall, and her head—from her nose up—was wrapped in bandages.

The first time I saw her I almost threw up, backed away from her little bed in panic, denial, and outrage, and thought *No, that's not her, that poor battered baby is not my sister, it can't be,* but then Beale leaned down over her, touched her arm, and started to cry and I surrendered, staying with her day and night, refusing to leave, sleeping in the chair, eating whatever Beale or the nurses brought me, praying, begging, whispering to her, trying to call her back to me, crooning my "Ellie, Ellie" song, and telling her she had to get better because we had to go home, we did, all of us together, and so please, Ellie, please get better, and the unbroken silence made my head pound and my stomach sick, and tore my heart to pieces.

I thought about Aunt Loretta, too, as I sat there, and of what the doctors said about a brain stem stroke. The headaches had been a warning that something was wrong, but the stroke had followed fast, hitting her as she was doing the laundry. I shouldn't have listened because their words made it so vivid in my mind, and I couldn't stop thinking of her lying there terrified and alone, paralyzed and struggling for breath, unable to scream or move or get help, knowing she was leaving us, leaving everything she loved, leaving the baby upstairs alone . . .

I whispered her name to myself, sitting alone in that chair, whispered, *Come back, please. We need you so bad,* and missing her more than I ever thought I could, the pain tearing another jagged hole in my already damaged heart.

I thought about my mother, too. She was on another floor, her back wrecked, and almost totally out of it on pain medication. She wouldn't open her eyes or talk to anyone, not even Beale, and wouldn't eat or drink, so they were hydrating her by intravenous, and calling in a grief counselor.

I didn't care. I really didn't.

I had smelled her breath, I knew the truth.

My baby sister, Ellie Joy Galen, died at 5:16 on Monday afternoon, with me and Beale by her side, stroking her cheeks and holding her limp little hands.

She was fifty-nine days old.

A Double Funeral

Ellie's casket was small, and white.

Aunt Loretta's was mahogany, carved and beautiful.

We had framed photos of them both on the tables around the room.

The funeral home was stuffed full of floral arrangements, the room where the wake was overflowed with mourners.

It was the worst tragedy Sullivan had seen since Miss Mo's murder.

My mother was out of the hospital and at the wake, propped in a chair on one side of Beale, sitting pale, drugged and silent, as the mourners offered their condolences. She didn't even look up when Jillian's mother came over, dabbing at her dry, bright, inquisitive eyes with a tissue and hugging Beale so tight he grunted.

I stood on the other side of him, numb, dry eyed and hollow inside, an empty shell being hugged and released, kissed and released, fussed over and released, and hardly remembering anyone except Jillian's mother and Reverend Ganzler, the new youth minister, because he had a bright, reddish-orange beard and brought me a paper cup of water.

Yesterday we had given the funeral director Ellie and Aunt Loretta's burial clothes, and now all I could think about was that Ellie was lying inside that coffin wearing a T-shirt under her lambie pajamas that said SAYRE'S MY BIG SISTER because I never wanted her to forget that.

I would have been such a good big sister.

My mother didn't make the funeral. She didn't say why, she just wouldn't get up no matter how Beale pleaded and, finally, losing it, said Ellie was his daughter, too, and Aunt Loretta his mother. He had twice the agony to deal with and if she didn't get up and go, he didn't know if he could make it through without her.

My mother didn't say a word.

Didn't even crack an eye.

So we went to the funeral, me clinging to his hand, and at the gravesites, when the Methodist minister had finished the solemn service, I picked up my big bouquet of Queen Anne's lace and stepped toward the caskets that were holding the people I loved, the caskets that were going to be buried in the dirt and would stay there forever, through all the seasons, and I would never get to see or touch Aunt Loretta and Ellie again, and that's when the numbness cracked and the tears spilled over, raining down on those lacy flowers as I set them on the caskets and, sobbing, returned to Beale.

They were gone.

And three weeks later, so were we.

The Betrayal

Accidents happened.

That's what the grief counselor said, not without sympathy.

People made choices, some conscious, some automatic, and like pebbles dropped in a pond, the reactions from those choices expanded, uncontrolled, like ripples drifting in all directions. We could never have predicted that everything would go wrong at once.

It was no one's fault.

It was a terrible, tragic accident. That was all.

I heard her, but all I could think of was *if*.

If Aunt Loretta had gotten her stroke upstairs, instead of in the cellar.

If she had gone to the doctor sooner.

If Beale hadn't left for the auction.

If my mother hadn't gone down to Candy's that day.

If she hadn't drunk. If she hadn't worn flip-flops.

If I hadn't just stood there mute, wracked with shock and unable to speak.

If even one of those ifs was different, then Ellie might still be alive.

And we would be happy again because now we weren't.

Not at all.

Without Aunt Loretta, the farmhouse was an empty, cheerless place.

My mother would not get out of bed, wouldn't talk to me, Beale, or the counselor, only lay in the room with the shades drawn.

Beale was miserable, his gaze still stunned and desolate. He would come into the house and stand there dazed, like he was waiting to wake up from a nightmare, waiting for Aunt Loretta to be in the kitchen and me to come barreling down the stairs saying, "Guess what we're having for supper?" and Ellie to be waving her arms and kicking her feet and cooing at the sight of him, and my mother to come in and give him a kiss.

But there was no waking up because it was real, and everything was gone.

The fridge was full of hearty, homemade casseroles, cakes, and pies, all brought by Aunt Loretta's friends, but somehow they were too rich and nourishing, and we couldn't eat them, so we choked down bologna sandwiches for supper instead, and then afterward, when there was nothing to say and the silence grew deafening, Beale would rise, kiss my cheek, and go out to the barn. I followed him once, needing to be close, and discovered him sitting on a stool in the shadows, shoulders heaving, hands over his face and crying great, wrenching sobs as if his heart was broken.

I didn't interrupt, only went back to the house, went back up to Ellie's room and sat there in the rocking chair in the dark, too, as the wail inside me howled and howled without relief.

I heard him talking to my mother at night, heard him knock on his own bedroom door before going in, heard him bringing her food and asking how she was, telling her how lost he was, how overwhelmed, how every single thing he looked at reminded him of his mother or Ellie, and then his voice would break and he'd tell her he needed her, that he didn't blame her for what had happened, that he didn't blame anyone, but he couldn't do it all himself, just couldn't focus, didn't care, was lonely . . .

I never heard her say a word in reply, and sooner or later, shoulders stooped and footsteps dragging, he would come out of the bedroom, slowly closing the door behind him, and plod down the hall to the guest room to sleep.

I didn't tell him about smelling the alcohol on my mother's breath. I don't know why. Maybe because he would have looked at me, bewildered, and asked why I'd waited so long to mention it, or why I would be cruel enough to say that about my mother when it wouldn't bring either of them back.

He was a stable, good-hearted, hardworking man from a good, stable family and he'd never lived with a full-blown alcoholic or an addict, never saw the depths to which they'd stoop to get what they needed, and had no clue as to how bad it really got. He'd thought the motor court was a hellhole dump when in reality it had been one of the better places we'd stayed and I could never have made him understand that. Could never have told him the way it really was.

Or maybe I knew that if he knew she'd been drinking, he would ask her about it, and once he did that, it would all be over.

Maybe I didn't tell because I loved him, and I could see how much he needed my mother, how much he needed to know that he wasn't alone, that somehow she would end her silence, and open her eyes and her arms and comfort him.

Or maybe my omission was automatic, and as simple as blood winning out.

I didn't know, but I never said a word.

Days passed, and it was all I could do to get out of bed in the morning, feed the cats, and find food. I didn't want to go back to school yet, and since Beale had to work and didn't want to leave my mother alone all day, he didn't make me.

I brought her toast in the morning and Campbell's soup for lunch. She never finished anything but her pain medication. She never answered anything I said, and after a while, I just stopped talking. Life became a dull, gray, block of ice and I just couldn't bring myself to care.

The world was falling down around us.

And then, two and a half weeks after Ellie was buried, when Beale had gone into town one afternoon to the lawyer's to talk about Aunt Loretta's will, I heard my mother get out of bed, but not stagger directly into the bathroom.

I ran upstairs and stood in the bedroom doorway, watching as she got dressed, moving stiffly and with no emotion on her face at all. She didn't look at me, only said, "I'm leaving. Candy will be here in fifteen minutes. Go get me some garbage bags from the kitchen. If you're coming, pack your stuff and be ready when she gets here."

I gazed at her, thinking dully that I should be more surprised, that I should be horrified and angry and trying to talk some sense into her, or cry and plead that this was our home now and Beale loved us, and we couldn't just walk out and leave him . . .

But I wasn't surprised, and I didn't cry, only made a small, help-less sound and sat down on the edge of the bed, dizzy. I'd been afraid this would happen, that it would end, that somehow she would wreck it because it was just too good, and I'd been right, I'd been right, and God, a furious flash of hate shot through me, drove me up and out of that room, down the hall to Ellie's nursery where I stopped, sagging against the closed door, my hand on the knob but unable to turn it. Her soft, sweet baby scent lingered here, her powder and her lotion, and my knees gave way and I sank to the floor in despair.

Ellie hadn't hated our mother. She'd loved her, she was *of* her, and so was I.

Oh God, my heart.

When Candy came I only stood back and watched, numb again, as she invaded the house and hauled half a dozen bulging garbage bags into the car, as she carefully helped my mother down the stairs, the bag of pills in her hand rattling with every step.

I took only one picture of me and Ellie off the fridge, and tucked it into my garbage bag. Made myself take one last look around, one last look at the best home I'd ever had, at Aunt Loretta's room, at our First Family Christmas needlepoint piece hanging on the living room wall, at the terrible, one-line note I had penned—*I'm sorry. I didn't know we were leaving. Love,*—and then I'd paused, wanting to write *Miss Sayre Bellavia* but it seemed like a pet name from a different time and using it now was a violation, so instead I just wrote *Sayre* and left it on the kitchen table with my mother's house keys, right where Beale would find them when he got home.

I looked at everything except myself, and then I picked up my bag, stepped out onto the front porch, and closed the door behind me.

Seven Years Bad Luck

The garbage bags my mother had taken from Beale's held more than just her things.

They held some of Beale's and Aunt Loretta's things, too.

"You stole from him," I said tonelessly, sitting on the couch in Candy's cabin and watching as she and my mother emptied the bags all over the living room floor, examining their loot.

"No, Loretta *said* I could have her jewelry—"

"Not all of it," I said, holding her gaze. "She said you could have the amethyst promise ring if you gave it back after you got a real engagement ring, and her pearl earrings."

"Well, I never got that engagement ring, did I, and I didn't take everything," my mother snapped back. "I left her wedding bands and her watch and most of the stuff she wore while we were there. And besides," she said, tucking her hair behind her ear and giving me a warning look, "I don't exactly remember you trying to stop me, so you'd better just sit there and shut up, or get the hell out of here so we can concentrate."

So I sat quiet and watched, sick at how she twisted things, and when she pulled the ruby velvet blazer out, Candy looked at the embroidered lapels, snorted, and said, "Wow, where'd you wear that? To a quilting bee?"

My mother laughed and said, "Yeah, right?" and tossed it over onto the pawn pile.

Stone-cold fury ripped through me and I vowed right then to steal that blazer back from the thieves, to ease it out of that pile before it could leave this dump, because Aunt Loretta had spent days embroidering those flowers, and they stood for love and sanctuary, and it was our first family heirloom that was supposed to be passed down to me, and so I would make damn sure that it was.

And I did.

I took it and kept it in my locker at school, along with the picture of me and Ellie, because that was the only place my mother couldn't rifle through, looking for stuff to steal and sell for her pills. Her addictions were alive again and hungry, and since technically she'd been on leave from the factory when she fell down the steps, she was now on disability. The money wasn't enough, though, so she and Candy had started shoplifting and stealing, writing bad checks, and indulging in the occasional credit card fraud.

I'd gone back to school right after we'd moved in with Candy and then lingered at the library afterward, mostly because it was better than being stuck in that cabin with them, but the three-week absence had been long enough for me to fall behind in my school-work, and for Jillian to make a new best friend. She still talked to me every so often but it was only to try and find out all the juicy details of what had happened between my mother and Beale, and when I wouldn't give her that, her conversations got fewer and fewer until they dried up completely.

I didn't care. I didn't care about much of anything, except for losing my family. Beale, Aunt Loretta, and Ellie filled my mind, they were all I could think about, and most of the memories were good, the kind that left me sitting in homeroom alone after the final bell rang, my head lowered, my hair falling in front of my face and silent tears dripping off my nose.

But there were bad ones, too, images of Beale walking into that empty house after we'd run out on him, standing bewildered and disbelieving in the silence, sitting at the kitchen table in the dusk, my note in his hand and an untouched sandwich on his plate, the old, happy pictures of Ellie and Aunt Loretta, of me and my mother, still on the fridge.

And then there were the daydreams that started out good because I thought Beale was coming for me, and I couldn't wait to see him, but when I let him into Candy's he saw all his stolen stuff piled high on the table and then he looked at me, his face filled with sadness, betrayal, and disgust, and I covered my ears but I still heard him say *You knew she was a liar and a thief. You knew, and you never even warned me.*

And it was awful because it was true, I hadn't warned him, but if I had he and my mother never would have fallen in love, we never would have lived up at the farm, never would have had Ellie, and trying to stop any of that had been unthinkable. When my mother got out of rehab, I'd wanted to believe she would stay sober. I'd wanted to believe that when she said Beale knew about her past, she'd meant he knew *everything,* not just *some* things, but that had been stupid, a wishful, childish, eyes-shut acceptance of her lie because I'd so wanted to believe. I should have realized she would *never* have told him the truth, should have guessed from the way she'd whitewashed all those Candy stories at supper, making her sound like some high-spirited girl who just always happened to be at the wrong place at the wrong time instead of what she really was.

The only consolation I had, and it was an unsettled one, flip-flopping between shame, relief, and miserable longing, was that as time passed and Beale never came for me, I began to understand that he never would. He would have come for Ellie because she was his blood, his birth daughter, and he had a right to her, but I wasn't, I was only my mother's and he'd only been her boyfriend, and boyfriends came and went around here, and they never left with their ex-girlfriend's kids.

Holding on to that hope, even just one illogical, smoldering ember of it had been bad, but when that last little bit of it died, it was worse.

My grades plummeted, and I didn't care. I squeaked by with

Cs and Ds that marking period and when I showed them to my
mother, she gave a derisive sniff and said, "Yeah, you're a real
genius, all right," but that was the only time she ever referred to
Beale.

She never mentioned Ellie at all.

Ever.

I whispered her name to myself for a while, walking to and
from school where no one could hear me, and sometimes I would
pretend she could see what I saw, like the snow and a cardinal
and icicles, all things she'd never seen before, but that was harder
because the grief would rise, making my arms and legs and heart
heavy, making me feel slow and stupid and dangerously near tears.

I took my first drink—a screwdriver—that New Year's Eve in the
company of my mother, Candy, and a bunch of their friends. I was
eleven, the youngest one there, and most of them thought it was a
real hoot to see me knocking 'em back.

Until the drinks hit me, that is, and then I lost it. My shoes
annoyed me, so I pried them off and threw them in the bathtub.
Took somebody's cigarette and put it out on the rug. Drank vodka
straight from the bottle and almost choked. Crawled over and told
Candy she was white and gross like lard, and when she told me to
go fuck myself, I laughed and laughed, but it wasn't funny. Nothing was funny; it was terrible and tilted and wrong so I laid down
on my stomach and scrabbled around under the couch, pulling out
the dusty picture of Ellie and me. I'd brought it home from school
for winter break so we could be together on Christmas, and had
hidden it there because I knew no one would ever find it, but when
I looked at it, instead of making me feel better I started to cry and
couldn't stop. The world spun out, filling my mind with flashes of
Ellie and Stormy, Beale and Aunt Loretta and even Grandma Lucy,
Miss Mo and Mareene, all the people I'd loved and lost, and it
made me hysterical, made me stagger up and push and shove and
try to run out of the cabin.

Furious, my mother grabbed my arm, ripped the picture from

my grasp, and shook me, slapped my face and yelled, "Stop it! Stop it! Don't you ever bring them up again! EVER!" and then she whipped open the door and pushed me out onto the porch in the snow, and said, "Now stay out there till you sober up," and slammed the door.

"I'm sorry," I blubbered, sinking to my knees and then down to all fours, snow swirling around me, freezing my tears, my skin, making me shiver and moan. "I'm sorry, I'm sorry . . ."

I blacked out after that, and woke up the next afternoon in my bed on the couch, sick, feverish, miserable, humiliated, and done with drinking.

I never saw the picture again.

We had a late snowstorm that spring and I got bronchitis. The cough was so deep and uncontrollable that I would hack until I threw up, and when the school nurse found out that my mother hadn't taken me to the doctor, she told me to have a seat, pulled up my records, picked up the phone, and squinting at the computer screen, said, "Is this the right number?" She read it aloud, and I got light-headed because that was Beale's number at the farm and for one blinding moment I wanted to say yes, and let her call it, wanted to sit right there and listen to her tell him that I was sick and needed care, to hear if he was worried and what he would say . . .

Unless he told the nurse that I wasn't his problem anymore, and then exactly why.

I started to cry, and that made me cough and I threw up again. Once I could speak, I choked out my mother's cell phone number and the nurse called and got her, and told her I'd been sick for a week, and that she really needed to get me to a doctor by this afternoon. My mother must have said something rude because the nurse stiffened, visibly startled, then straightened up and with ice in her voice said, "I'm sorry you feel that way, Ms. Huff, but this child is ill, and the fact remains that she will not be allowed back in school until she has proof of a doctor's visit with her. Come to the office when you pick Sayre up, and they'll page her. Thank you. Good-bye."

An hour later my mother showed up in a car driven by a guy I didn't know, and signed me out of school. She didn't look at me, only pointed toward the backseat and told me to get in. "And for Chrissake if you have to puke, hang your head out the window or he's really gonna be pissed."

But I didn't throw up, only sat huddled amid the trash and a smelly, hairy old dog blanket, breathing as shallowly as I could so as not to cough, listening to the snow crunching beneath the tires and gazing out the window at the heavy, gray sky until we got to the clinic, where he dropped us off and went down the street to wait in the Colonial Pub.

The waiting room was loud, hot, and full of sneezing, stuffy-nosed people and whiny little kids. By the time we got called to see a doctor it was already getting dark, and my mother was rabid to leave but the doctor listened to my heart and lungs, took my temperature, made me cough up some gross phlegm and confirmed bronchitis. She told my mother to feed me chicken soup and plenty of fluids, use a cool-mist vaporizer and cough suppressant at night if the cough was keeping me awake, and not to let anyone smoke around me, which was a joke because I slept on the couch in Candy's living room, and everyone there, including whatever friends dropped in, smoked.

My mother got me a doctor's note and then I followed her down the street to the Colonial Pub, where she told me to go sit in the car while she ran in and got him.

Ninety minutes later, when she still hadn't returned and I was freezing, coughing so hard my chest ached and desperate to pee, I got out of the car and sidled into the pub. The hot, noisy, boozy air hit me in a rush, blurring my vision, sending my nose into an immediate thaw, and making me frantic to find a bathroom. I stood on tiptoe, searching the crowd, and spotted my mother sitting at a table in a corner of the room with a bunch of other people, a pitcher of beer nearby, her coat slung across the back of her chair.

I was heading her way when I saw the ladies' room sign, and my mother was busy laughing and slapping the table and didn't even notice me, so I went on by and into the bathroom.

I lingered awhile, thawing, and when I was finally finished, went back out into the pub and over to the table.

Three people were still there, but my mother and her coat were gone. So was the guy driving.

I hurried back through the crowd to the door and burst out onto the street in time to hear the car *vroom* to life, to see it start to pull away from the snowy curb. Panicking, I ran across the sidewalk, slipping on the ice, pitching forward and landing hard on the passenger-side door.

My mother's head snapped around, startled, then she said something to the driver. He stopped the car and, fumbling with the handle, I opened the door and fell into the backseat.

"What the hell were you doing? I thought you were back there sleeping or something," my mother said irritably, tucking her hair behind her ears and turning to give me a look. "You're lucky we didn't leave without you."

I was coughing so hard I couldn't answer. Coughed the whole way home, rolling down my window twice as we drove to throw up, but nothing but bile came out because my stomach was empty.

The bronchitis lasted almost a month, thanks to the smoke and the cold air. I stayed home for about three days, using the shower as a vaporizer before I went to sleep, but my mother and Candy's constant cigarette smoke was killing me and we had no chicken soup, so I went back to school and had two bowls for lunch every single day. I tried really hard not to cough on anyone and visited the nurse's office when I had a headache or was feverish. She called my mother again and got permission to give me children's Tylenol, and let me lie down on her couch until I felt better and could go back to class.

My birthday passed the way it always had before Beale, without notice, and then Ellie's birthday passed the same way. She would have been one year old, and I wanted to spend the day with her, so on her birthday I took all the change I'd been collecting from the bottom of the washing machine, money I figured I'd earned by volunteering to do Candy and my mother's laundry, especially their jeans because they always left change in the pockets, and setting out early, walked all the way into town.

I was starving when I got there, so I went to Dunkin' Donuts first and got a banana-nut muffin and a strawberry Coolatta, carried them down to the little park by the river, and ate them sitting at a picnic table in the shade, trying to imagine Ellie was there with me. I couldn't actually see her face in my mind anymore, but I always felt warm and happy whenever I thought about the beginning and the middle of her life, never the end.

Memories of the end came at night in the dark, when I was too weak to stop them.

From the park I went to the convenience store and tried to buy just one rose but they wouldn't let me because they were sold in bouquets, so I walked to the florist, the same one we had used for the funerals and the only one in town. It made my knees watery, walking in there, and all the flowers blurred to brilliant masses, overloading my senses, and there was a line of people and the air-conditioning was way too cold and the whole place smelled like her funeral but it wasn't, it was her birthday, and I just couldn't take it.

I left the florist's sweating and empty-handed, and walked all the way across town to the cemetery. When I got to the main gate I stopped dead, staring in shock at all the gravestones stretched out before me, hundreds of them everywhere, row after row of white, black, brown, gray . . .

I had no idea which one was Ellie's.

I'd never even thought of it.

How could I lose her? My memory of the funeral was so narrow, so focused on her casket, hers and Aunt Loretta's, that I thought

I would always recognize her grave, that it had become a forever landmark in my mind . . .

I curled my fingers into the chain-link fence surrounding the cemetery and closed my eyes, trying to remember everything about the day she and Aunt Loretta had been buried. The ground had been flat because there were chairs set up in rows under a tent . . . and it was a family plot because Beale had said something about it and I hadn't known what he meant, so he'd had to explain it.

Ellie and Aunt Loretta had been buried near his father, in a family plot back by the fence near a big old oak tree, where all the past Galens had been buried.

I'd never seen their gravestones—we'd left before they were done—but Beale had said they would have angels on them, smaller versions of the towering angel statue that marked Beale's great-great-great-grandmother's grave.

I opened my eyes and scanned the cemetery, ignoring the hilly side. There were two big trees in the distance, near the opposite fence line, one to the left and one to the right, but the one to the left had a monument by it that looked like an angel, so I took a deep breath and followed the fence line all the way around, stopping to pick the scattered clumps of Queen Anne's lace growing wild at the base of the chain link.

When I got closer I saw gravestones with angels on them, but two of the white ones looked newer than the others so I headed toward them, legs heavy, footsteps slowing. Someone had placed a vase full of little pink and white roses on one of the graves and I knew that one was Ellie's before I even read it, knew it must have been Beale who had been here.

What I hadn't known, what I never could have imagined and what brought me to tears, was the photo of my sister on her gravestone, cradled in the angel's embrace. She was laughing, her eyes bright and her hair damp and wispy, and I recognized that picture, knew exactly when it was taken because I'd been holding her after her bath and singing my "Ellie Ellie" song, and she'd stuck her fingers in my mouth and chortled and Beale had snapped the picture.

I could *see* her again.

He'd made sure she existed in more than our minds, made a place where we could see her, and I sat there for a long time whispering her song, carefully tucking the Queen Anne's lace into the vase with the roses, memorizing her sweet face all over again. The photo wasn't taped onto the headstone, it was somehow a part of it, and I would have given anything for a camera of my own so I could have taken a picture of her picture and had her with me again.

But at least now I could always come here and see her.

It was almost midnight when I finally made it home. The long walk back had been scary, the night alive with mosquitoes, bats, and unseen animals rustling alongside the road in the woods. I was tired, hungry, and all I wanted to do was collapse and go to sleep, but my mother was lying on the couch, snoring.

I stood there looking down at her for a long moment, at her slack mouth and the thin line of dried drool across her cheek, at her greasy hair and stained T-shirt, at the near-empty bottle of vodka and the pills on the end table, then turned away and picked up my blanket.

Normally when the couch was taken I just curled up with my blanket on the floor but not tonight. Tonight I went straight into her room, skirted the pile of used tissues, empty liquor bottles, and dirty laundry, shoved the overflowing ashtray away from the side of the mattress on the floor, looked at her stained and wrinkled pillow, and then lay down across the bottom of the bed, cradled my head on my arms, and closed my eyes.

Today was Ellie's birthday, and we'd spent it together.

I would always love her.

Would always be her big sister.

Nothing in the world could ever change that.

The Downhill Run

When my mother first injured her back, the doctors in the hospital had put her on strong pain medication, and when she left the hospital, they gave her a prescription for Oxycontin to manage the pain. She'd taken those pills willingly, faithfully, only one or two more than the prescribed dose at first, but then, as her body got used to them, she started needing more and more, going through the prescription far too fast because she'd been chewing or snorting them to get around the time-release action, renewing the prescription over and over until finally the doctor refused, suggesting she'd become addicted and provoking an ugly scene, with my mother being escorted out of the building by security.

She moved on to another doctor then another, sometimes two and three at a time, filling prescriptions for Vicodin and Oxycontin and anything else she could get, using vodka or beer as a chaser, and when she was finally denied by every doctor and drugstore in and around Sullivan, Candy called up her brother Bobby who turned her on to Buck, a guy who lived in a trailer down by the river and who dealt mainly in pills.

He always had more Vicodin than he did Oxycontin, which he called Hillbilly Heroin, and my mother was willing to take whatever she could get, but she needed money for them now, a lot of money, and so she started shoplifting in earnest, stealing anything and everything she could get her hands on to hock, including wallets and credit card numbers. She never got caught for the credit card fraud, but was arrested twice and banned from all the stores downtown for the shoplifting, pleaded addiction, and was sent back to rehab.

I saw it all happen, but from a distance, pulled back so far inside that sometimes I wasn't even there anymore. I slept, I ate, I breathed, but I couldn't afford to feel anything because Candy was vicious with my mother gone, resentful and bitter, hammering me all the time, venting her poison from the kitchen table, reminding me daily that I was living on her charity and so I'd better not fuck up or I'd be out on my ass.

I tried not to let it get to me, but it did.

When my mother was finally released, the first place she and Candy went was straight down to Buck's, and when they got back to the cabin they put a big bag of Vicodin, a quart of vodka, and a quart of tequila on the kitchen table, and commenced partying until they both passed out.

The next night they went down to the Colonial Pub and hooked up with Harlow Maltese, who'd done his time in the county mental hospital for Miss Mo's murder, moved out of the halfway house and was free and looking to party. My mother seemed driven to stay stoned now, even more so than before. She was never sober, never, and when Candy got home from work she joined her, and I was the only one in that cabin whose hands didn't shake and who could walk without stumbling.

I visited Ellie's grave on her birthday and holidays, somehow never running into Beale, although he always left proof of his existence behind in pink and white roses, a teddy bear, and once a *Merry Christmas, to My Beloved Daughter* card tucked carefully into a plastic Baggie and set at the base of the angel headstone. I crouched in the snow and stared at that Baggie for a long time, even reached for it once, but in the end, I didn't open it. That card was from a father to his daughter, and it was none of my business.

When I was a junior I hooked up with a senior named Carter who was second cousin to the Fees, and after his prom we all went out to a summerhouse on the river. We got one of the bedrooms, and in that musty, damp-smelling room on a lumpy twin bed under worn, faded, pinecone-print sheets, Carter kissed and stroked me, peeled off my clothes, and ran his hands everywhere. It felt good to sink into him, to have him sink into me, skin against skin, hot, sweaty, burning, it made me feel alive and wanted and close to someone again. He cared about me, I know he did, and so I stayed with him all summer until he got a job with the gas well drillers and left in the fall.

He'd used a condom that first time, and then I went to the clinic and got the birth control ring that only gave you four periods a year so I didn't have to worry about getting pregnant. I didn't want a baby, couldn't even look at one without thinking of Ellie, her short life and her brutal, wasteful death, and every time that pain started to resurface, the ice wall inside me would descend, trapping the memory in a frigid stasis and holding it there so I wouldn't have to feel it.

Losing Ellie might have been the only thing that kept me from following in my mother's footsteps, though. It was too hurtful a road to go down more than once. That part of my heart was done.

But I worried about other things as I listened to my mother complaining about her constipation and her headaches, as I watched her stumble around the cabin, dizzy and nauseous, as I endured her drunken tirades and insults, and watched her stagger into her filthy bedroom with Harlow or any number of wild-eyed guys so twitchy and sick they were little more than walking cadavers. I fretted and worried, and every single day when I came home to find her lying out drunk, stoned, and going nowhere, I wondered *Is this who I'm going to be, too? Does history have to repeat itself? Has living with my mother imprinted so deeply, without me even knowing it, that no matter what I do differently, I'll still somehow end up following right behind her?*

No. No, I wouldn't. I would rather be dead than be like her. I was positive of that.

But . . . what if I had no choice?

The thought scared me.

Haunted me.

I had to make sure I was different, that my path would be different, better, only I didn't know what to do, and each passing night at the cabin only made it worse. I couldn't sleep, listening to my mother, Candy, and Harlow clink the bottle to the glass, the slow, slurred babbling, and the crushing and snorting of pills right in the next room. My nerves were raw and I felt like I was leaning forward all the time, muscles tensed, actively waiting, all revved up but spinning my wheels because I didn't know which direction to go.

I worried so much that a solid, heavy knot lodged in my chest, down between my breasts, near my stomach, a frantic knot all tangled with confusion and anger and anxiety, and it stayed there until the day I got my grades for the semester.

I sat in my seat in the back of the classroom while the other kids talked and laughed and joked around me, staring at all Ds, at the failure warning made out to me, Sayre Bellavia, right there in harsh, hard-lettered black-and-white print, and with a sharp piercing the knot cracked and something inside me rose up and said NO.

No.

I would not fail.

I'd been smart once, a man I'd loved dearly had told me so. Smart, with a good head on my shoulders. A survivor, a kid who'd managed to make it through a rough childhood.

A kid he was proud of.

A keeper.

If he could see me now, what would he think?

The thought gnawed at me. Shamed me.

And so it was that memory of Beale telling my mother that I had a future of my own ahead of me, that I was a different person from her, that I had the grades to go to college and make something of myself, that I could leave Dug County like he had and go out and see the world . . .

That beautiful year, the one I couldn't speak of to anyone, became a smoldering ember in my heart, warm and alive, a golden memory I hung out before me so when everything became too grim and all I wanted to do was stop, I could close my eyes, turn my face to it, and feel loved again, even if only for a little while.

That memory made everything change.

I made everything change.

I started spending all my free time in the library and brought my grades back up to As and Bs. It wasn't easy, but it got better once I started trying again, paying attention and turning in homework.

I got a job busing tables at a local restaurant, and paid the other busgirl, Marisol, gas money to haul me back to Candy's after work.

I was away from the cabin a lot, which was good for the life I was trying to build, but bad in a way I hadn't foreseen, as Candy decided that since I was out anyway I should stop by Buck's twice a week for the Vicodin. And I did it, not because I wanted to but because Candy got enraged when I first said no, picked up a steak knife, and yelled that she couldn't do it all and if I wouldn't do that much for them, then I might as well get the fuck out since I was living rent free anyway, which was actually a joke as anything I didn't want stolen I had to keep with the ruby blazer in my locker at school.

So they got plenty of money off me, and I became a goddamn mule.

I hated it, really hated walking down that dirt path to Buck's, handing him money and waiting outside where anyone on the river could see me while he counted out the product. I didn't want to be linked to him, didn't want people to think I was just like my mother, and for a while I was tempted to tip off the cops and let myself get caught just to bring the whole stupid, ugly mess crashing down, but I didn't because I couldn't stand the thought of being led off in handcuffs, of maybe having Beale hear about it on the wind and forever thinking differently about me.

Because I'd heard something on the wind about him, too, something that split us farther apart but that made me happy for him, in a bittersweet kind of way.

He'd gotten married.

It was old news when I heard it—they'd met when she'd bought Miss Mo's old house and married two years ago last fall, out at her church in Wilkes-Barre—and the waitress who'd mentioned it didn't know much more than that, only that she'd come in once to pick up a takeout meal under the last name of Galen and they'd chatted for a few moments. The waitress remembered that Beale's new wife had dark hair, what she called a "good face," and a modest but pretty diamond engagement ring and wedding band on her finger.

I was glad to know that he had actually made it through and moved on, but the gladness I felt was mixed up with a dull, aching sadness for what could have been.

It could have been us.

I bought a card that Saturday, and a box of plastic freezer bags, and went out to Ellie's grave. Sat there for a long time trying to decide what to write because there was so much I wanted to say but in the end only scrawled *Congratulations! I just heard. You deserve all the happiness in the world.* And then, because *love* was impossible and *xoxo* too frivolous, I signed it simply *Sayre,* put it in the Baggie and left it tucked up against Ellie's headstone.

When I went back that next week before work on Thanksgiving, my card was gone and I searched around some, hoping, but he hadn't left anything other than flowerpots of copper-colored mums for Ellie and Aunt Loretta. I'd warned myself not to expect anything, that too much time had passed and too much pain had been left unresolved, that if he'd wanted to get in touch with me he would have done it a long time ago, but the disappointment hit me hard, sent me hurrying out of the cemetery, head lowered against the wind, telling myself I was still a keeper, I *was,* and struggling to believe it.

And later that night, while I was lying on the couch in the darkness, drifting, a quiet calm settled over me, a feeling like I had discovered something that had been there waiting for me all along, that I *did* believe I was worth something, and that somehow the faith Beale once had in me had rooted deep and grown strong without me noticing. He had said I was a keeper and I still believed him, believed that I was worth the effort, and even if I was the only one *making* the effort, I was making it for *me* and that had to count. He had given that to me, and even if I never saw him again, I would still believe it.

I would always believe it.

I slept like a rock, and when I woke up I felt steady again, like I was standing back on solid ground, and that was good because everything else around me was disintegrating.

The snow started right after Thanksgiving and it never seemed to stop, which only made things harder. The restaurant was in full holiday swing and had upped my weekend hours, so I had no chance for a social life or to even visit Ellie's grave. Candy was working the day shift down at the factory, so it left her plenty of time to bitch at me at night when I was bone tired and trying to do my homework.

My mother was sicker than I'd ever seen her. She kept falling into sleeps so deep she would pee herself, ruining the sheets and towels, and staining the whole mattress orange, and have to be shaken awake, hard. She trembled nonstop, was always cold and even skinnier than when she was addicted to meth. She hardly ever ate but was always drinking and pushing me to get her more and more pills. She had been in and out of the hospital every winter these past years, but that had been self-induced and somehow, this was different.

I took a day off from school and got us a ride down to the clinic with Marisol, where the attending doctor examined my mother, took blood, listened to me recite her problems, and armed with a very grave look and the blood test results, told us her liver was failing and that he would make an emergency appointment for her to be evaluated by a transplant team.

I was so shocked by the news that I couldn't think of anything to ask, and so I just followed them back to the front desk and waited while the receptionist made my mother an appointment two days later at the closest transplant hospital, which was over sixty miles away.

I had no idea how we were going to get there. My mother didn't have a car, and even if she did, she was in no shape to drive. I didn't have a car or a license. Candy was on the day shift and needed her car. Marisol was an option, but when I got to work and asked her, she said she was working double shifts and couldn't do it. Sullivan didn't have any commuter buses, only the little blue-and-white senior citizen bus that went to the grocery store and the bank. We didn't have any train stations, either. For that I'd have to get my mother out to Wilkes-Barre or Scranton, which was just as impossible.

I called Carter, my old boyfriend, prepared to beg, but it turned out he was in Colorado and didn't really want to prolong the conversation. Called two of his friends, but they were unavailable. Called Bowden, a guy from school who I thought might like me, but his parents were on his case about all the days he'd cut out of school already, and so he didn't dare do it again.

Finally, in complete desperation I took my mother's cell phone and scrolled through the numbers, asking Bobby Fee, who said a flat-out no because she still owed him for some product she'd stolen years ago, a phone number for Harlow that was disconnected, and a woman my mother used to party with whose kid told me she was in jail.

I looked at my mother, pale, emaciated, slumped and snoring on the couch, and then back down at the phone, scrolling up to the one number I really hadn't wanted to call.

Buck.

But I did, and he said fine after I told him I'd give him gas money and a little something to cover his time, and so two days later I took off from school again, loaded my surly, hungover mother into the front of Buck's SUV, and drove sixty-eight miles down to the huge, clean, bustling hospital where we met with the transplant team, a very kind and serious group of doctors, and where my mother, scornful and sarcastic, willfully destroyed any chance she might have had to get on that list.

"Why did you do that?" I cried on the walk out, violating all the rules and taking my mother's arm in a desperate, bewildered gesture. "What is WRONG with you? That was your only chance, Mom, and you blew it on purpose! Why?"

"Because who the fuck do they think they are, telling me how to live? God? 'We don't give livers to addicts, Ms. Huff.' Where the hell do they get off talking to me like that? Self-righteous bastards."

"Mom, they told you the chance of the transplant failing is a lot higher for an addict and they don't have enough donated livers as it is, but if you just got sober again—"

"Shut up and get off me," she snapped, wrenching her arm away and trudging straight out the hospital door.

I was furious on that ride home, madder than I'd ever been at her, disgusted with myself for scrambling so hard to get her there, for missing school and wasting my hard-earned money on Buck, for beating my head against the wall over and over and over again for a woman who did not give a shit whether I lived or died, or whether she did, either. I was so mad that I didn't say a word for the rest of the night. The next day I woke up still angry, and it was hard to spend the day smiling and busing tables with that resentment smoldering in my veins, burning deeper and deeper, the hot ash igniting layer after layer of old anger built up inside me.

I didn't know it at the time, but I was heading for a meltdown.

The Explosion

We might have made it through Christmas if my mother hadn't gone and stolen the wad of tip money I'd hidden under the couch, and spent it all on pills, because when I woke up and found it gone, and saw the big plastic bag of Vicodin set square in the center of the kitchen table, and my mother passed out in her bed, I flipped. I threw on my clothes, grabbed that bag and my coat, and stormed all the way down to Buck's, who just shrugged like he knew he'd be selling them back to me in a couple of days and gave me my money back.

I stayed down at the library all day, steaming, knowing my mother would wake up in the afternoon and go right for her pills, and when she found them missing would freak and have to find a way to replace them on her own. I knew that if I waited long enough she would pass out again and maybe Candy would, too, so I stayed out till late and when I got back to the cabin, they were both laid out and snoring.

I avoided them for the next couple of days, so angry and disgusted I couldn't even stand to look at them, but on Wednesday night, a week before Christmas, when Candy was out helping one of the woodcutters deliver cords of firewood to people who could afford to buy them, and it was just me and my mother alone in the cabin, it all came to a head.

It was my night off work, and I was sitting at the table trying to finish my homework before winter break. My mother was lying on the couch under a blanket, muttering, twitching, and giving me the evil eye.

"Where the fuck do you get off taking back my pills?" she croaked suddenly. "Those were mine, and you had no right to touch them. I'm in a lot of pain here. You think *this* is gonna do it?" She picked up the ten or so pills left in the little plastic bag next to her on the end table and shook it. "This won't even get me through tonight."

I shrugged and kept writing.

"Wrong answer, *genius*. Now get your ass out there and get my goddamn pills back."

I caught my breath, went still for one shocked heartbeat, and then shook my head and tried to keep writing but my hand was trembling and the answers weren't making sense anymore.

"Goddamnit." She pushed off the blanket and eased her awful, stick-figure legs down onto the floor. "You're really pissing me off, Sayre. I don't need this shit tonight. Now go back there and get my pills!"

"No," I said quietly as the simmering anger flickered, then burst into flame. "It's done, Mom. I'm not getting you any more pills. The doctor said you shouldn't—"

"Fuck the doctor. He's as useless as you are. The two of you can go straight to—"

"NO!" I pushed away from the table and stood up, shoved my chair back so hard it fell over and the crash was huge, damaging, and irreversible and I did . . . not . . . care. I crossed into the living room in one stride, fury unleashed, and stood over her, fierce and unstoppable. "Stop it! Just stop it! What is WRONG with you? If I had a daughter I would never, ever treat her like this! I would love her and protect her and take care of her every single day, Mom, the way you're supposed to, so no, you're not going to talk to me like that anymore, do you hear me? I'm your *daughter* and you're not going to treat me like some piece of—"

"Wrong again," my mother said in a cold, flat drawl, and staring up at me with mocking, bloodshot eyes. "I'll treat you any way I want, and if you don't like it you can get the fuck out of here right now." She cocked an eyebrow, her lip curled in derision. "What do you think of that, *genius*?"

It was the *genius* that did it.

"You are so *stupid*!" I shouted and when she drew back, shocked, it only infuriated me even more. "You make fun of me for being smart but look at you! Look! You're disgusting. You smell. You live in a dump. You can't hold a job, you don't have any money, it's just you and Candy getting high every day, every night, like it's the only thing in the world! You never go anywhere or do anything. God, you're so screwed up that you can't even go to the *bathroom* any-more, and *you're* making fun of *me*?"

"You better shut your mouth, little girl," my mother growled, leaning forward again. "Who the fuck do you think you are, talk-ing to me like that?"

"Are you kidding?" I cried wildly, the words surging in an un-stoppable torrent. "You talk to me like that every day! You don't care if you hurt me, you never have. All you ever do is blame your shit life on me, like I ruined it just by being born, but I never did anything against you, *ever*, and I could have, you know. I could have done a lot, but I didn't because you're my *mother* and I kept thinking that meant something but I guess it didn't. Not to you." I stood there and watched as she grabbed onto the arm of the couch and struggled to rise. "I didn't ruin your life, Mom. You did it to yourself and you didn't even care that it wasn't just you, it was *me*, too. You wrecked it for *me, too*. God, we had *everything*, do you understand that? We had *everything* up on that mountain—"

"That's it!" my mother yelled, abandoning her attempt to rise. "Goddamnit, you shut your mouth *now* or I swear to Christ I'll shut it for you." She pushed her hair out of her eyes and glared at me with venom and fury and just a hint of panic. "You know what I said about that."

"About what?" I said, staring right back at her. "Oh, you mean about when you were sober and fell in love and we moved up into the farmhouse—"

"Sayre," my mother warned, breathing faster.

"—with Aunt Loretta and Beale—"

"Shut up," she ground out.

"—and you got pregnant—"

"I swear to God if you don't stop, I'm going to kill you," she said, voice rising.

"—and Beale gave you Aunt Loretta's amethyst promise ring because he wanted to marry you—"

My mother grabbed her bag of pills and threw it at me.

I sidestepped and heard it hit the wall. "—and then Ellie was born—"

"Motherfucker," she swore, pushing herself off the couch and pitching toward me, arms flailing and lips pulled back in a snarl.

I didn't move, didn't duck or run or cringe, no, not this time and not anymore. Her first slap caught me across the face, rocking my head back and making my eyes tear, and then she grabbed a fistful of my hair and yanked me sideways, panting and swearing from the effort and I was so enraged that I almost hit her back, but I didn't, only grabbed her wrists and dragged her hand out of my hair, her fingers raking strands out with them, twisted away and got behind her, locked my arms around her like a vise and hung on while she writhed and cursed, kicked at my shins with her bare feet and bashed her head back against my collarbone, stomped and pinched and tried to bite me, until finally, exhausted, she just went limp.

"Let me go," she grunted, panting.

"Not yet." I stood there breathless, heart pounding, holding her, hating her, and in a low, ragged rush, said, "We had everything up there at the farm, Mom, everything in the *whole world*. I had a real home and a family who loved me and I was happy, and so were *you*, I *saw* it, and I just don't understand why you had to go and start drinking again." I tightened my arms around her, hard. "You knew you weren't supposed to but you went and did it anyway, and I knew you were, I smelled it on you and I should have told someone but I never did because I was afraid it would ruin everything, and then when Ellie . . . after Ellie . . ." My voice shook. "Why did you leave him like that, Mom? Why did you have to steal from him? Why did you want to hurt him so bad when he was already in agony? Because he made you happy and you just couldn't stand it? Well, what about *me*?" I let go of her then, shoved her away from me, wiped the feel of her from my arms, and watched as she lurched over and fell onto the couch. "He was the closest thing to a father I ever had. Do you know what that did to me? Did you ever think that maybe I *loved* him, and would have liked to see him every once in a while, instead of making sure he would never even want to *see* me again? God, I used to pray every night that he would come and knock on this door looking for me." Head splitting, I shoved my damp, tangled hair from my eyes. "I would have given *anything* for that, and it killed me when he never did. Did you ever think about *that*, Mom? Did you ever think about anything at all besides yourself?"

My mother made a strange, strangled sound, then pushed herself upright on the couch, looked at me, and started to laugh.

"What?" I said, unnerved because it was an ugly humor, harsh, hissing, and weirdly triumphant, and the glee in her eyes was far too sudden and bright. "What's so funny?"

"You are," she said, pulling the rumpled blanket out from under her and spreading it across her lap. "You sound just like my mother." She laughed again and shook her head, as if the similarity was just too much, and when she stopped laughing the viciousness in her gaze nailed me to the wall. "I think maybe it's time for me to let you in on a few things, genius." She leaned forward, her glittering gaze riveted to my face. "He *did* come looking for you, four, maybe even five, times. How do you like that? Stood right out there on the porch while you were at school, looking all hurt and depressed, wanting to know how you were doing and if you needed anything."

My jaw dropped and I stared at her, unable to breathe.

"You know what I told him?" She settled back on the couch, her smile sly with malice. "I told him to get his ass off this property, that it was over, and you didn't want shit from him anymore, but he didn't want to hear it. He kept coming out and bringing you stuff, and the last time he came he was gonna wait till you got home and see you for himself but I told him straight out that you weren't his business anymore and there was something really fucked up about a grown man chasing after a pretty little girl—"

"No," I whispered as my knees gave out and I slid down the wall in a heap.

"—and that if he ever came sniffing around you again, whether it was here or anywhere else, I'd call the sheriff and report him for—"

"No," I moaned, doubling over. "Oh my God . . ."

"—fucking with you."

"No! You know he wasn't like that!" I scrambled to my feet, saw her watching me and smiling, and I just couldn't believe it, couldn't believe what she'd said and done, couldn't believe he'd actually searched for me, come for me, and she'd turned it into something so unthinkable and disgusting. Couldn't believe I was still standing here, in this room with her. "You're sick, Mom, you really are, and I can't even stand to look at you anymore. You deserve what you get, so go ahead, hate me some more, do whatever you want, because I don't care. Merry Christmas. You're finally getting your wish. I'm out of here for good."

"Good," she said, shrugging and turning her face away from me. "Go."

"I will," I said, and I did.

Those were our last words to each other.

Chapter 26

"We had everything, Mom," I mumble, drifting in a thick haze, caught in the shadow land between asleep and awake.

Something brushes across my arm once, twice, three times in a light sweep, then settles down over my hand, trembles against my skin, fingers curved and clinging to me, the grip weak, not tight but with a feeling of final, mustered determination and somehow I understand that it can't stay long.

I don't want it to leave, though; deep inside I have waited forever for this moment and it's finally come, finally found me, like a battered, faded, end-of-summer butterfly, flitting, lighting, leaving, and returning again to sit quietly as its strength is slowly sapped and its wings forever stilled.

But for now, right now, its quivering warmth is mine.

I hear the faintest whisper— "Saa . . . Saa . . . Saayyre . . ." — and still drowsing I mumble, "I'm here," because I know what it wants, it wants sanctuary, and I pull the soft, ruby velvet blazer closer so the intricate, Queen Anne's lace embroidery touches both our hands.

Our hands.

I open my eyes, groggy, and stare at the ceiling.

The light is different.

It's morning.

I talked all night.

I lay there a moment, puzzled, trying to gauge how I feel because . . .

I feel calm. Peaceful.

I feel all right.

And someone is holding my hand.

I lift my head, only my head, and stare down at my hand resting on my stomach, and at my mother's hand, covering mine.

It takes a moment to sink in.

She'd reached for me.

I look over at her, see her eyelids fluttering, her lips moving. Lean closer, and hear a faint, hitched, "Say . . . Sayre . . . Sayre . . ." I murmur, "What, Mom?" and her lids flutter faster, her brow wrinkles like she's in pain, and her trembling fingers twitch then tighten around mine. On a quavering exhale, she whispers, "Sor . . . ry."

And then she deflates, as if saying it cost all that she had left, and as she sinks back into her world I stroke her forehead and kiss her cheek, stay close beside her because she is my mother and I am her daughter, and this is our bond, whittled down to its purest form, its only form, and so with my lips still pressed against her skin I whisper, "Love you, 'bye," and slipping my hand out from beneath the diminished weight of hers, I get off the bed and, taking my bags and the ruby velvet jacket with me, go down the hall to the waiting room.

Candy is still there, red-eyed and grief stricken.

"Go ahead in," I tell her.

She rises slowly from her chair as if terrified and says, "Is she . . . ?"

"Not yet," I say, "but soon. Go ahead."

Candy chokes on a sob and rushes past me.

I turn and stare out the window into the cold, gray morning. The air is still, the sky opaque with snow clouds, heavy and on the brink. It's New Year's Eve and I will end the year as an orphan. A ward of the state. A person with no parents, no car, no money, no one to call, and nowhere to go. A person with no idea what to do next.

A snowflake drifts past the window, then another and another.

I watch them fall, dozens and then hundreds, thousands, all fat, white, and fluffy, lacy like the embroidery on the ruby velvet blazer, my blazer now, and so I put it on, pull the soft velvet close around me and I can see by my reflection in the window that it fits, it suits me. I nod at the Sayre gazing back, and we exchange small, crooked smiles. Take a deep breath, turn, and gather up my stuff because there's a beverage station across the waiting room and I'm hoping the coffee is free so I can—

"Sayre?" someone says from behind me.

It's Red. I recognize his voice before I even turn around and when I do, I discover he's standing there with someone else.

Another man.

A man whose tired face is grave under the brim of his cap, a man who stands back a ways, with his hands in his jeans pockets as if he's not sure he's welcome.

A man who is seven hard years older and whose dear, steady, hazel gaze shines with tears, and in that split second of realization the heartbroken wail that's been waiting inside me all these years comes out as one small, yearning, whisper.

"Beale."

Chapter 27

"I'm sorry," is the first thing I say to him, and the tenth, and the twentieth because when we finally end the tight, tearful hug and step back, I can see by the lines of his face and the shadow of pain in his eyes that what we did to him seven years ago was not easily overcome, and will never be forgotten.

For me, either.

Red embraces us both and leaves, called away to bring comfort to someone else.

We sit, Beale and I, knees turned toward each other.

"I'm sorry about your mother," he says, glancing down at our joined hands, and when he looks up, his eyes fill with tears again and all he says is, "Why, Sayre?"

And that is the question. It has *always* been the question.

I tell him that, and more.

A lot more.

I tell him all I know about my family, about our real life before him, and then about it afterward, and he listens hard without interrupting, he hears the story beneath the story and when I'm finally done, he looks at me, shaken, and says he could use a cup of coffee. I'm forced to tell him I don't have any money, and he hugs me again and in a gruff voice says he'll buy, and so side by side we leave the end-of-life wing and head down to the bright, bustling cafeteria.

He buys breakfast sandwiches, too, and we find a table in the back where we can talk undisturbed, and as we eat he tells me what it was like, coming home that day and discovering that my mother had not only abandoned him but had stolen from him, too.

"I knew it wasn't you," he says, even before I can ask.

My eyes fill with tears. "This was all I managed to save," I say, touching the ruby velvet blazer's lapel.

"My mother made that," he says, swiping a quick hand across his eyes.

"I know," I say hoarsely. "It's my family heirloom."

We sit silent a moment, remembering.

"I tried to see you, you know," he says, glancing at me from beneath the brim of his hat. "It took me a while to find out where you'd gone but once I did, I went out there every week, but no matter when I got there you weren't around. And then it got pretty nasty between her and me—"

"I know," I say, becoming very busy neatening my side of the table. "I mean, I didn't know about you coming by—"

"What?" he says, sitting up straighter. "She didn't tell you?"

"No, I never knew. She never said anything about it until, like, two weeks ago, when we had our big fight." I can see by his astonishment that he still doesn't understand the way it was. "I had no idea you ever came to that cabin. I just thought you, I don't know, gave up on me, I guess. I mean I wasn't your kid, so what could you really do? Nothing." I catch his wounded gaze and say, "I'm not saying that to be mean. It wasn't that I didn't *hope* you would come because I did, every minute of every day. I waited and waited but as far as I knew you never showed up, and I thought it was because of how we left and that you couldn't even stand to look at me again." The tears in his eyes are killing me. "There was no one I could ask, Beale. We never talked about you or Ellie or Aunt Loretta after we left. Never. I wasn't even allowed to say your names! The one time I did, she slapped me right across the face and told me never to bring it up again."

"Jesus Christ," he says softly, "I didn't know."

"I know," I say, and reach across the table for his hand. "And I know what she threatened you with, too, and I don't blame you at all for never coming back. I swear."

"She told me that *you* were the one who thought it was weird, me still trying to see you," he says, averting his gaze as if embarrassed. "She made it sound like you thought I was some kind of pervert, and that she was gonna call the law to report me and protect you and that was just . . . too much. I . . . I couldn't . . ."

"All lies," I say, releasing his hand and sitting back.

"Dear God," he mutters, shaking his head.

The silence stretches.

"The gravestones are beautiful," I say finally. "And Ellie's picture . . ."

"Yeah," he says, and then with affectionate regret, "little baby girl."

I stare down at the table, trying hard not to cry.

"I got your card," he says, looking at me. "It meant a lot. Thank you."

"You're welcome," I say and try to smile.

"Did you see what I brought you?"

I frown. "No, when? After Thanksgiving?" And when he nods, I say, "No, I haven't gotten the chance to go back yet. What is it?"

"If I tell you it'll ruin the surprise," he says, with the ghost of his old grin.

"I know, but what if it's not there anymore? What if somebody stole it?"

He gives me a good-natured look that says he knows what I'm doing, but tells me anyway. "Well, I remembered you only took that one picture off the fridge when you left, so I printed you out all of them, everything I had from that year and made up an album for you."

He looks so pleased with himself that I laugh through my tears, and run around the table to hug him. "Thank you," I whisper, burying my face in his neck and breathing in his familiar, woodsy smell. "That's the nicest thing anybody ever did for me."

"You're welcome," he murmurs, and wipes his eyes when I pull away and sit back down. "And damnit, now I have to admit that putting them in the album was Terrie's idea. My wife. You'd like her, Sayre. She's a vet tech out at the Scranton SPCA and she wants to rescue every animal she sees." He smiles. "She's got a real good heart."

"I'm glad," I say, plucking a napkin from the dispenser and blotting my cheeks. "So then you guys still live up on Sunrise Road, right? You kept the farm?"

"Well, it was touch and go for a while," he says, tilting the brim of his cap up and leaning back in his seat. "I almost sold it. Too many bad memories."

"So why didn't you?" I say, toying with an empty coffee creamer.

"Too many good memories," he says quietly and gives me a small, sideways smile. "It took me a while to remember that, though. It was pretty bad until Terrie bought Miss Mo's old place. I thought she was nice and all but I wasn't looking to get involved with anyone, so we were friends for a while, getting to know each other, and one day I just woke up and realized I couldn't imagine my life without her." His smile widens. "Turns out she knew it way before I did."

"Good," I say and it's all right this time, having two violent emotions at once, being over-the-rainbow thrilled that the person I love more than anyone left on earth has found happiness, but at the same time knowing that his happiness can't include me. I'm yesterday, and at best, the bearer of bittersweet memories. His new life is tomorrow, a bright and beautiful future stretching right out ahead of him.

The door to the past we just managed to open is slowly clanging shut again, and I am powerless to stop it.

"So, enough about that," he says, studying my face. "You still in school?"

"Graduating in June with all As and Bs," I say and manage a smile. "I work, too, down at the Candlelight busing tables."

He nods, impressed. "What about home? Where are you living now?"

"I have no idea," I say and tell him about Harlow and my unfortunate exit. "Which reminds me, I have to stop back there. I left a stray kitten and a coffee can with my seventy-three dollars in it under his trailer." I try to keep my voice light but it isn't working, and I can hear the worry setting in. "Not that he knows it, of course. He'd shoot the kitten and take the money if he did."

"And this is where you've been living," Beale says in a flat voice.

"I didn't have anywhere else to go," I say, shrugging. "I turn eighteen in five months, though."

"Where are you going to go until then?" he says.

"I don't know. I guess I'll think of something." I give him a weak smile. "There's always good old foster care."

"All right, that's it," he says abruptly, thumping a hand down on the table like he's come to some kind of a decision. "I don't know what you're going to think of this now, seeing as how you've gone through some pretty hard times these last years, or what you're going to think of me for the way I handled it, but . . . what the hell. There's no point in waiting. Remember back when you and your mom moved up to the farm, and she insisted on paying me rent?"

"Yeah," I say, puzzled.

"Well, I knew there was some animosity between you two, so I never told her what I did, but I didn't need that rent money, Sayre. The farm was doing fine, so I went down to town and opened a savings account in your name, and put it all in there. I figured it could go toward your college—"

"Because I was such a genius," I whisper, my eyes flooding with tears.

"And because that's what my father did for me, opened me a secret savings account and just kept dropping extra money in so that when I graduated high school and went out into the world I'd have a little something to fall back on." He clears his throat. "So that's what I did for you, Miss Sayre Bellavia, and I, uh, added a little here and there over the years, so . . . It's not a fortune, right around six thousand dollars or so, but it's there, and you can have it right now if you want."

I nod and fumble for his hand because I can't speak, can't do anything but pluck handfuls of chintzy little napkins from the dispenser and wad them up to stem the flow from my eyes.

"You know what?" he says when it becomes apparent that I'm a lost cause. "This place is starting to get to me. Let's take a little break. What do you say to a quick ride out to the farm? It won't take long. I just want you to meet Terrie and, uh, see what I've done with the place."

"Sure," I manage to say. "I have to come back, though, and visit Evan. I told you, the guy who went over the cliff so he wouldn't hit me."

"Tell you what," Beale says, rising and stretching. "Why don't you run up and see him while I go get the truck, and I'll meet you out front in fifteen minutes? I want to call Terrie and let her know we're coming."

"So she knows who I am?" I say hesitantly.

"Of course," he says with a gentle smile. "She knows pretty much everything."

"Okay then," I say, blotting my face and blowing my nose into the tissue. "Fifteen minutes. And, Beale?" I wait till he turns back to face me. "Thank you."

He reaches out and gives me a quick, solid, one-armed hug. "Anything I can do, Sayre. I mean that." He steps back, and cocks his head, studying my face. Nods to himself, and breaks out in a wide grin. "Okay. Fifteen minutes." Pulls his keys and his cell from his coat pocket and heads out the door.

I stop quickly in the bathroom to wash my face and smooth my hair. My mascara wore off ages ago and my eyes are swollen from the wind and the snow this morning and all the crying today. I know I look awful but I don't feel that way.

Patient information tells me that Evan's room is on the third floor but when I get there, the curtain around his bed is closed. There are voices coming from behind it, though, and so I knock on the door frame and call, "Evan?"

There's a scrambling sound and panicked, he calls, "Uh, wait. Uh, who is it?"

"Sayre," I say. "From this morning?"

"Now?" he yodels. "Oh, come on, God, are you *kidding*?"

I fall back a step, hurt, and then an elderly, gray-haired nurse's aide pops her head out from behind the curtain, waves a wet washcloth at me, and says with a grin, "He's a little busy right now. We're getting him all cleaned up for surgery and he isn't exactly fit for mixed company, isn't that right, Ev?"

"Your timing is killing me, Sayre," he says with both frustration and laughter in his voice.

"God, I hope not," I say, smiling and leaning against the door frame. "You sound pretty good. How's the knee?"

"Heading for surgery," he says, and then the bed squeaks and he yelps. "Whoa, that's cold! Here, let me do it. Hey, Sayre, I'm on some pretty potent painkillers, can you tell?"

"Yeah, but don't make a habit of it, okay?" I call, only half joking.

"I won't," he says, sounding suddenly solemn. "Did you, um, see your mom?"

"Yeah," I say quietly. "She's going fast."

"Aw man, I'm sorry," he says, over the sound of splashing water. "That really sucks."

I nod even though he can't see me. "Well, I guess I'd better get going. I'm really glad you're feeling better."

"Hey wait, listen," he says and then to the aide, "Is she still there?"

The aide pops her head out, then back in. "Yup."

"Sayre?" he says and now his voice sounds a little funny. "Uh, I know you've got a lot going on right now and if you can't, I totally get it, but, uh . . . could you maybe come back later and hang out for a while? I mean if nothing happens with your mom and all. Or even if it does, and you just want to talk or something. My surgery's not till four and I uh . . . look a lot better now than I did last night."

I straighten and clap a quick hand over my mouth, hiding the sudden, astonished smile. "Well, that's a relief. Um, sure, I can probably come back. And if I can't, I'll call and let you know, okay?"

"Okay," he says, in a voice that sounds way too happy for a guy going under the knife. "Then I'll see you later."

"'Bye," I say, and whirling, take off down the hall as fast as I can because it's weird and strange and totally inappropriate but there's a brand-new bubble of delight rising inside me and when I start laughing I really don't want him to hear it.

Chapter 28

Beale's cell phone rings when we're halfway out of town.

He takes it, and I sit there, still as a stone, listening to him say, "Uh-huh, yes. I see. I will. I know. Thanks, Red. Good-bye." He hangs up and turns to me, his face solemn. "That was Red. Your mom passed away seven minutes ago, at eleven thirty-four this morning. She went peacefully. Candy was with her, and is taking care of the arrangements." He reaches across the front seat and takes my hand. "I'm so sorry, Sayre."

"Thank you," I say, trying to decide how I feel.

I don't know.

She was so sick for so long, and now her pain is over.

But her life is over, too.

I'm actually an orphan.

Sometimes I've felt like one and once I wished I *was* one, and now I am one.

Bellavia, an unconnected name for an unclaimed person.

"You know, we don't have to go out to the farm right now," Beale says, glancing over at me. "It can wait. We can go right back to the hospital and I'll help you with whatever paperwork you need to do."

"No, let's keep going," I say, because *that's* what I need to do.

"Candy's there, and she knows more about my mom than anyone, even me."

"You sure?" Beale asks, gently tugging my hand so I look at him. "Because it's no problem, Sayre. I don't want you to worry about stuff like that. I meant it when I said if there's anything I can do, I will, okay?"

"Yes," I whisper, with tears in my eyes. "Thank you."

We drive in silence for a while.

The snow is coming down hard and Sullivan's plow trucks are out in full force. We're heading slowly up Sunrise Road to the top of the mountain and I quick clean the condensation from the window with my hand, staring out as we pass Miss Mo's house nestled in deep drifts of snow. The sidewalk isn't shoveled and the carport is empty. It looks dark and deserted, and that makes me sad because that's where it all began for me, with her kindness, in that cozy little house.

I turn to ask Beale about it but we crest the hill and there's the farm spread out before me, acres of raspberry canes and fruit trees blanketed in snow, and then the house, golden light shining from the windows, a pine Christmas wreath on the front door, and smoke coming from the chimney.

I knit my hands together in my lap and glance over at Beale.

"It'll be fine," he says, pulling into the driveway and parking the car.

I follow him up the steps and for a moment, a ghostly strain of "Stormy" drifts through my mind, and suddenly I don't know if I can do it, don't know if I can walk into this house when I don't belong here anymore.

He notices my hesitation, slides his arm around me in a quick hug, smiles, and opens the door. A warm rush of apple-and-cinnamon-scented air greets us. "We're home," he calls, ushering me into a foyer that is familiar yet thankfully different at the same time.

It feels strange being here, but good, too.

Welcoming, in a long-lost friend kind of way.

"You changed the wallpaper," I say, blinking hard to clear the tears and glancing around. "It looks nice."

"Yeah, we redid a couple of things," he says, shrugging out of his coat, hanging it on a hook and doing the same with mine. "Terrie is pretty good at—"

"Daddy!" A little girl with wispy brown curls and wide hazel eyes runs down the hallway toward him, face alight, and arms outstretched. "Daddy home!"

"Hey there, pumpkin," he says, laughing and swooping her up into his arms. "Did you miss me?" He kisses her and she laughs, then squirms upright and sits in the crook of his arm, looking at me.

"Hewwo," she says, reaching out a damp, curious finger and touching the delicate white embroidery on the lapel of my ruby velvet blazer. "Pwetty fwowwus."

"They're Queen Anne's lace," I say faintly, because I know she isn't Ellie but she could be, if Ellie had lived to be two, she could be, and I stand there reeling, mute because I don't know what to do with this thought now that I have it.

"This is Sayre," Beale says, and he's speaking to his daughter but holding my gaze. "Sayre, this is my daughter, Livy. Olivia. Would you like to hold her?"

I step back, heart pounding, wondering if he has any idea at all of what he's asking me to do. I haven't held a baby since Ellie, can't even *think* about getting close to one, of ever loving someone again as much as I loved her without the ice wall inside me descending, protecting me because I never want to go through that kind of pain again, so no, no, I don't want to hold her, don't want to kiss her soft little cheek or have her nestle against me so trusting. I can't do it and I won't, I won't risk it, ever, because wide-open love hurts, it leaves you vulnerable, and terrified and . . .

Oh my God.

I sway, dizzy, and put a hand against the wall to steady myself.

"Sayre?" Beale says, closing the gap between us. "What's wrong?"

I can't say it, can't tell him that I closed myself off just like my mother did, that history is repeating itself and the realization just hit me, that I'm scared of the way he holds that baby so close to his heart, so tight in his arms, like he has no ice wall inside him, like he's somehow managed to heal and love that hard again even though he knows, like I do, that pain that strong can numb you, cripple you, shut you down inside forever, but he's done it anyway, opened his heart and risked everything and now he's offering me that chance, too, even if he doesn't know it, and I'm afraid to take it, I am, but if I don't . . .

"Sayre?" he says, touching my arm and looking at me with concern.

"Yeah, sorry, I just . . . I haven't held a baby since Ellie," I say, and with great effort I hold out my hands, gasping, laughing and crying as Livy comes into them, slings a sturdy arm around my neck and gently pats my tearstained cheek. "Paw Saya. Saya is cwying. Don't be sad, Saya. Be happy."

Be happy.

"Sounds like a plan," Beale says gruffly and then he gathers us close, holds us tight, and when he says, *Shh, it's okay, Sayre. Everything's gonna be all right,* it feels like a promise, forgiveness, a future.

Chapter 29

Waking up early on Saturday morning with the May sun streaming in my bedroom window is not the best part of my life right now, which, since my bedroom is in the familiar, cozy little house that I've been renting from my next-door neighbors Terrie, Beale, and Livy for the last five months, really ought to say something.

I stretch, feeling luxurious under the new blue cotton sheet, and down at the bottom of the bed Misty crouches, wiggles her back end, and pounces on my foot. "Ow! Come here, you, and be careful of your scar," I say, patting the sheet and smiling as she comes to me, eyes bright and tail high, then collapses, purring and nuzzling me under the chin. She's been spayed for cost, thanks to Terrie's connection down at the SPCA and her incision is healing nicely, but still, I worry sometimes. I just don't want her to get hurt.

What's better is that I liked Terrie the moment I met her back on New Year's Eve, when she came in from the kitchen with mugs of cocoa, a heaping plate of leftover Christmas cookies, and three tumbling, frolicking Sheltie puppies at her heels. They'd been rescued from a puppy mill outside Lancaster, she said, setting the tray on the coffee table in front of me, and she was fostering them until they found their forever homes. She stood there a moment, watching as they romped around her feet, seized the flared bottoms of her jeans in their sharp puppy teeth and, growling, commenced a lively tug-of-war, then looked over at me, her dark eyes bright with amusement and yes, assessment, too.

"Hi," she said, and smiled. "I'm Terrie."

"Hi," I said and couldn't help but smile back because the waitress had been right, she *did* have a good face. "I'm Sayre."

She invited me to stay the night and I slept in Aunt Loretta's room, listening to the soft, garbled hum of her and Beale murmuring in their room down the hall, gazing at the framed needlepoint pictures on the walls, the rocking chair in the corner and finally closing my eyes and snuggling down under the quilt Aunt Loretta had hand-stitched way back for her own wedding.

In the morning I woke up with a startling idea, and so at breakfast, when the three of us sat down at the kitchen table, and Livy sat on the floor and shared her oatmeal with the puppies, I summoned my nerve and asked them about Miss Mo's house, who owned it now, why it was empty, what they thought it would rent for, and how I could go about renting it. They looked at each other, surprised, and then Beale cleared his throat and said that he and Terrie had talked last night, and I was welcome to stay there in the farmhouse with them.

It was a good feeling, knowing that, and I said so, but I also knew this wasn't my home anymore, it was theirs, and that was the way it should be. So I asked again about Miss Mo's, and I know they understood because Beale didn't argue or try to change my mind. Only nodded and said that Terrie still owned the house, and the former tenants had left back in the fall, claiming the mountain was too bleak and lonely, and they wanted to be closer to town.

But the mountain wasn't lonely for me. No, it was the one place in the world where I'd never felt lonely, and so we talked about rent, rules and responsibility, school and work, graduation and boyfriends, and I got more and more excited because it would be hard, really hard, but I could do it, I knew I could. I'd done far more for less, and in far worse circumstances. So we agreed, struck a bargain, and although my mailing address for school records and all had to be Beale's because technically I was still a minor, I moved into Miss Mo's house that weekend, after standing alongside Candy at my mother's short, quiet funeral.

I sit up and swing my legs over the edge of the bed, careful not to step on Sunny, who is sprawled out on the floor. My bare feet brush against her soft, thick fur and she lifts her beautiful, pointy face and yawns at me, thumps her long, feathered tail in acknowledgment, and heaves a giant, doggy sigh the way only a Sheltie can do.

What's better is that I don't have to go to work today because the Candlelight always gives its waitresses—yes, I got a promotion—their birthdays off, and so I'm hosting my first party, not because Terrie didn't offer to but because I'm eighteen now, and I wanted to. It's not going to be big, friends and family only, and there will be plenty of food but there won't be any alcohol. Beale didn't care when I told him, and Evan, who gets way more enthused about saving his river than drowning his brain cells, only limped over to kiss me sweet and long, and whisper, "It's not the beer I come here for, Bellavia, just in case you don't know that yet."

I'd been so busy making plans with Terrie and Beale that I never got back to the hospital to see him before his operation, but I'd called and we spent a good hour on the phone, and then I went in the day after and sat with him all afternoon because he'd opened his eyes, groped for my hand and asked me to stay. He's had three operations on his knee so far, and should be done now, except for rehab. He's missed a lot of school and I feel bad about that but he doesn't, claiming school will still be there when he goes back but right now he wants to make sure that I will be, too.

What's better is that he thinks I'm a keeper, and the feeling is mutual.

I make a pot of coffee and while it's brewing, run in, take a shower, and get dressed. I don't have a lot to choose from, don't have much stuff and hardly any furniture, but it's coming on garage sale season and since I make better tips now down at the restaurant, I plan on getting out there and finding some spectacular bargains.

What I do have, though, are photos, and it doesn't matter that their frames were a quarter apiece down in one of the Salvation Army store bins because it's what's *in* those frames that counts, all the pictures from the album Beale had made and left for me on Ellie's grave, pictures of him and me and my sister, my mother and Aunt Loretta, Miss Mo and Mareene, starting with my first time here as a foster kid, and then skipping to our year up here on the mountain. I have pictures of Terrie and Livy, too, and even one of Grandma Lucy, standing out in front of the church and holding my hand, both of us getting ready to board the bus to go to Radio City Music Hall for the Christmas show. Red Ganzler found it for me in one of the old church event newsletters, and had it enlarged. It's grainy, but I can still see her fine.

What's better is that Red was right, pain isn't as heavy when it's shared, and airing it gives it a chance to heal, rather than stay festering deep inside, and so I stop in at the church office to see him twice a week after school. We talk and sometimes I cry for the way my mother and I might have been, but in the end I understand that life holds no guarantees, and, in a surprising bit of comfort, that if even one moment of my past life had been different, a different choice or reaction, then I might not be where I am today.

That thought usually leaves me feeling two distinct emotions at the same exact time, regret and relief, and it isn't confusing at all.

What's better is that I've laid flowers on my mother's grave, a mixed bouquet left on the flat, bronze marker Candy had made to mark her spot next to my grandfather, Big Joyner Huff. It has my mother's name on it, her birth and death dates, and down at the bottom in small print it says A FOREVER FRIEND.

And that's fine.

I spot Stormy at the edge of the field, stalking something in the weeds and put Sunny out on her lead so she can roll in the grass and bark at squirrels for a while, then go back in, have a cup of coffee, and straighten up for the party. There isn't much to do except put away all the toys I have here from babysitting Livy, make my bed, and get my part of the food ready. It doesn't take long because Marisol is bringing appetizers from the Candlelight—they have the best spinach-artichoke dip ever—and Terrie the birthday cake. Beale donated his old hibachi and some charcoal to the cause and has promised to play grill master for the hamburgers and hot dogs. Red is bringing buffalo wings made with an old family recipe, and Evan's in charge of the Snapple and soda.

I am making the salads: potato, pasta, and ambrosia.

What's even better than all of that is the sound of car doors slamming outside in the driveway, and voices raised in cheerful greeting, Evan's broad smile and the birthday kiss that leaves my knees weak, Livy barreling into the kitchen, squealing an excited *Happy bufday, Saya!* and throwing herself at my legs.

What's better is lifting her high in my arms and kissing her chubby, pink cheek, stroking her curls and laughing when, impatient with all that loving, she squirms to get down.

What's better is the love on Beale's face when he walks in, carrying the scents of sun and earth and newly mown grass, hugs me, and says, "Happy birthday, Miss Sayre Bellavia. I'm so proud of you," and then he hands me something, a sheet of three-inch high, black, stick-on, alphabet letters and grinning, says, "Come on." He leads me outside, down the sidewalk to the mailbox and when I look at him, puzzled, his grin widens and he says, "Well, go ahead, honey. You're eighteen and this is your legal address now. You're going to be getting your own mail delivered to your own house from now on, so . . ."

What's best of all is standing there in the sunshine surrounded by the people I love, peeling those letters off the sheet one at a time, the ones that spell BELLAVIA and sticking them to the side of that big old farmhouse mailbox, smoothing them down tight so that they never come off, putting it right out there for all of Dug County to see that I made it through, that I live here, responsible, happy, and on my own in this beloved little house up on Sunrise Road, and while that might not seem like anything special to the ones who have always had warmth and food and shelter, deep roots, a promising future, and a family who cares, while to them this might seem like nothing more than basic or normal or ordinary, to me . . .

It's beautiful.

Ordinary Beauty

Laura Wiess

INTRODUCTION

Seven years ago, Sayre Bellavia had everything she could ever want. But when her mother's relapse meets with unexpected tragedy, Sayre's life is consumed by her mother's addiction and neglect.

When fate lands Sayre in the truck of a wounded stranger with an out-of-service phone, she finds herself reliving some of the best and worst memories of her upbringing, including the year that changed everything. And time is running out—not just for Sayre's mother, but for Sayre's chance to finally speak her piece.

TOPICS AND QUESTIONS FOR DISCUSSION

1. One of the overarching themes in *Ordinary Beauty* is identity. How would Sayre describe herself? What does she think of her last name, Bellavia? How do other characters in the book struggle with identity?

2. Why is Sayre so intent on feeding the kitten in the beginning of the story, especially when she barely has enough food for herself? What kind of symbolism do animals represent throughout *Ordinary Beauty*?

3. When Evan swerves into a ditch to avoid hitting Sayre, she stays with him until help arrives—even when Candy tries to take her to the hospital to see her mother. Why does Sayre consider her promise to stay with Evan so unbreakable? How do the themes of trust and loyalty develop throughout the story?

4. Discuss the relationship between Dianne and Candy. Does their friendship resemble any relationship anything in your own life? In what ways is it healthy and unhealthy?

5. How would you characterize Sayre's self-deprecation? How does her mother influence it? Which other characters have a powerful effect on Sayre's self-esteem?

6. Red tells Sayre "There is no grief like the grief that does not speak." (p. 107) Why is Sayre so hesitant to talk about her pain? Can you pinpoint any events with her mother that may have influenced this reluctance?

7. After her brief time on Sunrise Road, Sayre clings to the blissful memories of life with Beale, Aunt Loretta, and Ellie. Do you have a happy memory of your own that you feel you can never reclaim? How does living in the past affect Sayre's emotional health? Is it helpful or hurtful?

8. In what moment does it become clear to Sayre that her mother is really dying? Why is this realization significant?

9. Sayre refers to Queen Anne's lace as "clean and pure and safe." (p. 156) How does this description fit into the larger themes of *Ordinary Beauty*?

10. When Sayre brings home an A+ on a homework assignment, Beale calls her a "genius," but Sayre's mother is not impressed. Why does Sayre's success bother Dianne so much? Can you think of any other reasons why Dianne would resent her own daughter?

11. Can you name any redeeming qualities about Sayre's mother, Dianne? Why is it so difficult to see beyond anything but the addict—even during the time she was clean, sober, and happy? Can you think of other identities that cloud our judgment of someone's true character?

12. How did you react to the narrative structure in *Ordinary Beauty*? How do you think it relates to the story itself?

13. Why did Sayre decide on her last words to be *Love you, 'bye* to her mother?

14. After reading *Ordinary Beauty*, has your understanding of addiction and its influence on those involved changed in any way? Why or why not? Have you ever known anyone

who has battled this disease or do you yourself have any personal experience with addiction? If so, where there any parts of Sayre's story that especially resonated?

15. Discuss the title, *Ordinary Beauty*. What were your assumptions about the book when you began reading? How would you characterize the title now?

ENHANCE YOUR BOOK CLUB

1. Volunteer for a day at your local animal shelter. Like Sayre, who loved animals of all kinds, spend time with and care for strays and other unwanted cats and dogs. You might even find your own Stormy.

2. Bring your book club on a wilderness adventure and find a spot with Queen Anne's lace. Discuss *Ordinary Beauty* in the company of its most prominent symbol.

3. Read one of Laura Wiess's other books, *Such a Pretty Girl, Leftovers,* or *How It Ends.* Discuss any parallels it has with *Ordinary Beauty*. Which one did you like better?

4. Visit Laura Wiess's website, www.laurawiess.com. Learn about her past works, favorite activities, and upcoming appearances.